The Buried God

The Buried God

Hermann Stehr

K A Nitz
LOWER HUTT

Der begrabene Gott first published
in German 1905

This translation by Kerry Nitz
Copyright © K A Nitz 2012
All rights reserved

ISBN: 978-0-473-22798-2

National Library of New Zealand Cataloguing-
in-Publication Data

Stehr, Hermann, 1864-1940.
The buried God / by Hermann Stehr ;
translated by Kerry Nitz.
ISBN 978-0-473-22798-2 (pbk.)—ISBN 978-
0-4732-2799-9 (Kindle)
I. Nitz, Kerry, 1971- II. Title.
833.912—dc 23

For my friend Moritz Heimann

PART ONE

The Buried God

1

Three hours south-east of Glatz, aloof from the traffic in a valley of the foothills of the Eisengebirge lies the little mountain village Steindorf. The actual village, a small number of humble cottages and farmsteads lying hidden under the fruit trees, is set at the foot of the Little and Big Hedwigstein. Its dependencies hang and crouch in the hollows on the margins of the surrounding mountains.

"Our village has five parts!" every Steindorfer boasted, but nobody was richer for it. The stone debris was laboriously wrestled from the meagre fields, then piled up into walls stretching between the fields. They are grey, weathered, covered in moss and lichen, overgrown with scarlet elder and dog roses, like the walls of a ruined town, like the forgotten material of a great building whose plan has been lost.

The last October days bring deep fog over Steindorf both morning and evening. It climbs up from the valleys of the basin of the Grafschaft Glatz on whose south-east edge the little village lies. The exhausted wind rustles it up sleepily like misshapen, grey giant beasts. Then they gather lazily, push themselves at the steep, blackly forested slopes of the Rollenberg and the Hedwigstein to try and clamber over them, but fall back lazily and roll their plump bodies down into the valley which is soon filled with their woolly, restless movement. The wind, their shepherd, goes back and forth for a while yet on the crests of the mountains, praises the peace of its grey flock of giants with high, contented singing or roars its displeasure in raw screams into the valley and finally digs itself in late at night with growling sounds to a short rest in the forested heights.

In such foggy nights in late autumn, life in Steindorf's street stops even earlier than usual. Even the little bell tower on the Lord of the Manor's estate, which is otherwise always peering over the rooves as a steadfast watchman, hides away somewhere quite early. It sleeps quite softly. Only with the wild scream of the raging wind does it awake, and its little bells strike a few times stammering like the pounding of a fearful heart that is conscious of forgetting its duty. Then the little tower rushes every time to the high, steep roof of the house, dissipates the sleeping fog with its flags, looks up and down the village and hops calmed again into its nest deep in the darkness.

The little houses of Steindorf are a well-bred mob. They also quieten down early on bright evenings. But on these foggy nights, they leave their inhabitants hardly enough time to clear the supper from the table, calling them to their beds and blowing out the lights.

August Klose, called the cobbler Guste, has an awake little house though. It always bears the light of the little lamp longest in the village.

All the residents are indignant over it.

"The cobbler is simply never sensible! Was does he do for such a long time? Sitting with the costly light and reading foolish things from books, simply nothing will come of it", they reason.

Only the cobbler stays up in defiance of them, often until ten o'clock, sometimes even longer.

The Buried God

But today he has society in his humble sitting room. The well-thumbed tomes lie undisturbed on the shelf above the wooden bench running along the table, and he is looking, his elbows propped up leisurely, through the small circle of light at his opposite.

He looks across tensely, with every vigour in his countenance, like that which hardship carries in defending a right.

"No, there you might not come to it at first, stupid boy," he cries agitatedly, "there's water there. Tell me, I went surveying with the forest assessor Winkelmann for who knows how many weeks. I know the stone, that's why I know it! And for that reason alone it's essential. But at your place, the best stone on God's earth is for a well. What do you think then! Gushing — a base! There's nothing more beautiful! That is stone for you, hard like a hearthstone. A water drip could sit on it for ten years and not sink in.

Courage! Shovel and axe and out! Before you are snowed in completely."

His guest had been sitting there quietly during the speech, his head bowed over his chest, his hands clasped between his knees.

Now he raised his face, stared across the table and nodded his large head thoughtfully a few times. Then he replied, "And if I pocket the money and it doesn't happen ..."

The cobbler stroked his thick, yellow walrus moustache angrily, "Now, Karl, if you do, and you will just never believe it, then nobody will be able to help you! Nothing more will remain for you, you'll sell your concern, because a house without water is like a head without a mouth. A jaw you'll find. The Lord of the Manor simply won't look after you. Sell, move away and swear off Marie."

Karl Exner's beardless face became sullen like a gnarled branch.

"You shouldn't take her name in vain!" he shouted angrily.

"I wouldn't entice her away from you. Even if I wanted. I am too poor a devil for that. She wants someone who can provide for her. That I know."

With a bitterly serious air, he looked down in front of himself while chewing on his moustache.

With deep breath, as though casting something off, he began anew.

"Well, she can too, as suits her. Like a petunia flower and hair direct from the goldsmith. Marie!!"

Exner's cheeks were clenching grimly. He swallowed forcefully. Suddenly he thumped the table so that it boomed.

Behind the little door on the right wall there was a stirring, and quietly wavering words, escaping from a hidden soul, silently walking their way through the air, came aloud around them. Shapeless speech which seemed to stir from the room in which the cobbler's old mother slept, and yet it sounded as if the forged breath, far from the lips which it arose, was stirring randomly into audibility.

"Did you hear it!" Exner stuttered. "Didn't you hear it then?" he asked more urgently in fear, since the cobbler remained composed.

"Oh yes," he finally answered, "mother talks in her dreams."

The clock struck the hour, the "twelfth" in fact.

"Guste, it's midnight. That's a sign", Exner said, still in deep fright and staring into emptiness.

"For who then? Mother? Now, yes, it's a sign that she will be awake soon if we sit here any longer and chatter."

"Don't make a racket, cobbler!" Exner admonished the mocker. But he was getting angry.

"Ass! Wanting to speak to me. Do you really believe then in such foolishness?" he asked disparagingly. Then he came out from behind the table and stretched his hand out to him.

"But it's buried!" he admonished again. "Which I want to make otherwise!" answered Exner, still stupefied, and went without saying farewell.

Outside the thick fog was hanging between the trees so that it was completely dark.

Exner was still quite beholden to what had happened and took a few steps forwards haphazardly. When he felt the soft grass under his feet, he remembered that he wanted to go home, sought in the darkness vainly for the path and looked up to find his bearings. Then he saw between the dark treetops the route he had to take lying as a pale stripe. He followed it, groping his way forward with his feet on the stony, steeply climbing road. The higher he climbed, the brighter the pale band above him became, and the clearer a number of shimmering patches stood out in it. Now he was stepping out of the fog and the stars were glittering sharply above him in the deep blue of the night. Under them the milk-white, thin sickle of the moon was swimming like the shimmering fragment of a shattered cup. "Home", he murmured relieved as just at that moment a solitary farmstead by the forest became visible in the dark.

As dismal as the background from which it stood out, it had no companions far and wide. It lay there silent and reserved. Its little glittering windows stared like greedy eyes at its meadows and fields. Even during the day, it stepped for only a few hours out of the twilight of the forest and into the happy, peaceful light of the earth.

Exner had grown up within the spell of this spirit and, not for nothing, he carried his father's house around in his soul.

Twenty years ago, he had been a cheerful, wild boy. No stone was too high, no ditch too deep: he had always ventured the leap. Then one day, hours-deep in the forest, he had broken his foot in his foolhardy rambling. For a long time, he had lain there and screamed helpless and alone, until only a hoarse groaning had come from his sore throat. Towards evening woodcutters returning home had found him and carried him home on a bier of green fir branches. When the father saw the boy, he flew into a rage, beat him soundly and walked out angrily. The next day, he took pity on his son and looked at his foot, which was even more of a bloodshot clump. "Chamomile and lukewarm water on it", he growled wearily and left without once looking back. After half a year, the boy was walking upright in the sitting room. But his foot was clumpishly stunted. His mother weeped when she saw him hobbling across the floor. His father blanched all the way to his teeth and hurriedly left the room.

Karl, however, sat for hours in one place and stared silently at the floor. If someone timidly grabbed his attention so that he "lost his thought", he looked around himself with a hard expression on his face. The wild cheerfulness had disappeared from him since his accident, he became sullen and taciturn and backed away from contact with boys of the same age. His shyness and reserve took him further and further from his comrades so that they gave no voice to their pity and made his defect the target of their ridicule. They gave him various nicknames, but, after weeks of dithering between the description "hoppy" and "clod", they stuck with the last because it contained not only his defect but especially also the inelegance and coarseness of his

entire being. Karl Exner defended himself with the
boundless fury of his lonely soul against this unkind-
ness, struck his tormenters ferociously, spat and
scratched, stabbed with knives and lashed with whips. It
was no use, the name "clod" remained with him for his
entire life. As though with a jolt, he walked away from
the community of his schoolfellows entirely. Self-
secluded, he silently went his way, sat in the sunshine in
shunned places, played in hidden spaces and looked at
the laughing, loud, colourful realm of the other children
from eyes numbed by the drilling with envy, denied
spitefulness and secret, turbid sorrow. Never again did
he attempt to leap or to run, because through that his
defect had made him look a fool not only to others, but
also more clearly to himself. With morbid painfulness,
he struggled to prevent the twitching droop of his body
whenever he settled on his right leg which had the
clubfoot. So he was in the habit when walking, which
remained steady and measured, of hanging his head to
the left side, because with that he enjoyed the sensation
of a regular step which did not distinguish him from
other people. That he believed. But in reality his gait
looked quite strange.

In order to not expose himself to ridicule, he also
avoided the play in the breaks at school. Then he holed
up and watched with burning eyes and blanched cheeks
the sporting of his schoolfellows, but immediately moved on indifferently if he thought he was being observed.

Once the teacher surprised him in this observation
post and attempted to lead him with mild words and
gentle force towards the loud cheers of his comrades.
Karl sank his head silently, stared in front of himself
and held himself back against the pressure of the
teacher who was slowly shoving him forward. Suddenly
he threw himself to the ground, cried out shrilly as
though for help, contorted his frightened face as though

in spasm, beat with his feet and hands like a madman and just screamed continually the agonising, accusatory, "No, no, no! Let me be, let me be!"

From that day on, he was also transformed at school. His eyes observed the teacher covertly and mistrustfully. His indifference to schoolwork increased more and more and finally, despite use of the cane, gave way to thorough dislike for any intellectual work. The hardest punishment yielded in the end nothing but cold fury in his face, which soon always merged into a contemptuous air. Hence his schoolfellows began fearfully to go out of their way to avoid him, since they saw he was endowed with powers which the boldest of them lacked.

His parents were too immersed in their work, and also lacked the gentle, soft souls to be able to wrest him from this alienation. They certainly saw that "the boy's quite strange", but let it go in their rustic fatalism, for "what could you do?" And the little clod, because he needed people with whom he could sit down without exposing himself to ridicule, became a visitor to the retirement homes of the old wizened women and the doddery, dull eyed old men. But his arrival did not lead the way to the delightful play of longing shyness and shamefaced tenderness with which children solicit the affinity of grown-ups, nor did he reward the imparted love with his stirring, full dedication, but rather, silently with downcast eyes, he penetrated into the dark little rooms of the old people, greeted them irritably as he spat, took a seat in silence, remained sitting wordlessly, shut himself off from all questions, left after a few hours just as he had arrived, repeated his visit and then stayed away entirely without reason. From the wrinkled hands, he took neither sweet slices nor oversweetened coffee, he just waited raptly until the old people spoke of their lives. They talked of it gasping, with thin, wailing voices in that enraptured confusion, like the telling of fairy tales, then fell silent, waggled their bald heads and groped across the table with their fleshless hands as though grasping after the lost. The clod sat hidden in the dark, absorbed all the superstitions of these reminiscing people as though thirsting and then left noiselessly. The rapture of his eyes was his only thank you.

In his lonely, hidden walks, he pulled together from those accursed stories a doctrine detached from the world and opposed to life. But it remained his secret. Only sometimes did it smoulder hotly from his eyes and twitch around his unattractive, thin lips. He grew up thus: distant, serious and alone.

Later a love of money which bordered on greed was also added to his unhappy traits. He lent to nobody. "The clod has no money to lend out." In this way, he dispatched loan seekers.

Only the cobbler Guste could ask for what he wanted from him. He never asked in vain. For he had always taken his side at school vigorously and screaming loudly when others had mocked him, and he still defended him just as well. That's why the clod was attached so ardently to him. This single person was his entire humanity. For the others, he remained as bleak and inhospitable as a stone. Over time, admittedly, this relationship had also loosened.

Thus he had become twenty five years old. He then laughed from the depths of his heart for the first time since his accident.

It was at night. He was torn from his sleep and called downstairs. His father lay dying.

"Come here, Karl", the sick man said when he heard the clod's irregular step on the floor. "You are lame, but I am guilty — I alone", he concluded with anxious, failing voice.

The clod paled and remained silent.

"Come here, Karl", he asked again.

He came closer and struck heavily with his clubfoot. With that the dying man started as though from an unexpected blow and groaned, yet asking urgently, "Give me your hand! — Aren't you angry at me?"

"No." It sounded defiant, spiteful. He stretched the words between his teeth.

"You were punished by me", with these words, the sick man retrieved himself from a state of fatigue. "You should have the best too. — With the Lord of the Manor's forest — the concern — is yours. — I have already had it — committed to you. — Be industrious as ever and pray for me ..." Then it rattled in the chest of the old man. It was gone forever with him.

His brother wrung his hands. The women threw themselves down weeping. The lame one stood there stiff as a stone and smiled.

He probably meant, "Now it starts."

And today he was laughing again as he tardily wrapped himself in the blanket. He closed his eyes to be able to see better. Light and soft, like in the distant days of his joyful childhood, it skimmed over his heart. In silent blessing, his inner being quaked before this wonderful visitation, and smiling he finally sank into sleep.

2

Exner's thoughts lay in his blood. He did what he had to. Slowly, mechanically, reluctantly, like a claw, his spirit embraced an intention and never let it go again. If his wanting had thus become instinct then he only looked forwards, and there was no pause for breath before then for him, none before its fulfilment lay behind him. After a short rest, he was on his feet again the next morning. His sister was just then walking across the yard with the milking gear and lantern, when he stepped out the door, his head hanging to the side and front as always, serious and reserved, without greeting her. He strode down the street to the village and summoned old Freiwald, a good, wise old man with whom he had already discussed some things earlier, to his land at Freibusch so that the long planned building of the well would finally begin.

At seven o'clock, just as the sun was forcing a red haze, the light of its immediate vicinity, through the dark treetops, the pair arrived at the place of work.

After long deliberation, bound up with all kinds of mysterious, very intricate measurements by old Freiwald, two strikes were made in the lawn by the left corner of the house, not very far from the front door. After the third strike, however, the old man shook his head and turned to the clod, "But that is a bigger well than a farmer needs."

The clod looked at him ill-temperedly for a while and then answered with poorly hidden anger, "I just think too much water is better than too little." "But look ..." "Dig, Freiwald, dig now!"

He thus shook off the needless questioning and then struck his pickaxe into the ground with vehemence.

"He is a rough obnoxious fellow", the well digger thought to himself and resumed the work again.

Several times he tried to induce a conversation with the lame one in order to obtain the opportunity for a leisurely pause, but his taskmaster was deaf in his industriousness. Only now and again did he straighten up and look furtively at his house.

It resembled his father's house. Nothing distinguished it in construction from the other farmsteads of the village: living area and stables under one roof, one part from square cut timbers, the other from stone. A narrow hall from which a steep staircase led to the loft, "the stage", separated both parts internally from each other.

To the right of the hall, a door led into the living room. A small little door to the left was the entrance to the stables, above which the hayloft had found a place under the joint roof next to a small woodshed.

It was a tidy little house with its white-washed timbers and the brown painted alternately in between. But the same spirit of inhospitability and joylessness lay around it. Instead of turning its windows to the street to watch in comfortable curiosity the sparse life developing on the way between Steindorf and Erlengrund, the small openings stared in sullen dreariness at the nearby forest which stretched towards the east-facing front of the house. There a metre high wall of field stones arose towards the street, a wall, as the Steindorf villagers say, which deters every curious look over it and only allows a view of the roof.

But the clod liked it just so. And deep homeliness came over him every time when he, striding down the narrow path, stepped through the gap in the wall into his realm. Grinning, he then looked up and down the long, narrow home field.

Here his lonely brooding assumed shape, and in his eyes it smouldered, around his lips it twitched. His ownership was free of debt and he even had a thousand talers over and above. Was it then not possible to push out the boundaries and take his cows over the wall to graze on the other side, because the land there had also become his?! Then, before his eyes, a portly farmhouse enclosed with walls like a city grew in place of the poky house, a pigeon loft next to the giant compost heap and double doors at the entrance. Then no man would dare anymore to give him mean nicknames or make fun of him.

But he spoke to no one of his desire. His sister, his mother, even the cobbler were strangers to the world of his soul. But he nursed it in all his silent hours so that it finally turned into a clear, driven plan.

Meanwhile it had struck ten o'clock. They were already standing up to their hips in the earth. The clod struck his mattock into the stones and straightened up. Freiwald immediately broke off his activity too and looked at him surprised.

"Will it have water?" the lame one asked. The old man wiped the back of his hand over his mouth and, with a superior smile, got ready for an intricate explanation,

"Wells are not just wells," he then began, "they're of two types: ground wells and spring wells. The ground well is the true one, it has soul water direct out of the earth. The spring well is also good. Because down there in the earth, there nothing is dead, there it's alive in the darkness and water goes back and forth, it flows, makes pools, all kinds of things. With the spring well, the water goes straight through. When it rains a lot, it has a lot. When it's dry, the well remains empty."

"So and my well?" the clod asked impatiently.

"It is just that," Freiwald unswervingly continued his long-winded explanation, "it is just that. It is a spring well which gets its water from the Rollberg. But if we break through the yellow stone on which we are now, the white comes and lastly the blue in which the soul water lies. See, cl... Karl, soul water. It is so, your soul is the most inward thing. For that reason and because the groundwater comes from the deepest place of all, there where we almost like to say ..."

But it was taking too long for the lame one. He pushed the fine wisdom of the old man away with his foot, while he asked, "So, will it have water or not?"

"Sure enough, sure enough. But it will be deep", the old man returned and smiled compassionately at the clod. —

In rough, reckless industry, the lame one drove the old man through the days. He became more and more irritated, since the brutish zeal of this activity took his entire soul and left nothing but empty grasping which fatigued and agonised him. He hacked away with fury in order to get as soon as possible to a depth where daylight stopped and he could just work alone. And when he was alone again in the turbid night with the little red light in the lantern, all the enigmatic deliberations and stories awoke with which he usually accompanied his leisurely diligence. He filled the basket with the loosened stone, and, on a signal, the load was wound up from the lame one on a rope running over an axle. Now a friendlier relationship occurred again between the pair, even if the clod often grumbled gruffly down into the hole, since the signal for the winding up was in his opinion often too long in coming. Freiwald then gave the appearance of not having heard it in the depths, and the clod got accustomed to filling the long pauses with his hidden dreams. Often he stood still and listened to the pounding of the mattock which from day to day became harder to hear. But the water was not forthcoming, although already two fire ladders had had to be bound together.

One day fury overwhelmed the clod. For he had tallied up the costs, and he screamed down,

"Will you be at a gusher soon?" — "Dawdler!" he added softly. "Hey!" he growled even more furiously because he received no answer, and repeated his question using so much lung power that his voice cracked.

"Well, gusher!" came murmuring up scornfully. Exner held a fist-sized stone in his hand and threw it down angrily when he heard that.

"Karl, leave off with the stupidity! It came straight down on my arm. If you do that again, I'll come up and let you lie in the rubbish", Freiwald screamed incensed.

"To the devil with you", the clod growled, crouched on the hoist and began again to arduously total up his expenses for the well. It became no less whether he placed the small posts first and the large at the end, or did it vice versa, and he looked down ill-temperedly. The frost had begun, a snowless, grim cold in which the entwined, damp stone froze together instantly. "If only the snow stays away", the lame one thought. But over the Rollenberg, grey-white heavy clouds had stood since yesterday. The air only had to warm up, then the driving snow would kick off and the work would have to rest until spring.

Finally, after two days, the cry came dully from the well, "Water, water!"

The ladder clattered and heavy stamping rose from below. The clod threw away in happy shock what he held in his hand, rushed to the well and called down, "Bring water with you! Water! Water!"

After a while, Freiwald surfaced and handed a bottle of muddy water to him, at the sight of which the lame one recoiled. The old man laughed, "Now, now, take it! The water is never any different to begin with. It'll settle down when calm has come to it again. Take it and tell me it tastes pure!"

The lame one tasted it. The water was turbid and loamy. But over his pale face went a shimmer, for he was swallowing his future drink.

"Will it hold out?" he asked afterwards, darkening again.

"Well now, I think so", the old man answered hesitantly and, after short deliberation, directed his eyes gravely at the questioner. "I can say for myself: yes. But what's the point of that. I have helped it out, and it came, for my hand is pure and my nature good. Whether it stays there, stands with God and you. Good luck!"

With childlike emotion, he reached out his hand to the clod. While they were walking away, the air began to fill with fine, white particles which pricked like tiny nails when the heavy wind drove them against the skin. "Over night it'll become white", the old man said.

"It doesn't upset me anymore", the clod replied in cautious joy. After that they separated silently from one another.

3

Since New Year, a new maid had been working for Mr Wende on the Lord of the Manor's estate. Her arrival took place in winter. Hence few in the village had set eyes on her.

Her presence particularly excited the eligible, young fellows of Steindorf, and the most exploratory of them approached her to take up an everyday romance. After a short time, they were calling the girl a "silly goose" and cursing loudly.

At the beginning of spring, they did not yet know any more than that she was called Marie Alke and came from Silesia. They resented her imperious being and called her the "Silesian Marie". It was a put-down, because the Grafschaft residents thought everything that came from Silesia was heartless and crude.

Marie did not worry in the least about this carry-on. She did not treat her fellow servants as her equal and spoke to them as though from another class, with restrained friendliness which brought about the hate and the persecution of the servants. The greatest rudeness left her seemingly calm.

"You are just now still being a little too backward", she would say shaking her shoulders and leaving.

But when the hostile hustling of her fellow servants assumed nasty forms, she stepped quick and decisive before the Lord of the Manor and declared she had to leave his service if he did not bring her peace. Wende had then gone with furious "blessed cursing" among them. Since then nobody dared to go near her anymore and, without looking up, she continued to carry out her work and take no notice of any scorn. She just exerted herself even more and did not let herself be discouraged by her doubled industry, although it fetched her the titles "mule" or "snake". Consequently she excluded herself from all the amusements which her fellow maids sought out. When, after their work was finished, they scrapped with the boys laughing loudly in the smoky servants' room, she sat at the massive table and mended her clothes by the light of the small hanging light or washed her clothes.

When talk and fun then assumed repellently sensual forms, she left the half-lit room silently and lay in bed or went to the hill behind the farmstead, from which she could see across the valley to the deep ravines of the Wartha pass.

If, on clear evenings, the shadowy outline of her homeland climbed up out of the fine haze in the distance, then her large, blue eyes gleamed and she bent down, picked a flower and stuck it in her hair as though she had to adorn herself with the thoughts which then came over her. She saw on such evenings more than a distant land. With that far-off lying region, a life arose for her, lovely and sweet, which had once been her's and had looked different from this existence in the constrained hole of servitude.

She descended from a rich farming family of Frankenstein County. Her father had been seized by the intoxication of millions in the seventies, had taken off his honest leather trousers and torn the short pipe from his mouth. Windowed coaches and uniformed coachmen, pleasures of the hunt, wine and cheer. He rode on the rolling talers through the mad garden of consumption, and behind him bankruptcy silently appeared and followed him. After a few tumultuous years, it caught him up, and the schemes of his short wind were abruptly lost under the hammer.

He disappeared without trace, and meanwhile sorrow dug a grave for his small, delicate wife in a corner of the cemetery. When it was finished with digging, it was a twilight evening, it came in from the graveyard, quietly opened the door and tapped her on her left breast. Her tired heart obeyed hurriedly and instantly hung still as a silenced bell. Her face smiled and her soul stretched its gait and fled to the Father. The wind of fate scattered the children about and ploughed harsh memories of bleak, joyless years into their young natures with its stings.

Marie, the second-oldest child, was at that time just seven years old, full of sunshine. She found lodging with a brother of her father, a hard, stingy man who despised and oppressed her for the sake of the brother's debt. He did it to drive the flippancy out of her, so he said. But that was only an excuse to be able to deprive her of food more often and overload her with work. Only the dull man did not know that children live by their soul and that it can also erect its shimmering palaces in the most squalid corner. So the child prospered nevertheless into ever greater beauty and strength. This beauty had grown still more with the years, and Marie had built all her hopes on it. It was meant to leverage her back into the life of her early childhood which seemed so desirable to her because she had not consciously gotten to know it. That's why she guarded the long, heavy, golden plaits of her hair, never exposed her fine, fresh face to the burning sun and adorned herself with all the cheap finery peddled by hawkers.

With longing heart, she stood in the corner of her humble position and patiently awaited her saviour. If she was becoming discouraged, then she only had to look secretly in the light from the dormer window of her chamber at her face in the small mirror. She was thus again confident in the certainty that one day a rich, well-dressed farmer would step up to her and lead her as his wife to his wealth. She did not know him, but he was present and secretly desired her, and she made herself precious to him with her pride, the doing without all the usual pleasures, the joy in her beauty and her unflagging industry. In the middle of summer, she saw the man to whom fate wanted to chain her.

It was at the time, as the rays of the sun were cradling the ripening ears of corn in their glow, a Sunday afternoon. The crickets were already sensing the twilight and beginning furtively to chirp. The forest stood steadfastly rapt. Life lay in the field margins and slept. Marie was walking between the fields, all alone, and always looking down in front of herself like someone who expects happiness to run across the path to them, hurriedly and unexpectedly like a little, white weasel. Suddenly a shadow fell on the quiet stalks next to her, and when she straightened up startled, a large, heavy-boned man stood before her, whose unusually long legs were stuck into shiny, knee-high boots. His arms were hanging slackly by his short torso as though they were weighed down by the weight of the overlarge hands. In his pale face, there was a helpless joy, the empty eyes stared helplessly from the yellowish whites, and although something oppressive, fear-awakening lay about the entire image, Marie was touched pleasantly for a moment, despite the beating of her frightened heart, because of the silent admiration which the ugly man was paying her beauty through all this. A strange pain hindered her from being able to stride past him as fast as she wanted. Beset by a mysterious cramp, she was unable to turn her gaze from him. Only when the glimmering of his eyes, small creases around his lips and an incomprehensible murmur proved clearly to her that he wanted to talk to her, did she find the strength to proceed, but still noticed how he nodded his head a few times so that the cap rode over his brow. This movement suddenly changed the entire scene for her into a funny incident.

Responding to the man's silent greeting with quiet caution, she scurried away. Finally she ventured to look around. Between the expanses of corn, already so far from her that his body only stuck half out of the ripe corn, she saw him moving away jerking oddly. His head was hanging to the left as he moved.

She breathed out relieved and smiled, as she again pictured to herself how he had stood before her and nodded with his head so that his cap had ridden down to his nose. But it did not free her from a mysterious cramp, a fear which, as groundless as it probably was, did not go away from her. To scare it away, she sought to think of her "beautiful time", of the "long Sunday", as she called her future. Only the images which she called did not stand up, the songs which she yearned for did not ring out. From across the village, she heard cows bellowing, children clamouring, a pushcart creaking, dogs barking, and in between the shouting of a furious man occurred in sections. Sad, she went home.

4

The residents of Steindorf, like almost all Grafschaft residents, hang on Catholicism. This is not just piety, but also accords for the burdensome journey to heaven many a day in which they can shed their work clothes, put on the Sunday fleece, smoke a cigar leisurely, put on a little play and drink a schnaps to it. What time would they have otherwise had away from their toilsome life if next to Sundays, which exist anyhow, there were not a few holidays!

But when you take your fingers and count them, the beautiful days which come in the middle of the week, ones to take the mattock, the plough or the rake quietly out of the hand, like a dear friend who likes to prepare some fun, and to say quite rightly, "My good man, stop! stop! Take a breather and let your soul catch its breath again". When you count them, unfortunately a few fingers still remain on both hands on which the sun does not shine.

That's why nobody resents a good Christian that he helps this defective arrangement somewhat and, on his own initiative, plants in the middle of the whirl of the week such a day of laughter. If it has enough saints, then it will not be too difficult. This rational view also found adherents in Steindorf, and although the small place has no church and therefore no choir singers, on the 17th of November every year, the festival of St Cecilia was celebrated.

Even this year, "Franke, the fat innkeeper" notified the community that, as usual, the celebration was happening from seven in the evening onwards.

The tavern's saloon is adorned with fir sprigs, the four lamps on the timber ceiling are cleaned up, and the stately row of beer casks narrowing even more the already narrow hall testify to the steady faith which the old man is accustomed to place in the devotion of the community members.

With the increasing darkness, the guests arrive. When eight o'clock is past, a colourful, cheerful crowd fills the saloon. The four ceiling lamps are already struggling desperately with thick clouds of smoke. Two boys and two girls, with white aprons and cloths of the same colour in their hands, are trotting back and forth to the tables. They are in high excitement and draw their eyebrows and ears up in their serious travails. With an order, they run around frightened as though receiving a smack from a whip, extract an empty drinking mug from the noisy mob and hurry to the barroom. The "Melittes' Club", nobody knows how the village's musicians arrived at this name, are sitting in calm expectation behind the stanchions of the raised choir. The dance-lovers are looking with shining faces at them and giving them a friendly nod. As a thanks in return, each and every Melitte wrings from their instrument a note. The right side of the saloon is occupied by the married couples. The fathers are sitting there, drumming on the table and telling stories. The mothers are smiling. Some are holding small children in their laps, girls or boys of four to six years, and giving them beer or schnaps to drink.

On the left side, the singles are sitting. The girls sit on a long bench, pretty faces throughout, their hands folded on their aprons, turned to the front of the saloon. The young men, rolled into a thick mob, are smoking with all their might, drinking diligently, laughing and talking too loud in order to excite the attention of the girls to whom they sometimes gift from their glass.

Through the open door, many wistful faces, boys hardly escaped from the school desk, are looking; "half-skulls" as the farmers call them. They are pushed aside contemptuously by those going in and out, and laughed at as well, but take advantage of this exclusion by secretly smoking and drinking schnaps.

Shortly before the beginning of the ball, a small table is placed before the Melittes' choir, and a young man sits down at this spot visible from everywhere. The stranger wears a fashionable, grey suit. His heavy, blond moustache is turned in pert spikes, and his sharp eyes are surveying with a dismissive smile the row of unfashionably adorned women; he gives the girls a nod with a meaningful wink. Then he remembers with a start that he is in a tavern and must drink at once. Since he does not catch sight of a subservient spirit, he rises, makes a small knee bend to tidy his trousers and then walks with strides, to which he imparts elegance through a snapping of his legs, to the middle of the saloon, surveying everything anew with hurtful astonishment. He returned four weeks ago from his three-year-long military service to the coach business of his father in the four-hours-distant Tannerau, "with the buttons" and even greater disrespect for civilians and all bourgeois occupations, a disrespect which he clothed in the ridiculous copying of a second lieutenant of his squadron. He walks about in the bright circle of the four ceiling lamps in the middle of the saloon, two fingers of his right hand under the buttoned-fast jacket at his chest, the thumb of his left hand stuck in his trouser pocket, and is visibly sunken in deep thought from which he starts with a furious face when people go by.

In truth he refreshes himself with the excited curiosity of the guests, which is directly linked quite strongly with the girls and young men and with a quiet awe. But, be it now the big boots with the bands of excess leather alone; be it the shuffling stride which always finished with a heavy strike of the heels; be it the entire poise or the way his head stretches with cautious attention from his body, enough, some of the young people have recognised his true being through the clumsy imposture and call out, "The Lindenwalk von Plan!"

That unleashes a mad laughter. The grey suit makes a vigorous turn to the bar as though he has now waited in his goodness long enough for service, and shouts into the din, "Barman! damned barman!! A real one! A bit warmed up!!" Then he returns serenely to his small table, turns his back to the saloon and stares at the Melittes.

"Barman! dammit, barman!! a bottle of wine for a Bohemian, but a full one!!" is called out after a while from the middle of the young men.

The stranger tears his head around fitfully and changes colour, without however paying further attention to the jeering that follows this mockery. After a while, a barman brings him a light lager beer and places it carefully on a spot of the table which he has cleaned with a towel beforehand. "Hm," the grey suit begins with a furious look at the drink, "I could have known that there was no real beer here." — "What do you have for novices back there?" he then shouts at the barman so that it echoes through the saloon. The young man being addressed turns the towel spasmodically and removes himself clearing his throat without answering.

The Buried God

At the table of young men, someone toasts noisily, "I think the real beer tastes good, it's a little thin and it scratches in the throat too; but it does no harm, it costs only half!" The stranger addresses the girls out of revenge, "But today I want to dance with spirit!"

The tavern is already in uproar and observing the quarrel with rising fury, but does not know yet on which side it should discharge it, and besides, it is only talk.

Suddenly the teasing talk falls silent, and everyone looks to the door. The old forester, a spindly widower, in very narrow, green trousers and a grey beard lying like a cake on the coat of his uniform, is coercing a resistant girl by hefty shoving of the shoulders into the saloon.

"Go in, go in! they can well use such as you in here!" he spoke mutedly and looked fondly under his glasses at her. "That's right, ever lively, forester, right, it's beginning shortly", the innkeeper barged into the matter delighted over the sudden turn of the mood and concluded with a grin at the girl, "a being like a cherry!"

The heads of the party came up, astonished over the sudden break-off of hostilities. When they caught sight of the girl, the whisper went among them, "The Silesian Marie!"

The young men at the tables are amused, and Marie stands alone, still near the exit, because the forester has hurried away to shelve his things, and she does not know where she should seat herself or whether she would not rather leave again. She rues having yielded to the forester, but she feels restrained by the looks directed at her.

Just as she broke the power of these curious eyes over her and turns imperceptibly to slip out again unnoticed, the grey bearded chief Melitte counts buzzing, "One, two, three!" and the music starts up, the notes of a timeworn march passing animatedly among the guests, and Marie feels herself embraced and held from behind, spinning around frightened, by the old forester, who says something solemnly long-winded through his nose and thereby without further ado orders her body to dance in his arms and then begins to spin her through the saloon. As though by agreement, nobody joins in the dance to begin with. The young men look agog at the couple from their places.

The old men think, 'you respect your important civil office and seek to make as imposing as possible a figure', while he trots in stern soldierly deportment through the saloon, now and again gracefully kicking his legs back. The grey suit devours Marie with his eyes. The music falls silent, only a clarinet concedes a sharp sigh. The young men clap and shout, "Bravo!"

The green coat, standing in the middle of the saloon next to Marie, bows in thanks and then leads the girl after a short deliberation to the small table of the grey suit, approaching with an imperious "Excuse me". The stranger stands up saluting and stammers with a sympathetic smile, "Oh, yes, yes!" bows and moves to the short side of the table. Then he looks around the saloon, stroking his moustache, to see if everyone has noticed his dashing behaviour.

But now the unfettered dance is surging. A few are hopping like will-o'-the-wisps through the swirling waves, they surface circling and disappear again. Some shuffle in slowly, stiff as a wavering tree trunk; others gallop back and forth double-quick and thereby rub their foreheads on those of the female dancers. Some put everything into imitating a question mark; others hang every moment floundering between heaven and earth. The bass growls, the horn coughs hoarsely and sporadically, the clarinet screams shrilly like someone having a growth cut from their body and vies with the violin giving its anguished whimpering. With that the drum rolls as though someone is dumping field stones in a wooden tub to celebrate the day. The Melittes practise their art with the utmost effort. The innkeeper looks at them in awe.

The women's eyes seek to quickly follow every couple. The family fathers strike the beat with their fists and heels, and the half-skulls advance into the saloon in astonishment. The mood is in full flow. Everyone is doing their own thing with their entire soul. When the young men return to their places after a dance, they are not a little astonished to meet on the bench the clod and next to him the cobbler Guste sitting behind the table. They each have a glass of lager beer before them and the lame one is listening to the cobbler gesticulating and expostulating to him.

"Well it really has struck fifteen," shouts the joker amongst them, the redhead Klenner, a square-built woodsman with small, blinking eyes under bulging brows, "today anything is possible! Pay attention, either Hörner gets the Lord of the Manor's horses overnight or the innkeeper gets it in the belly; anything can happen today. Even Karl is here! Well, good evening, to every two!"

Everyone laughed their heads off, sat down at the table next to the pair and, after a while, they began, without naming names, all kinds of joking talk which obviously referred to the clod. He pulled his sullen face, and when that did nothing, he grasped his glass, drank a long swallow and then slammed it down on the table so that the beer splattered about. That perplexed the high spirited young men. With lightly sparring words, they backed away from the lame one and dedicated their exclusive interest again to the beer, the dance and the girls. The clod breathed out relieved and fingered his neck.

"Damn thing, such a collar!" he growled angrily. "Is the tie still right?" "Of course," the cobbler answered, "as it must be. If she sees you, you'll look right."

"You shouldn't talk to me of that!" "Well, we came here though for that reason."

"The mouth should be kept shut over that in case someone hears."

Then he stared bleakly before himself. He felt uncomfortable among the many childishly happy people and asked himself what it was all for actually.

"You have to thaw out a little," the cobbler began to instruct him again, "be cheerful, drink, talk here and there, try to help yourself. Otherwise ..." he made a dismissive gesture. Then he settled himself closer to his sullen ear. "I know my way around. You have to talk like a jew. The girls like some joshing."

The lame one succumbed to the agonising feeling of being excluded by everyone, and raised his face after a while to make some sneering remark, but let his head sink coldly.

The cobbler had talked him into visiting the Cecilia ball because he had to first get the necessary social refinement before he could think of starting with Marie. In truth, however, it mostly lay on the poor cobbler to dance neatly, to drink and to smoke at the expense of the lame one. So he clinked glasses with him again.

The clod swallowed imprecations over the "boozer" and lapsed, without stirring his glass, still deeper into his sorrow.

The cobbler waved to a barman, and when he did not hear, he rose with the empty drinking vessels and wandered, adding his jokes sometimes to this, sometimes to that table, to the barroom, had his pint filled, emptied it hastily, sought a second and then liltingly took his place again.

"Now," he suddenly poked the clod in his side, "see there how the man, the man with the grey suit, is talking with Marie and how she laughs! Watch, that's how it's done."

The lame one squinted under his lowered brows at the small table and surveyed the stranger sharply for a long time.

"That's a jumping jack," he then replied in grim contempt, "what he can do, I could do long ago. With one hand, I could beat him up like a young dog. You can count on that." He drank and emitted a raw sound of derision, looking at the cobbler from the side. The latter sat there silently, his elbows propped on the table and blowing long clouds of smoke. He was suddenly transformed and staring lost at Marie. His face bore at the same time a deep strain of distress.

"Cobbler", the lame one murmured because he had a vague feeling this conspicuous behaviour could compromise him. But the cobbler did not stir. "Cobbler", he repeated and, since his friend still did not hear, drove his fist into his thigh. "You shouldn't look in her direction!"

The cobbler Guste turned around quickly and smiled happily as though absentminded. Suddenly his face darkened,

"Let the bird fly, I'll never catch her", he said and shook off his heavy mood. "Drink, drink, Karl, drink, I tell you! No, no, have no fear either, I am a poor, miserable fool." The clod thought the cobbler was drunk, because he talked so confusedly, and flared up gruffly, "Guste, I can see where it's going. It's best I go home!"

In the same moment, the barman stepped up to the table and looked unsparingly at the clod.

"Well, what do you want?" he purred into the young man's face. The barman smiled. "Cleaning, cleaning should be done", he replied and motioned at the table with the thumb and index finger of his right hand as though counting money. In the same moment, he was pushed from behind so that he half flew over the table. The young men were returning from dancing and excitedly seeking their places. Most of them had irate faces.

"We have to strike the ass with teeth in the back of his neck!" shouted a small man with yellow face and straight, black hair.

"Yes, yes, if he was made of sugar, I'd say: everyone seize him, Tone, devour him", the tall Klenner scoffed.

"And, you giant lamb, didn't he rush you too, hey? and you put up with it, you who mocks the others", the yellow face gave it back venomously. The cobbler stepped between them to arbitrate, "Stop the bickering! What's happened? Who's pushing then?"

And now someone told him about the grey suit and how he behaved insultingly, running into everyone whilst dancing, said "unfriendly stuff" and danced away with Marie as though he had hired her. Nobody else came near the girl, and yet she now belonged to Steindorf. It was a shame on everyone to stand for such from a stranger.

But then Joseph, the Lord of the Manor's steward, entered on the side of the grey suit, "What concern of ours is the Silesian, that stuck-up bit, I won't stir a finger over her."

"Shut up," Klenner interrupted him, "you don't understand because you have no sense of honour. You're an ape."

The cobbler Guste took the general excitement into his hands.

"If you are all agreed, then let me deal with it. I didn't work on the main road into Berlin for nothing, I know what a collection of curios is. Let me deal with it,

I'll put a spoke in his wheels without a fight so that he takes off like a dowsed poodle."

"I'm of the opinion that you could easily tear the ears off that jumping jack." With that the lame one entered into the dispute.

Most of them were of the view to let the cobbler deal with it, and should it not work out then there was still time for a drubbing outside.

Laughing in high spirits, in the pleasant expectation of a stunning coup, everyone stood up and stepped up for a dance.

The pair remained behind alone at the table, the lame one and the cobbler. "And me?" the clod asked when the dance was in full swing. "You?" the cobbler answered, "leave it to me, it won't take long and Marie will be sitting between me and you."

The lame one blanched in cheerful shock, but moved his large head unbelievingly. "But I must have drinks, as I mustn't see a mark. Being stingy won't work." "Haven't I ...?" "Yes, yes, you have paid indeed, I don't mean that. But now it really begins proper. And then you'll see that it was lucky for you that we came here today. I certainly wouldn't have dreamt that Marie herself would be here."

As though by a signal, both looked to the small table before the Melittes' choir and saw how the stranger was leading Marie there by the hand because a round had just ended.

"Take care, they do it like this in Berlin." The cobbler seized a glass violently, emptied it, breathed out heavily, shoved the others to the side and walked diagonally across the saloon directly to the small table.

The clod swore full of admiration. The other young men raptly follow the whole affair. The devilish cobbler talks with the old forester, even with the grey suit, and then bows to Marie and speaks laughingly to her face, whereat he elegantly moves his feet alternately back and forth. The girl finally nods. Then he jumps up and claps his hands.

The chief Melitte blows a leading note in his trumpet and the other instruments follow. A trot clatters through the saloon. None of the young men stir, in order to miss none of what follows. The cobbler seizes Marie and shoots into it like an arrow.

You have to say, he can do it like no other! Now he is hunting to the left around the saloon, then again to the right like a thoroughbred, with sharply clattering heel steps; now he is whirling on a spot in the middle; then he leads the girl forward with rocking upper body, then back, now he is hurrying around teetering; sometimes he leaps like a rider; other times he turns with outstretched arms like a windmill; he scurries like a wagtail, he gobbles like a turkey and scratches mincingly like a hen. The Melittes squint over their sheet music at him and work themselves up into a fire. The beat gets quicker, wilder. Finally every instrument is blustering in wild fervour. In the frenzy of ferocity, the piece breaks off abruptly.

The cobbler stamps his foot and remains standing a while, exhausted. The young men break out into jubilation, "Up with the cobbler! Hey, up with the music! Up with Marie!" The Melittes blow a fanfare.

In this noise, Klose leads the girl back. His eyes are shimmering, he presses her hand fervently, and in ecstasy he whispers to her, "Dear Marie, dear Marie, oh God, Marie!" The girl did not understand a word, but understood the pressure of his feverish hands, broke free and ran the few steps to her seat, alone and quick.

The cobbler followed her with a long stride and had already raised his right hand to teasingly capture her again, when the old forester turned to him and said disapprovingly, "Cobbler Guste, know that such a thing is not dancing, it is murder."

That tore the cobbler from his intoxication. He raised his right hand higher and caressed the hair on his temples whilst he made a deep bow out of embarrassment and left. The grey suit smiled contemptuously, then bowed to Marie and loudly asked, "But the next dance, we will dance again. You cannot smell such old shoes for long."

Walking away, the cobbler heard this mocking and, with the fury of a rival, he tramped to the clod's table where they surrounded him joyfully. "Let it be! But it isn't over yet, now it really begins", he said, working his way to the clod.

A long argument followed in which the cobbler finally convinced the clod by mobilising all his volubility and stock of expressive gestures. The lame one pulled his wallet out of his pocket in a moment when the attention of most of the young men was directed elsewhere, dug indecisively around in it and handed the cobbler something which he turned down after a scrutinising look. Painfully animated, the lame one added something more, and the cobbler stood up and triumphantly climbed the choir of the Melittes. After a short negotiation with their chief, a trumpet blast resounded, and the chief Melitte announced, "A half hour of free dancing for the residents of Steindorf!" Then a long pause took place.

This extraordinariness in itself put the men at the tables in a great commotion, but the young men were happy in their high spirits. The clod appeared like a demigod to them. But he paid no attention to any praise, to any astonished exclamation, instead he sat there stiffly with prised elbows and stared silently into the noise with grimly clenched face. The shimmer of his small eyes was angry with contempt.

The grey suit stared now and then darkly into the emptiness and then forced himself into spasmodic cheerfulness with Marie.

When the Melittes finally gathered their instruments again and the cobbler stepped decisively up to Marie, the redhead Klenner shouted, "Go and fetch your broom!" The music devoured the whinnying laughter of the entire saloon. The grey suit turned pale with fury, clenched his teeth, smoked so that the sparks flew and drank hastily and a lot.

With every dance, the same taunt repeated. Finally the grey suit could not hold himself any longer and shouted into the silenced saloon, "Long live the smuggling, wood stealing and hold-ups! It harvests something!"

The affair was taking a turn which did not suit the cobbler. He considered what to do to bring everything to the end he had promised his friend. But, then the battle of words broke out even more acrimoniously. It sounded from the corner, "In Tannerau everyone goes fencing except the steward. He stays at home and patches his beggar's sack."

The stranger asked the forester, shouting, "Hey, you must know best of all, does everyone here milk the green cow!" The forester, who had heard the words quite clearly, gave the impression that he did not relate the address to himself, took a deep swallow from his glass, then interrupted his drinking suddenly and asked him as though amused, "Do you mean me, young man?"

"Now really, there is no other forester here in the saloon." He said it insolently, but only because he thought he would make himself ridiculous by a friendly answer.

"Where do you have your handkerchief?", the forester asked in an authoritative way, without letting his anger show. The grey suit became confused, tore his handkerchief out and shook it right in front of the forester's nose, "Here! Ha, ha, I never knew that a hand-kerchief was such a strange thing around here."

"I didn't think you would have one", the forester now replied with cutting sarcasm. "For one does not see it near your nose, and when you have time, you can dry behind your ears." And as the stranger was rising to incivility, the long restrained fury came over the old green coat. The veins on his neck were swelling as thick as a thumb.

"Shut up," he shouted and sprang up, "do you know who I am? I am the royal forester Knölle of Steindorf, and where I am there is no talk of wood stealing or hold-ups ..."

On the innkeeper's nod, the music blew a fanfare during which both men shouted at each other. Then the fanfare segued into a dance.

The cobbler stepped up and asked Marie for a dance. When the girl rose, the grey suit tore his head around and measured her for a moment with his furiously sparkling eyes, then turned back to whoever was standing behind his chair. He recognised the cobbler and shouted, "Go forever!" and, with the exclamation, "Such a man would not be worth my ... such a dry!", dealt the girl such a hefty blow in the side that she floundered a few steps and then abruptly fell over.

The music fell silent as though with an outraged scream. A moment of stiff anxiety followed the crudity. Everyone looked silently at the incomprehensible.

A scream, similar to that a wild steer makes in bursting the chains of its stall, rent the silence. A table fell dully to the ground, glasses smashed on the floor, and with hobbling step, the lame one hurried in front of the choir. At the small table, he stopped. His face was ashen; his eyes stood deathly in their whites, only their trembling betrayed life. His breath was whistling through his half-open mouth. Fury shook his entire, bony figure. The stranger tried to laugh, but paled up to his clammy hair. A pause. A seconds-long measuring up. Now the lame one's fist was swishing like a giant stone at the head of the grey suit.

Noiselessly, overflowing with blood, he collapsed. "That is from the beggar!" "And this is from the wood thief!"

With this second raw cry, the clod seized the impotent man and threw him with a powerful swing into the hallway.

And then he looked down astonished at himself as though curious, as though he was not seeing himself but someone else.

Then his eyes fell on the swooning Marie. With her face against the ground, she was lying like a corpse. Blood was trickling from her brow and forming a small puddle.

He observed her attentively without stirring. Then he smiled happily and finally he bent down with a rough cheer, lifted the girl up, held her towards the light and covered her pale, beautiful face with fervent kisses.

His body was shaking as he cautiously turned towards the saloon door with his prey and disappeared into the darkness of the hallway.

Hardly had he got outside than the old forester Knölle sprang into the middle of the saloon and cried with commanding voice, "Silence!"

He had in a way been accused by the grey suit of superficial administration and considered himself as a civil servant to be obliged to defend the public order, in short, it lay to him to give a speech.

"Silence!" he repeated with threatening voice, since mutterings were rising, and murmured into his beard, "I will delouse your caps, you damned hounds!" "Silence!" he roared for the third time. But no one was looking at him to begin with. They were sitting at the tables and talking and violently gesticulating. Knölle looked around with concern. Finally he stirred himself up and harangued them over brawling, decorum, rabble-rousing, rough greenhorns, high fences, culture, conifers, Bismarck, logging, Luther and finished off with a triple cheer for "His Majesty, the most gracious Kaiser". After that he took himself back to his place with soldierly deportment. The Melittes blew a fanfare, the innkeeper thanked him for the "beautiful talk", and soon the couples were spinning under the red-lit ceiling lamps again.

The clod had carried Marie to the gate of the Lord of the Manor's estate and, because she had not yet recover-ed consciousness, wiped her forehead with grassy dew. Finally, with a yawning noise, she opened her eyes and looked around astonished.

"What do you want?" she said to the man kneeling next to her, holding her in his embrace and continually murmuring, "Little Marie, wake up, wake up." She broke free and sprang up frightened. The clod also rose. "Be quiet, look, little Marie," the lame one said to her, "I am Karl Exner from over there", and now he explained to her everything that had befallen. She remembered the scene, interrupted him with the words, "I have not been 'little Marie' in a long time, understand! I thank you deeply for everything and I'm well now", turned around and pushed on the latch of the small door leading into the yard in order to go in. The lame one seized her by the arm, "Little Marie, look, I think it will simply never be of much use to you, for I ..."

"Oh you! Have I not thanked you?" "Now, consider it; you must — on Sunday afternoon, come to the cobbler Klose, right. Then we can discuss other things."

"What are you thinking of then!" Marie replied indignantly.

"Around three, I'll wait for you", the clod said quietly but firmly, and when he saw how the girl disappeared behind the small door without answering, he set off home in silence without hope.

5

Marie was soon seeking to go to bed. Her bed, like those of the other maids, stood in a small room under the roof. A special partition had been made for her with boards, and in it, except for the bed, there was only a "store", a wooden chest for her clothes. She sat on it for a while, clothed only in a jacket in order to cool down a little, for she was feverishly hot. She thought it stemmed from the wound on her head and stood up to lean her head on the pane of the dormer window. It was mistily clear outside and the moon looked like a white chimney from which clouds of quiet, cautious smoke continually spurted and were driven staggering into the branches of the trees. They disappeared into the confusion of branches as though sucked up by the small, knotty twigs, and then every time a wave of mist heaved again cautiously and quietly from the pale, insecure moon to her. She stared unmoved at this monotonous, silent play of white night mist which not only dissolved the pain of the wound into a pulsing pressure, but also brought an, if also empty, rising and falling into the burden of her earliest experiences. But not for long, and her entire being swayed to the rhythm which was driving the pale shrouds outside. Marie bit her lips and held onto the roof slats at the base of the window with both hands. Meanwhile she had more and more tormentingly the feeling that this billowing mist was heaving her up and down and wanted to wash her away from there. When this sensation climbed to an unbearable certainty, she spoke strongly to herself, "No! I don't have to! — ha!" —

With that the darkness parted over her soul, and the power which was closing in on her in the night assumed the shape which had already twice crossed her path in such a mysterious way. She saw the lame one striding towards her in the shroud, but not in the clothes he had worn that evening, rather in high boots and the short jacket in whose shell his arms stuck out like long rods. His head leaning to the side so that his broad-rimmed cap rode down over his brow, he came up to her with his unequal steps, with a face full of steadfast determination. "It's all just foolishness", she thought to herself and headed for her bed. But when she felt how she was staggering, she steadied herself with her left hand on the wall and repeated threateningly and full of scorn, "No! I don't have to, take note!"

Then she threw herself roughly into bed with her face against the pillow, for the pain in her forehead had begun drilling again and its convulsions were passing through her entire body, and it seemed to her as if her whole life was injured. "Why do I have to? Where did the man appear from?" she asked herself again and again and, for the pain in her forehead, she just pressed her right hand vigorously to the wound over which she had bound a cloth. But if she was also searching all the scenes before and after the incident for an event which could perhaps give the clod the right to such an expression, she found no other ground for it than the unmoving determination in the unattractive face of the lame one, the immutability of his empty eyes. A mysterious spell originated from the entirely untoward man. She turned onto her side and closed her eyes with force in order to think of her "long Sunday", her golden sunny future. But she succeeded only very imperfectly, as she felt the inexorable presence of this man, who had arrived suddenly by his singular paths in the middle of her life, ridiculously, but also as secretively as ever.

It was probably still quite early, as the late moon's sickle stood directly opposite the small room's window, and the sky seemed to be filled with dancing particles of snow. The roosters were crowing everywhere. From the tavern, the closing fanfare of the dance rang out indistinctly. She thought, 'Tomorrow I will hear all about it', turned from the luminous window, drew the blankets over her head and, after an abrupt start, had the sensation of gliding down swinging deeper and deeper into a soft twilight between whose clouds the flying images of sleep were beginning to shimmer.

Then it seemed to her as though she was looking quite closely at the moon. It had left its distant place in the night air and come over to her with giant strides which crunched gently as though they were walking over old snow. At first this noise sounded from far, far away, quite softly, so that it could only be heard with the sensitivity of the skin. Then it became clearer, but a slow, cautious grinding, and now the moon crammed its gleaming, lean body into the doorway which it had opened just a crack. She knew that it only wanted to make sure if she was sleeping, for it paused half in the hall which led past the doors of the other servants' rooms, and it had only bent into the room its paper-white face on its thin neck and sought her with the gloating shadows of its eyes. Now she felt with an unease which enclosed her like a gentle net that it was watching her and observing attentively. For a moment, it seems to her as if it is the image of the steward,

Joseph, the number two on the Lord of the Manor's estate, but then she recognises that the illusion is not possible: it is the moon. Now a new doubt is rising in her, why the moon is not creeping in to her through the window, when a grating of the door lock banishes the twilight images completely. Awakened, she pushes the blankets down from her head and turns her face to the door which is locked as always. With a bewildered smile she turns her face again to the wall separating her small room from another maid's. Through a crack between the badly caulked boards, she looks into the deep darkness of the neighbouring room and notices two shadows which move past her a few times almost noiselessly. Then they both disappear, they must be to the right and left of her lurking eyes' narrow field of vision.

"She is sleeping hard and fast", a rough man's voice continued a conversation.

"No, go home. What else do you want? I'm tired and it's almost morning", a whispering girl's voice answered dismissively. After that the two flounder somewhere. Smacking kisses, the noises of skirts, a smothered call of distress from the woman, hard thrusting man's breaths. Then nothing is to be heard but the panting of two struggling persons. The loud racket in the night of some object being knocked over silences the pair's struggle. Marie listens in shame to her blood pulsing.

"Go!" the girls begins again, her voice is exhausted. "Did she do it then? Ha, and morning, then she'll look at him as if wanting to say: I know you, you're the right one for me."

"Oh, Paula, you are chaste and quite childish," the man answered, "you and the Silesian, she's clever but subtle! Ha! I was in the country down below, there they get together first, would you think! There, many a night there were more legs in the hay than shingles on the roof. What a one she was! Acts as if she was dead, acts out the comedy and lets the clod kiss her in front of everyone in the bright light of the saloon. What happened afterwards, that they'll, that is both of them, they'll know best of all. Otherwise she wouldn't be lying there like a sack of potatoes. What do you think, would the clod stop so easily! Hehehe!"

Then the pair laugh softly in mischievous merriment. It turns Marie, lifts her up and throws her down. It is embracing her inwardly with a twisting force so that her heart and breathing falter. She has to sit up in order not to suffocate.

"Psst!" the man in the other room cautions, having heard the noise.

Marie turns her head, but then directs her eyes into their room again. It seems like she is looking into the whirring gears of a merciless machine grinding and tearing everything up: her happiness, her pride, her good name, joy and peace. "Aha, that's why the dog said, 'you must', that's why — that's why — *so* —", she pondered and smiled coldly so that she became dizzy and had to hold onto the bed post with both hands to not fall out.

"Did you hear scraping?" the alert man asked the maid, as he had heard the digging of her fingernails in the wood. —

"Well ...!" "No."

"Well, then do it now and don't do it again for a long time!" he then advised impatiently. After that there is a quiet rustling, a cautious slinking as though naked bodies are pushing through wrinkles giving way and then a sense of beguiling oppressiveness. Then the sounds of passion arose. And all this groaning in heat, this hot, exhaling lisping closed in on Marie like an unavoidable incrimination. She clenched her teeth in despair, seized the hair at her temples with both hands and pulled her head down into the bed.

She lost consciousness and, after a long time, the faint turned into sleep.

The short hours of her sleep had been a constant affliction, had in a mysterious way created a clarity from the events of the previous evening and the images in her agitated soul, and when they, abruptly tearing away, drove Marie from her bed in the first grey of morning, the poor girl again found herself in the certainty of not being able to escape the clod.

Suddenly this numbness grew to a driving fear.

"What am I running up and about for; it's night, and everyone is still sleeping", she thought, put on her better clothes hastily and noiselessly, wound a woollen shawl around her head as low as her brow, took her shoes in her hand and crept on her toes down into the servants' room to wash herself and comb her hair. When she went past the apartment of her employer, she heard a creaking, disgruntled voice. Faster and quieter, she took herself down the stairs.

Wende was preparing for his first tour through the barn and yard. If Marie was hastening with her last preparations, then it was so she would be already on the street when the Lord of the Manor's heavy felt slippers shuffled down the stairs. Quietly and quickly, she hurried back and forth with the small light in the vaulted, sooty room. Meanwhile, Wende's voice seemed to become ever louder and angrier to her. His wife was talking soothingly to him now and again, but this happy, unclouded noise brought a stronger clatter into his voice every time. Wende had retained the practice from his long bachelorhood of inspecting during the night at intervals of three to four hours everything on his farm, but especially the horse and cow stalls, and was now desiring of his wife that she accompany him every time. She refused this, because it was enough if he alone pulled himself from sleep, and every night she brought into play a series of practical arguments opposing this fad and for ten years had sacrificed a part of her sleep to the struggle with her husband's stubbornness.

"Why doesn't she go as far as her legs will carry her?" Marie said to herself while she listened to the quarrel above. "Wasn't it better she had the boy and was contented as one can be, like now, since she has the old nurse?"

All that she pondered with the mechanical thought which always stands at our bidding and has nothing to do with our inner being.

The argument in Wende's bedroom was becoming louder meanwhile. It had the appearance of heading for its end, for the call and response was becoming more and more agitated. The Lord of the Manor coughed barking in-between, which he only did in a state of greatest agitation. Marie quickly extinguished the light so as not to come across the Lord of the Manor in the yard.

"What will he do first if he sees that I am gone?" she pondered and drew the door open, paused on the threshold, thrust out her head from the deep niche which formed the entrance to the servants' room and looked across the spacious hall up the stairs. Everything was still and the morning light fell through the night like a noiseless shower of ash.

Above, Wende's furious coughing sounded from time to time. Marie scurried across the hall, tore back the door's crossbar so that it drove back clattering into the wall and felt for the key which hung on a rusty chain. She had just grasped it and was raising it with her right hand to the door lock which she was feeling for with the fingers of her other hand, when the door above flew open and Wende stepped out grumbling loudly.

"No, no, stay, stay, you can lie in for my sake until fifteen o'clock!" he shouted back into the room and then slammed the door behind him. Marie let the key fall, fled across the hall again and hid herself behind the door of the servants' room.

Wende slowly climbed down the stairs, thrusting the sooty little oil lamp out in front of himself, and was still grumbling indistinctly all those furious thoughts which had brought him to slamming the door on his wife.

"I must pull her out sometime with her woollen coat!"

With these words, he continued the furious conversation with himself, standing in the middle of the hall below, raised the lantern to shoulder height and shone it all around.

"Why did I marry her! A good servant has never made a good farmer's wife", he said at the same time. "She knew boys then ..."

Here he broke off, and Marie saw through the crack in the door how he hastily stepped to the door whose thrown back crossbar was exercising his distrust. He growled something like "vermin", "vagrants" and "good-for-nothings", examined intricately the door lock which he unlocked and locked with the key, then considered with a searching look at the door to the servants' room whether he should look into that room, but contented himself with coughing a few times threateningly and then strode hurriedly out into the yard.

Marie listened tensely for the direction of his steps, believed to discern how the shuffling went to the right, to the barn, lost it, plucked up heart and was soon outside. She kept close to the cover of the giant compost heap to be sure of an exit through the small door out of the yard, and at the same time always looked to the long

row of grated barn windows which had to light up soon
with the weak red of the wandering lantern. The farm
dog rattled his chain in his kennel as she crept around
the corner of the house. She covered the few steps to the
door, whose uncertain outline she could already distinguish in the grey of morning, hastily and without regard
to discovery, because her flight seemed to be a success.
But she was just setting her foot on the large, well-worn
stone and raising her hand to the latch, when the little
door was slowly shoved open by someone who appeared
to have been waiting outside. Marie noticed a strip of
smouldering red light fall into the yard, knew that it was
from Wende's lantern and stepped with quickly beating
heart to the left, close to the wall of the house where she
was partly covered by the door, and left to chance
whether she was discovered or slipped away unseen.
Wende entered slowly, waited to see if the person whose
step he had heard would announce themselves, finally
raised his lantern and shouted into the darkness, "Now,
who is there?" When nothing stirred, he rammed the
door against the wall with a curse for no other reason
than to vent his fury. A smothered sound of pain added
itself to the clatter of the wood. Marie had been met by
the door on her wounded head and had to cry out.

The Lord of the Manor walked around and shone the
light in the frightened maid's face.

"It's you!" he said with friendly astonishment when
he recognised Marie, "you don't need to hide if you
aren't as lazy as the others."

"Oh now sir ..." Marie stuttered.

Then Wende saw that she was wearing her Sunday
clothes.

"When did you get dressed?" he asked slowly.

"Half an hour ago", the maid answered.

"Hm! and why were you hiding from me? And why
have you bound your head so that I hardly recognise

you?" he asked again after a pause, and his voice shook heatedly.

"Because I want to go — no, I must!" replied Marie, who began to her dismay to take the lead.

"To the seamstress or the church, right, is that what you mean by go?"

"No, completely, forever", Marie exclaimed in painful agitation.

"Yes", Wende turned sardonic with a short cough.

"Completely! Must! You don't say! Where in the empire will you go, hey Marie? Do you have enough food and drink with you? Aren't you allowed to complain of the work? Is some fifty talers still too small a wage for you?" "Must," he began anew and laughed sarcastically, "hmhm, we know. Yes, and I thought there that you were steadier than the others. Since when must you then?"

"Sir, I am as ever, but I must. If you don't let me go, I don't know what I ... I would have to drown myself!" Marie answered.

"But Marie, if it's nothing evil ..."

"I can't say a word, I would rather strangle myself", she cut into the middle of his talking. "I ask you for the sake of Mary and Christ, let me go! You will hear everything when I am not here anymore. I'll provide you with another maid. But I must. Oh God, oh God!"

So the girl asked. She had grasped the farmer's right hand and was pressing it because, in her despair, she did not know what she was doing. Wende felt the shaking of her entire body. Before he discharged himself, he grumbled half agitated, half irritated,

"Well, if it just won't work out, then go."

"God bless you!" Marie cried and hurried away.

The next moment, the farmer rued it. "But, what I wanted to say!" he called out.

Only her fleeing steps were already dying away down the street.

"Oh, then go. Women! Each one has their devil!" he called after her, took the lantern up and continued on his way. Suddenly he laughed out loud and shook with delight like a wet poodle, "She doesn't have her references with her!"

The red of morning was not there anymore. A deathly pale light, a frosted shine lay unmoving over the forests and in it swam the dying sickle of the moon. Shrouds of mist were knitted around the snow bestrewn bushes, grey swathes swayed lazily around the forest edges, and the mountains themselves looked like giant clouds which seemed to flow down noiselessly from heaven. No wings flapped yet, no animal's foot yet crunched over the first covering of snow. In the distance, the Kronerloch stream was humming and, deep in the forest, a yawning creaking sounded like that created by two trunks rubbing against each other.

Marie paused in her hurried walk and looked around fearfully. Movement had come to the high clouds with the morning wind.

"Why doesn't she go over the mountains instead", she pondered the fate of her mistress while she imagined Wende's furiously pale face with his rampant, brown beard.

"But it all comes to that, if we do what we shouldn't."

This thought quickened her steps even more. Almost running she crested the hill and dropped into the depression, the noise of the water quickly died behind her, bushes scurried past, and the lighter it became, the quicker her feet stirred.

"What we shouldn't do!" she whipped herself.

She hurries through villages, past lonely farmsteads; people encounter her; she springs over ditches; steps cautiously over stones; the railway drones in the distance: she sees everything and recognises nothing. Suddenly she comes across a flatbed wagon. The waggoner, who is scraping something off the back wheel, calls cheerfully, "Watch it!" She then comes to and notices that she is already in the outlying parts of Glatz with their long rows of small, dirty little houses. She hastily lets her skirts down again and crosses to the other side of the street. She stops at a shop window to arrange her cloth which has been displaced. With astonishment she observes her face which, red and glowing, shows none of her inner torment. The wound is hardly to be seen, it is a small red scab on the front, almost at the edge of her hair. Her right temple is swollen and bloodshot. She shifts the cloth further from her brow and brushes the hair on her temples over the blue bulging bruise. That way she at least does not look entirely like a "bush woman".

In a cellar restaurant, she drinks a cup of coffee and eats two bread rolls. After that she stays seated for a while in order to rest and kills time watching the legs striding past above her. The clock has already struck a few times, and the old woman behind the counter is observing Marie with more and more irritated looks because she makes no arrangements at all to pay or order something more. Finally she cannot keep herself anymore, lays down the knitted stocking so that the needles clatter, purses her toothless mouth and approaches the table at which Marie is sitting, with a washcloth to screen her intent.

"Would you like anything else?" she asks sharply and passes the damp cloth over the tabletop.

Marie says no, pays the twenty pfennigs demanded and asks after a good hiring woman. The old woman replies mockingly that the good hiring women live on the moon, here there are only vermin, she knows, for she served forty years with "princes and counts". It was best to contact the heads of families directly yourself, but if she wants to be referred to one it would be the Negwers in Schmiedegasse. They are "good, dependable and upright."

"But if you don't listen, they'll certainly belt you for it!"

With these words, she finished her unartful discussion.

When Marie is halfway up the stairs, the old woman calls after her,

"Say too, the Masingers give their best regards, then she will be set with you."

After repeated queries and going astray, Marie finally finds the Schmiedegasse. It is a steep, narrow lane leading to the Neiße river. Turbid water is running hurriedly down between the cobbles of the pavement. It is so dark that Marie can only decipher with difficulty the little nameplates next to the front doors. By a long wall with a weather beaten little tiled roof, she finally read: Malwine Negwer, Servant Hiring. Next to it is a half-derelict door niche. But nobody lives here, she thinks, presses doubtfully on the door handle, which looks like a long iron worm, and the next moment is standing in a dull little yard. A man, who she takes for a footman because of his blue apron, is chopping wood. When Marie presses the door shut behind her, the hasp squeals and the woodchopper walks around, examines her for a moment with his young, serious face, but immediately lays down the wood and axe and hastily approaches Marie while he replies to her greeting with a happy smile, affirms her question of whether this is really the hiring woman Negwer's place, and volunteers to be her guide. When they are standing before the sought-after door, he tells the girl she is very beautiful, presses her hand excitedly and runs off hastily as if he has stolen something. Marie stands a while in a trembling current, and it seems to her as if a light is streaming from her forehead into the night around her. Agitated, she steps into the room. After she has crept through a third of the room, she arrives at two doors lying opposite each other. She would have gone past them, if a heated argument between two women's voices behind the left-hand door had not excited her attention. It sounded as if the hissing was the battling of a small handsaw with the blaring of a child's trumpet. Marie thought, you are alone, brace yourself with both hands against the doorposts and bend your body forward listening. The small handsaw in there hissed furiously, "Nobody needs to wallow in muck at my place!", at which the child's trumpet only answered with a mocking whinny. Then a double-voiced laugh from the window scares Marie to her bones and turns her around. In a niche, two girls are sitting and thrusting their heads out. They laugh in her face, which is quite pale with shame.

Marie has the certainty after a few short moments of observing the two that they are gypsies, that is, belonging to that large family of servants who are found in chronic unemployment because of immorality or contentiousness and comprise a nuisance to hiring women all year round. She swallows a hard observation and contents herself with throwing them a deeply contemptuous look, which one of the girls replies to with a mischievous, cheeky face while she asks Marie if she would lend her a pfennig. At the same time, she shifts her stylish hat and puckers her withered face proudly. The other grimaces. Marie turns her back on them while she leans on a cupboard on the other wall.

Sorrow and fear are coming heavier over her again and their assemblage is making room for the old painful brooding.

"Why did I come here, where nothing will be if such things are here? Run away, I should desert everything. You can always buy clothes again."

So ponders Marie. It does not irritate her at all when one of the girls says to annoy her,

"Do you like blond hair? I can't stand it, it makes you dumb. Especially the quite light shade which village tramps have."

After a pause, the pair do not take any notice of Marie anymore and immerse themselves in their interrupted conversation.

A woman steps from the door on the left and sends a testing look up and down the room. Then she says to herself,

"Three. But still. I would not have thought it."

She replies to Marie's greeting with a kind smile,

"Now, my little treasure," she then says, "you have never been at my place. Look, you still have fresh healthy cheeks. That's right! No, no! And a good sturdy skirt. A wool mix, no?"

She says all that with her metallic trumpet-voice, more to win time for scrutinising the new arrival than to say something. After that she shouts to the pair in the window niche,

"I told you yesterday that there's nothing now." And before she turns back again, she reassures Marie, "Wait, little treasure. It'll work out." Then she closes the door.

Both the other servants ready themselves to go with curses on her life, and when the one with the stylish, big hat — the very type of an opportunist house servant — strides past Marie, she says in loud fury, "Watch out for Schleider. He's a sod, I tell you. You will have me on your conscience. There you'll have to whether you want to or not. Haha, I learnt it well! Right, Minna!" They disappear with noisy joviality.

Abhorrence, fury and fear are robbing Marie of calm deliberation. As though in a whirl, she begins to pin up her skirts and slowly creep out the door. When she wants to pass the next to last cupboard, the door opens and Mrs Negwer calls after her.

Marie quickly lets her skirts down and follows the hiring woman with the resolve to listen well. On a gesture, she took a seat next to the door.

Opposite her sits a lady dressed in the latest fashion. Her long silk-lined coat is open and letting her overly large bust protrude. She has a fat, red face and a hooked nose whose sides she is often dabbing carefully with a white handkerchief. When she is called, she begins the examination with her hissing, lifeless voice. Many questions. Whether she can clean up rooms. No. That will pass. How old she is. What her father was. She must show her references. After a long search to no avail, Marie had to declare that she has forgotten them, is dismayed and yet full of inner joy.

Both women exchange a meaningful look.

"Forgotten, hmhm!" Mrs Schleider hisses scornfully.

Now, she is hired in the hope the references will be found. The wages are ninety marks and ten marks at Christmas. But if there are many travellers at her hotel then the maids receive double. Here is the hire fee.

Mrs Schleider holds a one taler piece out. Marie finally declares she is not going into a hotel. In addition, she desires one hundred and twenty marks for wages, and she sticks to that despite all attempts at persuasion. Irate, the hotelier makes off.

The hiring woman returns to her chair and as the outer door slams, she breaks out into a cheerful laughter.

She is a quite well preserved fifty year old with pitch-black, parted hair on which a little mobcap sits. Her face is yellow and she has the large, lively eyes of a frisky cat.

"No, no, little treasure", with these words, she turns back from the window, where she was picking thoughtlessly at the leaves of the pot plants, to Marie, who sits motionless on the chair, rigid as if she has to keep herself upright because of many blows to the head. "You are too good for the work here. — — But the references, the references, that we must have!" she reminds in a motherly goodness after a pause and sits down opposite her on Mrs Schleider's chair. With pursed lips, she waits for an answer. Marie just looks silently and helplessly at her.

"Have you fallen, hey?" she finally begins to ask. The girl looks at her astounded. "Fallen to the floor of course, or down the stairs, I mean like that, hey?" Marie is getting hot. She nods hesitantly.

"You got a shove in the side, right, my little treasure! He must have been damned angry. You have a bump there like a hen's egg and a scratched bruise", she continues talking because she receives no answer, makes a pause after each sentence, purses her lips and rolls her cheerful cat's eyes. "I can't think what it was for. How pretty you are. That would be it. Isn't it?"

"Now talk then for heaven's sake, girl! You are not the first and will not be the last that it happens to", Mrs Negwer appeals to her and watches with anxiety Marie's face twisting in torment. "Jesus, little treasure, what is with you then? Just talk ..."

Suddenly Marie springs up deathly pale, looks around madly and then springs silently at the hiring woman. Mrs Negwer fled in good time behind the table. Marie sprung at the chair blindly. When she sees it empty, the paroxysm drains away from her. The agonising fury in her face makes way for an expression of deathly sorrow. She steadies herself against the wall and staggers out.

The Buried God

On the dark stairs, she again meets a man who holds her by the arm, lights her face with a matchstick and closes in on her. She strikes out at him, springs down the steps, sees the young woodchopper in the yard, throws herself at his chest, tears herself away again and rushes away. Men's voices close in on her; long rows of houses are running past her; the countryside is around her; water is running in front of her, in fear she kneels down and prays, wringing her hands at heaven; the forest is swishing, lights and shadows skim over her; she seems mottled like a cat.

Then she collapses. She has the sensation of having been tossed by a storm against a sky-high wall. Her inner being is trembling like a summer field over which the sun is cooking. In this flickering, she lies until evening. Then she awakes, sits up and looks around astonished. She is in the Hahn forest, deep amidst tall timber. Her dress is spattered all over with muck, the cloth is lost, her hair is loose and hanging mazily around her head.

As she recognises all this, she must grasp at the dry berry leaves with both hands to not fall over, then she braids her hair, as slowly as if there is no need for it to come to an end, and when she is finished, she begins anew and tears run slowly over her careworn face.

With the approaching dusk, she sets off on the way home. The Lord of the Manor's estate is already like a giant, sleeping night cloud when she reaches the house. On the threshold of the house, her mistress is standing, seeming to have expected her, and takes her warmly by the hand and leads her like her own child past the maids who by small lanterns are stirring the steaming beverage for the cows in large wooden buckets.

The living room into which they enter is empty and is poorly lit by a table lamp on a corner table.

"Sit here, silly girl!" Mrs Wende says and shoves Marie into a chair at the table. "My husband is not yet back from the market. I will speak with you again then."

"Mrs!" Marie cries, stirred by the kindhearted sympathy of her mistress. Her entire despair lies in this word which shakes with her sorrow.

"No, no! Crying is good, but you can do that alone up in your room. Now explain everything. When the tongue waggles, the heart catches its breath again."

Marie is baffled as to how it is possible to speak about these terrible things, but the more she talks, the deeper she gets into a form of intoxication, and she pours everything out.

"What should I do, Mrs!" Exhausted, she finishes her account of the wild day. "Wherever I look, pitfall after pitfall. And if nothing changes, I must go and drown myself. The matter is killing me. Whether I do it or not."

Mrs Wende's long thin face is grave, her eyes are full of tears. The slanting light of the lamp is illuminating her high bony forehead, long pointed nose and hefty chin with red strips. When she now brushes the corner of her mouth thoughtfully with her index finger and thumb, her composed hand with its knotted veins is shaking.

"Yes, yes, my girl", she then begins with a lowered nod of her head. "Everyone has a day on which they break. Especially us women. Nothing helps. We do it all ourselves, that which we don't want. How, nobody really knows. But suddenly it's there, standing outside the door and pounding so that we're terrified. If you don't go out and fetch it in to yourself, it climbs on your house and pushes the roof in. Death! Yes, death! Nobody knows whether we'll come through everything, whether we'll split in two or destroy ourselves for ever."

Her face is pallid, distorted unrecognisably. With a violent jerk, she springs up and steps to the commode, where she picks up and puts down an object. When she returns to the table, her step is certain again and her face is smiling quietly as ever.

"Marie", she says with painful voice and presses her hand, "don't take any notice of anything that I have said. You are young. But an old person is like an old pot. Whatever you pour in, everything ends up sour. No, no. I know well, because you are prettier, that you want to advance yourself. Don't talk now! But with pretty faces it is like fine days. The warmer it is, the sooner it rains. Nobody can cover their house with the sky, and red cheeks won't fill you up. You have neither a father nor a mother. You should be happy to find such a place to stay. Exner has his farm and money as well. That he doesn't throw his money around like the others is no disgrace. And his foot! Isn't he in other respects as he must be? Everybody has one flaw, you too. That one! Whoever he wants in Steindorf, he'll get. No, he wants you. I have made enquiries. Everybody in the village knows it."

"Everyone?" Marie asks terrified in-between.

"Well, after the past evening in the tavern certainly."

"But I didn't."

"Well! Go now and eat your fill and sleep. Go and consider all that I've said, and keep in mind one thing: no one recognises their own fortune. Good night! In spring you'll be the young wife in her own house, in her own fields, and then we will be neighbours." —

Marie pressed the good woman's hand heartily and sought out her room without eating. Soon she was standing undressed before her bed, godforsaken as that morning, and the entire storm of sorrow and despair had been of no use at all. With heavy hand, she tidied the rumpled pillows a little and lay down astounded that her eyes remained dry and her soul at peace. After a while, she sat up and grasped about. But wherever her hands groped, there were only boards. With dull stoicism, she accepted the illusion of lying in a box as certainty, and sinking down again, she thought of Mrs Wende's words as a rationale for these facts: "Everyone has a day on which they break."

After that everything that her mistress had spoken of went to her heart. And the thoughts went in and out of the raked-over bleak chambers of her soul like shadows in a cold, colourless light. Where yesterday her multi-coloured, fervent, foolish yearning had still bloomed, this grey, silent play was now dancing. Suddenly, between sleeping and waking, she started and asked into the faltering night, "Where is the sun shining?" A dull sound ran down the rafters.

Sighing, she sank down and went to sleep.

7

While Marie had been martyred by the hope of meeting her death, the clod was moving with the air of a man who has furthered some good business satisfactorily and is now dealing in comfortable ease with nothing but minor matters in order to await its conclusion in certain leisure.

Later than usual, but still so early that he saw the morning mist disappearing from the snow covered treetops, he rose in his small garret. In the room below, he met his sister who was placing the cleaned dishes from breakfast into the cupboard. She let her arms fall with his surly greeting and turned to him her large, flat face with its many freckles around the nose and its surrounding of overflowing red curly hair.

"Well, well, Karl," she then said with a semblance of mockery in her voice, "the tavern's beer makes for a heavy head", and she surveyed him with her grey, quiet eyes.

The clod sat down behind the table, emitted an angry sound and looked out the window at the yard where his brother was just then harnessing the oxen to the capstan of the threshing machine.

His sister, meanwhile, was placing the coffeepot and bread and butter on the table for him. When he turned around, she ran her hands across her apron as though she was drying off wet fingers.

"How was it all with the music yesterday?" she then asked timidly.

"Kath!" the clod answered and, at the same time, wanted to say she should worry about something else. But instead he added in response, "Apes."

"Well, but you were there too?"

"Jesus, yes! And if you know everything then you don't need to put on gloves first! I rammed it home to Laps from Tannerau, and the others opened wide their mouths, and the cobbler was drunk. Now you know and now you can go back to your work."

With a thrusting movement of his hand, he seized the bread and was not looking at her anymore. Kath walked through the room a few times, set a chair right, wound up the "Victor", the wooden wall clock, wiped the windowsill with her bare hand and, after she thought she had convinced the hard man that she had calmed down from his rudeness, she stepped into the hallway and waved secretly to her other brother.

"Joseph," she said quietly to him when he had walked over to her with slow orderly steps, "it's all just as the seamstress Mögler told me."

The beardless man just shook his head unbelievingly.

"Well, he rebuked me when I tried to get more out of him."

"No, no, I believe it. Trust him. But now we'll be on everyone's lips."

Then they wordlessly looked out into the yard for a while and talked over business matters, words which needed no thought, and in the silence of their souls, they suffered under the collapse of their hope that the lame one would remain unmarried.

"But didn't he talk about the rest of it with the Silesian maid from the Lord of the Manor's estate?" Joseph asked, returning from this silent agitation to the exchange of words.

"Well just the reason for it", his sister answered, still more depressed about something.

After some contemplation, however, her brother's face became still again and as bright as ever. "Let it be as it will be. To be is to be. That doesn't actually concern us. But I'll talk to him, and straightaway."

Before Kath could respond with more, he was inside with the lame one.

The latter received him with a roaring, prolonged laugh.

"It's going well for you", Joseph said and sat down next to him on the bench.

"So that the bench bends", the lame one replied mockingly.

"Well yes, yes! There's water in the well."

"Indeed. And if I had known everything, then I could have spared myself Freiwald. You know of course how to find a well", he laughed at the same time so that crumbs of bread fell from his full mouth.

"What do you mean, find a well?"

"You and Kath. Well, she has let it out!"

Joseph looked at him questioningly.

"The cat that you have in the sack, I mean", the lame one finished in mad cheerfulness. "But it appears to me, she never hops when you tweak her secretly by the tail. The mouse is too big. It's best you let her in completely." With that he lowered his head.

"Do I care about your Rollinger hanger-on?" he asked after a while, flaring up scornfully.

"I just think," Joseph replied bashfully, stricken on his raw spot, "if she should stick with me, everything will sort itself out one fine day."

"Rubbish!" the clod continued belittling him, "a fine day. Haha! The fine day! Seven years it's taken, hasn't it?"

It was true, Joseph has suffered as long in that sneaking love which is a characteristic of farmers. Every disgruntlement drove him behind the redoubts for months, but he never stopped hoping in the depths of his heart.

"See, it's such a funny thing", he finally replied with shy mastery.

"Am I not understanding?" the lame one asked, irritated over this tone.

Joseph pondered a little and then answered smiling, "Understanding. Oh, of course. But it doesn't matter. See, Karl, it's best we cut the grain when it's ripe. With your Silesian, every stem is still green."

"Take care of your hen's milk so that she doesn't sour it."

With these words, the lame one stood up from the table and walked into the middle of the room. Then he shook his head silently and jogged to the door.

"I'll drink from my pot," and with these words which he spoke in rising fury, he turned back suddenly, "and the flies which fall in, I'll eat. I don't need any skulkers. And when I leave the little yard here, it won't be ramshackle like your moneybag."

Joseph sprang up and stood face to face with him, forthright and serious. "Karl, nobody wants anything from you, not Kath and not me. Aren't we brothers? That you are harsh, isn't your fault. But people to you are good for nothing, and when you especially go and do things like last evening in the tavern then ..."

"Every bird picks its berries," the lame one cut his words of advice off in the middle, "one the red, the other the black. Leave me in peace!"

With that he went outside.

In deep agitation, Joseph set about his work. Kath joined him at the door to the house. He recognised from her face that she had heard everything and he said consolingly, "He gets it from father." With that he grasped her hand and they looked each other in the eyes silently.

They did not let go either when they headed across the yard to the barn.

The lame one was suspicious like all solitary men, and as he now walked along the gently sunken footpath from Fuchsloch to the village, his thoughts worked on the events with his brother and sister for a long time until they had assumed the nastiest forms. His soul was digging grey and passionately. The idea of having to go through the village lane, past people who laughingly watched him, became so unbearable to him that he walked across the dry meadow to the forest.

The treetops were breathing long and heavy, and their dull lament ran down the trunks so that the dimness became even denser.

The clod liked this air. He picked out a mossy stone which offered a comfortable seat and lapsed into brooding.

Until his leaving, his younger brother, who had presumed the patrimony, had to be given board and free residence, for which the three thousand marks, which were left behind in the will to the clod and were registered on the paternal estate, were interest free. In hard times, he had to help out on the farm, which yielded a pitiful living because everyone was disadvantaged in favour of the clod.

The lame one resorted to him sullenly in the hay or grain harvest, but incessantly belittled him over his "lethargy", as he called his brother's steady easy working method which stuck out so much from his wild, passionate industry which bore more of the mark of a furious struggle. "He has already in four years swallowed six hundred marks for the bread crusts that I eat and the rest of the milk," he pondered, "six hundred marks, thirty times twenty marks!" and he angrily kicked his boot into the moss. "Now he wants most of all my money and my farm and what I have sorely saved, all so he can continue lazing around in leisure."

This thought about his savings seemingly imperiled by his brother's sneaking avarice brought such an agitation over him that he had to spring up and walk about to get his breath.

By arduous, heavy forest work, he had acquired five hundred marks which he stored in a stocking under his bed's straw mattress. With fervent heart, he remembered his treasure, and from the golden glow of the double crowns, he wove his future, the large farmstead, the endless expanses of wheat and the row of fat, motley cattle.

The forest became lighter. After a few steps, he stood out in the sloping field over which the cautious winter light was lying like a milk-white shroud. "And in spring I'll marry her. Then you'll open your eyes, you ...!" he thought and looked with defiant eyes into the tired beauty.

With that he was again in the festive mood of his early years, and he advanced steadily and seriously with a lusty jog on a byway to the village. After he had entered his farm again and looked cheerfully in the well, he commissioned a little well house from Freiwald, painted a nice green, octagonal with red roof battens and a similarly coloured ball crowning the little roof.

"Indeed, indeed, it must be nice," Freiwald smiled artfully, "when will it be toasted then?" He meant the wedding.

"Perhaps before the starlings are calling before their nests, I think", the clod answered, ducked his head and walked to the small door into the cottage's narrow hall. The old man followed him.

"But have you considered everything well, Karl?" he asked before the lame one could open the front door. The latter looked at him furiously instead of answering.

"You have wooed with blood," Freiwald continued steadfastly, "and that can devour you all together if you don't have soft hands.

For blood is like fire. As long as it is in the body ..."

With a curse, the clod stepped out the door and walked away without farewell.

Freiwald watched him thoughtfully. His face had the mild seriousness of pure age when he turned back into his little room with bent head.

8

The deadly lightning bolts tend to fall from a blue sky, and often a cloud, alone drawing aloft, harmless and peaceful, turns so dark that a gentle twilight comes over our little rooms; often this silent cloud breaks forth, the storm springs up with the ferocity of a lion which had been sleeping in the glow, and in a few moments, the terrible cast transforms a strip of blooming land into a wasteland.

No green for far and wide. Like giant shovels, the storms dig the crumbs away down to the dead stone; the paths blur; the uprooted trees lie around lashed, and seldom does a bird visit this stricken place than it soon veers away from it with a timid cry. And the people hardly find the place where just before their crops were waving their ripeness to them. Their hopes are torn up like their houses. Where their hearts formerly tolled lustily, they now carry the dull pain of an incurable wound.

Such a quick storm had ravaged Marie's soul, and nothing remained from the entire world of her blossoming hopes than a turbid feeling.

She exerted herself in vain during the following days to overlook her situation. She got no further than a heavy sorrow and, when a power remaining in a corner of her soul still wanted to rear up passionately and call for resistance, she always sank back into melancholy in recalling her flight. Not once did the thought occur to her to ask after the true meaning of all her experiences, rather she just felt publicly insulted, slandered, desecrated, dishonoured. She walked about in grief.

The Lord of the Manor saw her shattered state and put it to her to go if she wanted. "Where would I go?" she said wearily, "my brothers and sisters are all in service, and my uncle! — — — What would I say as a reason for coming? No, no, sir, I see it is just going in a way that I'll come out ..."

In order to go easy on her, she was separated from the other servants and assigned to solitary work in the old extract house. There she shovelled the heaped up grain about in the dilapidated rooms. The deep humming of the threshing machine in the yard came muffled through the closed windows.

Here it was so quiet that life was draining away from every corner. Deserted spiders' nests hung in every corner, fluttering, bestrewn memories of a forgotten life. Her shovel stirred without rest in the grain, the heaps became no smaller.

So it fared to her thinking.

In the end, she came to the conviction that God sent her this test and decided as a practising catholic to go on Sunday for the Holy Sacrament and to pray for enlightenment after communion. She knew that the eternal often spoke directly to the pure human soul during this holy moment.

Like the water flowing into the weir, quieter than usual, so lustily that the hesitance under the surface is hardly noticed, she went towards the day of decision. Nobody knew of her intention. Nobody saw her leaving on the Sunday morning.

It was still quite dark, a wet chill, everything filled by a thick fog whose raw dampness soon dotted faces and hands with little droplets. Only by the echo of her steps did she notice the nearness of houses which all still lay in darkness.

When she turned around once, she saw behind her in the distance at eye-level a pale strip in the night which lapsed from time to time as though it was the breath of a trotting horse in the light of a hidden lantern.

She kept to the ditch where she saw the trunks of the trees by the main road seeming to drop down like ropes from above. But no clip-clop, no horse's wheeze rang out in the fog squirming soundlessly from the cold earth. When she turned around again, she saw in that place from which she had expected the approach of a companion a pale glow in the air like the white wall of a distant house.

Now she knew it was the light of the sinking moon and as she walked, she continued thinking about the sins she had to confess. —

It was quite dark in the church. A cold musty air filled the narrow nave which looked like a spacious cavern in the darkness. People were sitting here and there praying, sunken down before their little wax lights, and when the breath from their mouths skimmed through the red circle of haze like pale smoke, you could have thought they were weary fugitives and were huddling before the fires whose tiny flames they were endeavouring to fan in order to warm their hands lying there as though frozen. Sometimes they coughed subdued, and their eyes stood motionless like globes in the brilliance of the small flames.

The altar still lay completely dark, the eternal light glowed dully through the lamp's red glass.

Marie was becoming sleepy and heavy. She sank numbly onto a pew and buried her face in her hands. When someone coughed loudly, she stood up and walked as though called to the sacristy where the confessionals were. At the threshold she was met by the padre who was holding carefully a little candle stump whose light he was protecting with his hand. She stepped to the side and he raised his placid old face to her astonished. With a thrusting motion of his free hand, he pointed to the next confessional and whispered,

"The pastor is coming shortly!"

Then he carried his tall shape with slow dignified steps into the darkness of the church.

Marie hardly paid any attention to the two altar boys throwing white surplices over themselves behind the open double doors of a cabinet. She stepped before the grating of the confessional and began praying zealously from her book. While she was reading word after word so devotedly — of the baseness of human nature, its impotence and lust for vice — and touching her crucifix, it seemed to her as though the lines were a monotone draught numbing her soul with empty echoes. Her inner being was darkening.

But she had to pray devotedly to obtain from God a happy turnaround in her need.

She closed the book as if to rescue herself from the dull might of those pages, looked sadly at the floor and endeavoured to bring together her prayer of confession. "I, poor, sinful person ..." she murmured without break and got no further.

In the nave of the church, soft, long steps could be heard. The old farmer who performed the role of padre for the glory of God made a sign to her with his ice-grey, large eyebrows and then looked timidly through the door of the sacristy.

Like a seething jet of water, fear flowed into Marie's body. He is coming, she thought, and stuttering she wrestled with the prayer.

The steps paused before the altar.

Immediately afterwards Pastor Langer appeared hurriedly and unexpectedly in the candlelight of the sacristy and paused offhandedly next to the old man who should have been considering his holy vestments.

The old farmer raised his hand over his ear, carefully stroked the white hair which had curled into the form of a spiral there, and whispered, 'there is still someone there.' Without answering, Langer grasped his upper arm brusquely to indicate to the old man that now was not the time for it.

"You should, Pastor, it's actually a maid, from Steindorf it seems to me. You would probably want to", the padre said softly.

The Buried God

"So!" the pastor answered and turned around to her. He recognised her beauty and thought, 'Aha, one of those again.' Then he adjusted his stole.

Marie knelt before the grating and turned her face to the priest.

After Langer had been sitting there a while with his head lowered to his chest as though praying, he straightened up and described the sign of the cross to Marie with a murmur.

"I, poor, sinful person ..." the terrified girl began, and because she could not say the prayer entirely, she blew the air through her nose whispering in the rhythm of the words which had escaped her.

When she came to an end and wanted to begin with the confession of her sins, for which she took a deep breath, Langer exhorted her with pointed meekness, "Speak louder!"

Marie felt the suspicion in this demand, and trembling she began the confession of her guilt. The further she went with it, the more compellingly she felt that the pastor must believe she was hiding something difficult from him if she only confessed the usual evil. She also recalled that no one knows the state of their own soul. It seemed to her suddenly as though she had perhaps committed all the sins of which she had read in a book of sins.

After a short hesitation during which Langer had touched her lightly with a hard look, she confessed every human weakness which her memory could fasten on as her own defect, in order to deserve the pity of the priest and the grace of God.

She finally paused exhausted and looked beseechingly at the pastor who was quite pale with fury and looking at her from the side.

"Hmhm", he then uttered. "Are those all the sins?"

Marie nodded.

Langer straightened up as if he was stifled and swallowed violently. "The sixth commandment!" he then said with convulsive smoothness.

Marie recognised the contempt in his face and thought, 'It is all lost, I must drown myself.'

"The sixth commandment. What is the sixth commandment?" Langer asked again shaking. "Thou shalt not commit adultery", he finally answered and said it into her pale face like an accusation. "How old is he? — You will not have forgotten yourself so far as to seduce a child?! Answer! How often have you wantonly got together?"

But he received no answer. Marie had lowered her head, and the breath from her mouth was only moving the blond hairs which streamed through the grating. It was as though a radiance was running out from her innocent head.

"The devil has pulled you by your hair into the murky pool of lust", he continued. "Now he is hardening your heart with the shame you gave so easily to him."

Marie raised her face and stared in his face for a while.

"Pastor," she then whispered, "I am unhappy. That is all. The rest isn't true."

Her breath stroked his cheek like the bubbling of seething water.

"Are you that ruined?" he finally said coldly, because he believed she had confessed guilt. "How long have you been carrying the seeds of sin? I mean, how long have you been feeling it!?"

Marie's face had sunk down to her chest. Her hair trembled with the beating of her heart. When in immoderate agitation, he directed both these questions at her, he heard something fall and, at the same time, he saw her hands grasping spasmodically at the grating.

But he knew these "whores" and did not let himself be deceived by play acting anymore. He now spoke to Marie in the certainty which he was accustomed to use with the fallen. He forgot that he was sitting in the confessional.

The padre was hustling the ministrants into the church. Soon Langer's voice was filling the sacristy. He spat, called her a harlot, augured for her a cursed life, a tormented eternity and finally threw the absolution at her contemptuously like a crumb. She was hanging as though in a faint with her hands on the grating of the confessional and did not stir either when the pastor went out with loud steps into the church for the mass. Only with the echo of the opening chimes did she give a twitch.

The padre, according to his habit, had accompanied Langer to the door of the sacristy.

Then he turned back and looked for Marie. She was now kneeling there in upright rigidity and looking fixedly into the empty confessional.

He coughed a few times to move her to leave the sacristy.

Marie began to feel the grating with both hands.

Full of sympathy, he went to her and said full of love, "Girl! Hey, girl!"

She turned her face to him and remained in the kneeling position as though she did not understand him.

"Get up and go in now! Listen, the organ is starting", he said more urgently.

Then Marie raised herself, leant against the wall and stared haggardly at the old man.

"But, he did not absolve me?" she asked unmoving.

"Oh indeed. He just always does that. It'll be okay, there is still a Lord and He doesn't take it so neatly perhaps. Come, girl, come!" Trembling he grasped his spiral of hair and handed up to her the prayerbook from the floor.

Like going up a mountain, Marie walked into the church to her place. The sounds of the organ were roaring around her ears like a clamour, the heads of the pews were disappearing more and more below her, now they were only reaching up to her knee. With hurried grasp, she caught one and happily came falling into her seat.

The praying people in front of her turned around and looked at her disapprovingly. Marie had no sensation of it. A dead shell lay around her heart, and everything outside her was far away, entirely unimportant. The singing swelled and died, the clergymen and the ministrants turned back and forth mask-like in the candle-light to the sound of a bell before the altar, the red points of light before the praying people seemed to leap up and down the pews, and when the cantor was singing down from the choir, then all the light disappeared, and it became a night of human sound around her as she noticed everything with the indifference of a condemned man and continually thought, "The pastor! the pastor!", threateningly and accusingly.

At the sound of the bell, many of the believers rose carefully from their pews and strolled to the communion table. Marie, still doubting whether she had received absolution, nevertheless stood up too, grasped the prayer book with her right hand like a stone ready to be cast, and in the consciousness of her purity, she decided to wrest from the priest the body of the Lord with violence if it could not be done any other way. Collectedly, with mouth clenched shut, she walked to the table of the Lord and inclined her head over the white linen, clutching the prayer book convulsively with her hands. The clergyman approached her slowly from the right.

The Buried God

"Corpus domini nostri Jesu Christi custodiat animam tuam in vitam aeternam, Amen", he murmured and laid the host in the mouth of the communicants who inclined their heads deeply to the table immediately after receipt of the mystery.

Her heart was pounding to bursting.

"Lord God, take pity on me!" she prayed without break.

Now Langer was with her.

She stretched her head up unnaturally far and stretched her tongue out demandingly.

Her eyes smouldered in rigid brilliance. Her face was sharp and demanding like that of someone hungry. The clergyman muffled his voice as though watering down the blessing of the words and handed her the host.

Marie immediately closed her mouth over the holy fare. She hardly bowed. Her teeth clenched, without breathing, she hurried back to her place and buried her face in her hands.

The host stuck in her throat, it seemed to swell and the stronger she swallowed the more her throat narrowed.

Marie recalled the sins which, choking on the body of the Lord, were met as though felled down by an invisible stroke.

"Dear, dear Lord Jesus", she prayed and finally shoved the host down in despair with her finger.

After a few moments, warmth streamed into her body. Her soul began to shimmer, the blood flowed into her veins like beading light, her heart sang. Her eyes closed, her cheeks glowing in ecstasy, she lay there and enjoyed the miracle of God's becoming man in her body.

The organ had been silent for a long time. The church had emptied. Only in a hidden corner was a little, old woman crouching and spelling the words out quietly from her prayer book.

To Marie it seemed as though gently caressing, long vestments were passing far, far over her, and although she kept her eyes covered, she saw everything.

The saints stepped from their frames and strolled through the aisles, their long locks lifting with every step.

Suddenly it was quite, quite still. A spell came over the bodies of the saints in the aisles, and everyone stood staring. Every pale forehead turned upwards listening. And from far away, from infinite regions, a murmuring came and it became clearer and clearer.

The Lord was approaching. — —

She heard his voice as though it was carried on fluctuating winds. It was old and half decayed by the millennia.

"Go and follow him", it spoke over her.

She was paralysed by these words. A roaring developed by her ears and lost itself in the heights. — —

When she finally dared to raise her face, the grey light of morning lay in the vaults of the church. It was empty and dull as ever. Nothing betrayed to her that the Lord had been through this space.

Saint John was writing eagerly in his book and smiling while a black bird was rolling its eyes at his feet. One saint had folded his hands over his torso and was making a sad face as though something was ailing him there; another was ardently seeking somebody in the distance and pursing his lips as though whistling.

Disconsolately she struggled a while in prayer against their unsaintly eyes and then made her way home saddened.

In the afternoon, as God commanded her, she said yes to the clod.

9

Marie had become milder since she had promised herself to the lame one.

Her struggle against fate had been short, more like a foolish act of violence, senseless, inconceivable. Just as abruptly, she had provoked the decision which she had been denying God.

Now He had given her the peace of defeat. Her heart lay in her without will like an enchained slave and bore the change with unmoving resignation. She saw her changed life like a ghostly shape in the air around her. Every morning she climbed into it as though into an apparition. Taciturn as usual, she carried out her work. Only her industry was either weary or passionate as a delirium, and it would suddenly come to an end in a sort of torpor from which she could only tear herself irascibly with the greatest effort.

Once the maid working with her noticed it and said, "Marie, if you look at your husband like that then it will seem to him, I think, that his crown has fallen off."

"Husband?" she asked razor-sharp, "hm, husband … you, you …"

She swallowed a swearword, and her eyes flickered in fury. But she soon added smiling wearily,

"Oh, you mean it so? Now no, Exner is quite a good one. What do you think of me then! Otherwise I wouldn't have taken him."

At the same time, she paled and promptly bent down to her work. Although she bore her fate heavily, she had the frugality of a strong nature to conceal the greatest unhappiness from herself, to repulse her pride and every confidant, and to think of the relationship with the lame one not as a consequence of precipitate, brutal chance, but as a choice of free understanding.

It became especially difficult for her because of the cobbler, whom she now came across strangely often. He seemed to be doing especially good business that autumn, for sometimes he was walking by on the paths with the sole leather rolled up in a colourful hand-kerchief, other times with a pair of wreaked boots, he always caught sight of her red headscarf in the fields, shouted her a jovial greeting from a distance, then sauntered by to sit down in the furrows and chat with her. He helped her lift the scythed grass onto her shoulder or wrested the barrow from her.

Although she left him in no doubt that it was not agreeable to her, he forced his help on her again and again and restlessly talked to her. He liked most of all to speak about the Cecilia ball, how he danced with her there so that everyone on the benches had risen, how he had annoyed the grey suit to death and she had only him to thank that the clod had had the courage. He called the latter his "dearest, only friend" and told with satisfaction traits of his foolishness, his harshness and his ridiculous suspicion that the other girls were becoming "quite senseless with laughter".

But then he filled himself with indignation over "the geese" who could not believe he wanted to make fun of him, "for there wasn't a fellow like him in all the Grafschaft". He saw Marie suffering and laughed wanly and painfully with a joy that had something sneering to it. His eyes smouldered and when he offered her his hand in farewell, it was wilted, cold and trembling. She became anxious every time she saw the cobbler, but despite the anguish which it caused her when he fondly exposed the clod to ridicule, she experienced with the obscured grumbles against Exner a sort of satisfaction, a secret revenge at her fate.

The cobbler probably felt this instinctively, and his "mischievous trick" became more and more open, his visits more often, his smiles drunken and, often without reason, he took her by the arms and squeezed her passionately.

Finally Marie recognised where it was all leading and shoved him away.

"You're intoxicated, Guste!" she coldly said one day between his jokes.

"I haven't sniffed one for a week. Not even schnaps!" he answered in consternation to her unmovingly bitter face.

"No, no, I didn't mean that. Where would you get schnaps from. The mending of old shoes is hardly enough for dry bread. No, I heard that if a cobbler wants to get drunk then he smells the paste pot. That takes away his understanding for fourteen days and is cheap."

She was pale and looking Klose up and down scornfully.

"Do you want to scoff at me because I'm poor?" he asked sadly and sprang up out of the furrow.

"Indeed, that's what I want!" she replied even more cuttingly. "Sitting around in every furrow with patched trousers!"

With this exclamation, she turned to the maids who had stood up from their work.

"Marie!!!" the cobbler cried in the meanwhile, and tears rolled down his cheeks. When he sensed that he was crying, he bent over deeply and scratched at random on his trousers. As he rose again and, pressing the bundle tighter under his arm, prepared to go, his chest looked pushed in, his cheeks were hollow and pale. Suddenly he turned around, shook his fist at Marie for a while and made efforts to speak. For a long time, nothing but a breath broke forth from his lips. Finally he said mutely, faltering, quite softly, "I am an unlucky man!"

But his face looked like he was screaming with all his strength.

The maids laughed their heads off.

Marie called, "Jump to it, cobbler, meeh, meeh!" as he quickly fled to the path.

Because the pitiable man's words had struck her like a stab in the breast, she straightaway screamed after him in wild scorn. But she soon lapsed into silence, the absurd jokes of the maids over Klose became repugnant to her, she worked by herself inconspicuously to the side and fell into low spirits which she did not understand.

That same night, she awoke and suddenly heard the cobbler's clenched voice talking through the dark silence. Full of incomprehensible sorrow, she began reluctantly to cry.

From the following morning onwards, she had the intention of consoling the offended one, and did not shake it off for a long time. But even though she looked about inconspicuously, and asked this and that person after him, he seemed to have disappeared. Nobody was wanting to meet him. She only learnt that the light in his cottage was burning all night till morning again, and the entire time, he was walking up and down, from wall to wall, and suddenly laughing out loud. She became more and more discontented and listened for every little thing.

Even towards Wende, she was feeling a secret hostility, for in walking past, he taunted her with the lame one, because of the paleness of her face, or as future farmer's wife, and she always believed she noticed on his paper-white, morbid face a sneering aspect. Once she could not stop herself and gave him a pointed answer. Thereupon she looked at the estate owner for a while astonished, and then he slowly offered the opinion that Marie had turned pale. But he was not his father and knew to keep his hands for the fields. He alluded to the willy-nilly sale of that part of his estate which comprised Exner's concern.

Another time he said jokingly that she will feed herself in the future on the lice from his body, and implied how uncomfortable to him the lame one's presence in the middle of his estate was.

Wende found no peace in his marriage which was the consequence of a false step. For that reason, he took revenge on his fate through grumbling and the friction which he passionately enjoyed seeking and, where possible, developed into lawsuits.

Marie did not demand from the lame one any clarification over the Lord of the Manor's ambiguous words, but rather kept it to herself. For her last resort before the clod was the secrecy of her inner being. But although she lived so emotionally apart from him and wanted to live even further, she could not prevent a displacement in her breast, by virtue of which she equated his welfare and her own. Also on these grounds, she did not speak to her fiance about Wende's needling.

And every time, when the instinct of female wisdom had led her into it, it seemed to her as if she was tying herself to him with a new band. The ghost of this unnatural relationship sucked more and more blood from her body and became day by day tangible reality as if a lustful mushroom was growing rampantly from the deep crack in her injured being.

Then the impassioned intractability did not help her at all in the rare meetings with the lame one. She pestered him with crassness, needling and derision and waited with shaking desire for an outbreak of his ferocity. She was provoking him to the blow from which she expected with concealed hope a deliverance. But this untoward man's eyeballs barely rolled with the words of her bitter harshness, a smile hardly arose around his lips, he only looked at her from the side, paused a while in speaking and then led the conversation on again with a casual, "Well, yes, yes!"

Thus she became mad at him, and there were moments in which she mistook the lame one, against the opinions of all people, for a strong and quiet man whom only the blameless mutilation had made into an eccentric. He had certainly given a show of his beastly ferocity at the Cecilia ball, but that had only happened for her sake.

These friendly thoughts, however, always lapsed quite quickly and sufficed at most for a kind answer. But every time she felt as a result that her heart was becoming clear to the lame one and his soul was seeking to hustle into her life in clumsy tenderness.

One day, it was in the shed where she was sitting on a stump and cutting up beets which she let fall into the chaff basket in front of her, Mrs Wende walked across the yard to her, pulled her blue apron up with both ends and nodded to her kindly.

"I will see now whether the chickens have never forgotten to lay", she said and smiled her peculiar smile, whereby her lean face collapsed into dancing wrinkles and her long nose and large chin protruded even more and shoved against each other.

Marie hurriedly fetched the small ladder, leant it against the hen house and grasped a side of the ladder for safety's sake. Then she looked at her mistress as though to say, 'Now you don't have to worry.'

Mrs Wende shed her coat and placed her right foot on the first rung while she thanked her affectionately, "You are a good girl!"

Suddenly Marie dropped her hands slackly over her hips and said with a sorrowful voice,

"Mrs Wende, I'm suffocating!"

Then her mistress drew her raised foot back again and turned around laughing.

"Well now, bride fever! Where would you be, if you didn't cry before your great day!"

"Mrs Wende, how could you suffer me? I know that I have been grumpy, for a long time. But have I annoyed you?"

"But silly thing! Not at all!"

"I don't know how I have deserved it, that great day! ..."

"You are still young and foolish."

"Young and foolish, old and wise! — if the thought of wisdom already makes me so miserable then I just wonder why every white head isn't crazy."

"Girl, you are besotted with your sorrow."

"That could well be, because my sorrow is my life."

"Stop it!"

"Mrs Wende, how I like to listen. But say something lively, not like the others who just stir their tongues."

"My dear child, a pure happiness is seldom like a white cow. And always think of this: the Lord God deceives even a rogue less often than brothers deceive each other. And your soul is like your Sunday best."

"Yes, with brothers, but a stranger!" countered Marie, who had not grasped the meaning of the strangely ornate wisdom of her mistress.

"A stranger? Is Exner a stranger to you? Marie, then I just say to you, go and take your word back from him in person. Now there is still time before it's too late. And what that is, too late, my sweet Marie, that I can also say, God save you from that terrible thing."

Mrs Wende paused, and her breath was quick and short like that of children walking through the darkness.

When she began to speak again, her voice sounded dry, exhausted. "Certainly with what has been promised, it's such a thing. It is with him like with the hens who sit on the highest perch. If they want to go further then they can just go into the nest or they must climb down a rung. Do as you will, if you pray well you will lie well. But let go of the attitude. My dear, fate measures us on the body. What surpasses us, just makes us disaffected, but it doesn't help."

Then she climbed up the ladder and disappeared stooping into the hen house. Marie lifted the basket onto her back and carried it into the house.

For a long time, days and nights and yet more days and nights, her soul foundered in Mrs Wende's wisdom. It first became grey around her, full of fog, and if the experienced mistress's voice did not sound so real in her memory then Marie would just have to believe that it had all become an incomprehensible dream. It stood around her confused and yet an intangible certainty.

It seemed as though her old soul was slowly falling asleep, and disappearing with it was the old hope, the burning thoughts of a lordly life, of abundance and riches on a broad estate next to a smug farmer. But strangely, when these sweet voices were no longer sounding around her, she did not become smitten by a tormenting pain. She was barely shaken. She felt like she was saved, as nothing was standing behind her anymore and whipping what was lost into such un-deserving corners like in the recent past. The bitterness slowly fell from her. A white, gentle light came from her eyes, the soberness of her contemplation did infinite good to her distorted ardour.

She saw all the people exerting themselves, all stooping under burdens, in hardship and torment or in good living and sorrow. Her mistress with her shattered life was assiduous, laughed, bore children and loved them, carried a heavy lot and did not die. And when she went out, the tall, lean shape with the pale, wrinkled face and the quiet, soft eyes whose slow seriousness contrasted so strangely with the spryness of her entire disposition, then Marie often had the feeling that this woman was standing in an invisible light, and the possibility of a deep blessing with missing life came to her for the first time. This idea of an inexorably countervailing power behind the piecemeal nature of all existence fed back into her recognition that God had made her life his business.

She then lay an entire night in an agonised passion, she had strange visions, and when she awoke in the morning, she was smiling in calm fulfilment.

She gave herself to her work without worries. Certainly a fear was climbing in her, of what would happen if her faith was not fulfilled. But she recalled God's great love and might and put the doubt down as the needless torment of her concluded struggle. With constant step and steady eyes, she went and "followed him". Nevertheless she carried her great loneliness with God locked in her heart, a heart which she also did not open to the lame one after her deep change.

She was now walking more calmly next to him when they met and was taking all his words seriously and affectionately. And he looked at her from the side astonished, then answered her with a quiet smile.

Although this change pleased him, he felt a dullness towards her. Through the harshness, she had been more comprehensible, closer to his violent nature. Her patient mildness made her incomprehensible to him.

But when she looked at him, his rough soul was encouraged. For this girl, withdrawn into herself, paler and more delicate than usual, enticed words from his mouth against his will with her deep, still eyes, words he had never confessed to anyone but his own most secret hour. Her uncommon beauty tore him away from the mass of his intentions so that he shamelessly took apart the foundations of his violent plans before her eyes.

He always intended not to speak, always he succumbed, and he never enjoyed the certainty of being forthcoming when he had spoken again of his future, for he never succeeded in igniting the glow in her eyes which was filling his soul. A bitter smile, a lost staring into the distance, a tolerant sound was all the lame one longed for to betray her broken state to him.

But one time, the clod's lust for power became unbearable to her.

"Karl, what do you want?" she asked cuttingly, "is it everything?"

"What do I want?" he replied in passionate rawness. "Certainly everything! I want to have everything. Eight must be threshing on my barn floor; a farm like the Lord of the Manor; cows, row upon row; horses like planks; I will for you ... Everything is still out now, but it shall be in for me, you can count on me."

"You think so! Who will do everything then, hey?"

"I will, who else would do it?"

They talked over this together at the beginning of December on a Sunday afternoon while they were walking back and forth on a solitary cart track by the forest of the Rollenberg. It was bleak and damp, without snow. A pale mist was climbing out of distant river valleys and floating into the heights. Now and then, far in the distance, the Schneegebirge appeared, just like being breathed into a milk-white light, as if it was dawning over the shore of that dismal land in which, according to catholic belief, poor souls must wait for their blessing.

Marie looked out with eyes like a man drawing hieroglyphs in the sand with a stick, hieroglyphs that nobody can interpret, barely even his own captive life.

"Do you see the church tower over there?" she asked as though in a dream.

"No!" he answered with deliberate lack of grace.

"... and Bardorf there and Wirrwitz with the white castle and Leschkowitz with its church and parish ... do you know Leschkowitz?"

"Oh Marie," he answered after looking for a long time, "leave it! — Yes, you see that? — Don't laugh, it is nothing but clouds."

"And yet everything is there, the great farmers' Bardorf and masters' Wirrwitz and Leschkowitz together with the nice parish. Do you understand? — I have fed on all that and recreated it in me. *Because of that* it is in me, but like a dream which never was, never was — because — it was. Don't talk to me about that ever again, Karl, don't talk to me about it like just now and so often before! We will buy two cows and pigs, an ox too for my sake and keep what we have. That is all. No, no!"

She moved her head as though she was shaking something off for good. Despite her weary words, her face bore an expression of confident superiority. She was walking more upright than usual and for a long time did not pay attention to the clod jogging next to her with smouldering soul, looking at her covertly from time to time and always bitterly telling himself, "Excellent prize, just wait!"

Finally the girl turned her eyes to him and saw that he had a pale, weathered face like a washed out stone. They had turned around on their walk and Steindorf lay below her in its flat depression and was blowing pale threads of smoke from little chimneys into the empty branches of the fruit trees.

"Yes, is that there Fuchsloch?" Marie asked to break the painful silence and pointed to the right. The clod nodded silently. "But don't we ever see the yard?"

"Because the hill is in front of it and the trees", he finally replied dully.

"I would think," Marie said after some thought, "it were time that I got to know your brother and sister."

"Yes...ah!"

The clod tore his head around and looked at her astonished.

"Joseph and Kath — both of them? ... hmhm —"

"Is something not right there?" Marie asked, knowing nothing of the enmity between the siblings.

"No, no!" he replied with mocking laughter, "after I heard you say that, it's certainly time for that too ... now ..."

Suddenly the lame one began to run so that the stones flew under his clubfoot. He waited at a fork in the path for her.

His face was tense and shook from restrained twitching.

"Well," she asked, approaching, "what was that about?"

He looked for a while over the crest into emptiness. The expression on his face was painful. "Marie," he asked stuttering, "... see ... you don't know at all what they, ... when I ..." Then his words faltered.

With vigorous breaths, he waited a while and ran off again unexpectedly, on a deeply descending path between high walls then across the dry meadow, and Marie followed him slowly and calmly. At the small hill which separated Fuchsloch from Steindorf, at the crossroads of the line-thin steep path, he stopped again, and when the girl was standing before him, he said with arduous self-control after struggling for a few breaths, "Here we are now! See Marie, that is the way to the village and here goes up to them both. There I am and there I am not! — Now do as you want."

Without answering she stepped past him to the small homestead. Speechless with astonishment, the clod looked at her for a moment. Then he cried, "Marie!" It sounded like the call of a stag during the roar which a stronger stag has knocked back.

The girl turned around and said with self-control, "Now I've had enough of this dawdling. What is it all about then?! Now come or I'll go home at once and then ..." Without hesitation, as though gagged, the clumsy man followed her.

Joseph and Kath received Marie with the indifference in which farming people are accustomed to clothing their uncertainty. The simple friendliness and natural prudence of their future sister-in-law quickly transformed the cautious attitude of both the good people into open trust.

They walked around the buildings, stepped through the yard, surveyed the state of the animals and threw a glance into the filled barn. Everywhere Marie noticed lusty hands working in happy industry, order and neatness, and did not hold back with judicious praise. Lastly they sat around the table with coffee and chatted as though Marie had never been a stranger.

The clod was monosyllabic and irritated. In his eyes, a darkness lay lurking, and now and again, the line of a sneer disfigured his pale face.

When the hour was approaching nine, Marie rose to go home. The lame one followed her with the taciturnity of a suspicious guard.

At the yard gate, Kath threw her arms around the girl's neck, kissed her and said bashfully, "Marie, don't resent me, I am such an angry thing sometimes. I think, I thought you were proud because you are so beautiful. But now I see how people lie. No, I don't know how I could thank God for it."

The pair parted in fondness, and Marie walked in an unhurried air, her soul lying in the light.

Suddenly the clod, whose unequal steps had always been behind her, grasped her by the arm and tore her around. "Now say if you are happy with me!" he said in impotent ferocity with his entire body trembling. His bulky body was quite close to her. For the first time since the misfortune in his childhood which had maimed his body and his life, his subjugated heart opened and cried out for love, for tenderness and amicable coexistence. "Sweet Marie, sweet Marie", he stammered without knowing what he said.

The girl stood awhile as though numbed by the yearning of his soul. Then she said in cold sorrow, "You know that we have been forged to one another."

With that she pushed his cold hand from her arm and hurried off with a curt farewell.

The lame one stood for a long time like a stone still on the same spot. When, reaching the crest of the hill, she turned around, she saw him striding towards the forest.

Shortly before the beginning of Lent, the aloof couple entered into marriage with each other. It was a soundless wedding.

Apart from Joseph and Kath, only a few relatives took part in the depressed celebration. The cobbler stayed away. Marie sat in her black silk dress behind the table, quiet as ever. The lame one ate as though nothing should be left over.

"Nice weather on our wedding day," he said to her between his tireless chewing, "isn't it, Marie! The sun is shining, even the path, no snow, the air still, hey?"

Then she had to collect all her strength not to break out into loud weeping.

PART TWO

10

The storm poured from the sky. Exulting, it plunged down and shook the March snow from the fir trees. The trees staggered as though drunk with joy, flapped their branches as though they were green wings and sang a roaring song with their needles.

Marie stood in the living room of her new home and listened to the joyful unruliness of early spring. The nearby forest thundered, shadows and light ran over the white sand of the floor. She watched the silent play at her feet for a while, then she smiled, walked to the window and gazed up at the sky.

"Oh yes, now it's getting serious," she pondered, "I thought as much. It was humming and going on in the deep forest already the day before yesterday. — Now, it's time too. I am getting quite impatient."

And yet she could feel comfortable in her four walls. The large, brown tiled stove was mumbling cosy warmth into the room. The new clock with the red roses for hands was ticking clearly on the white wall. The pearls of irretrievable moments were falling ringing through the dreamlike silence.

A pale wooden bench whose age could be seen in its yellow colour ran around the walls of the room. Stools of the same age whose stiff legs were wedged steeply into their thick wooden seats stood around the large dining table whose scrubbed white surface took up an entire corner. The day peered in curiously through four windows, two per wall, as though there was something special to see in the room. Between the windows on the wall opposite the door, three wooden, crudely carved little deer's heads were mounted. From their ears and their jagged antlers, dwarf pumpkins hung strung on twine. Fir brushwood thrust out all around. Colourful pictures on card of the imperial couple and of the Pope completed the decorations. The corner shelf above the table was not missed out.

A blue and red painted Virgin Mary held her red heart before her breast and was always staring at the oven. Two angels knelt by her side and raised their red hands in humble prayer to the blessed, behind whose back was folded a yellow paper halo. A tiny hanging lamp made of red glass hung with its flickering little light on a cord from the little shelf. The wooden ceiling was painted blackish-brown. It hung over this room dismally, threatening, like a coffin which assiduous female hands had prepared for a pious, quiet life. The goldfinch in the middle of the room gave only broken off, wistful calls and fluttered against the wire walls of its cage, towards the light that danced up and down outside, now obscured, now prevailing.

On the right-hand wall, in the corner by the bulky oven, a door the size of a moderately large wardrobe stood half-open so that Marie, who went to it to close it, could with a light bend of her upper body look over the tiny little corner with the two high beds under hole-like windows. But while she was looking in, her face was not prettified by the sweet tenderness which usually over-comes every woman on surveying her bedroom unnotic-ed — with a hasty jerk, she closed the door in the meagre, poorly lit corner. The clod had allotted this narrow cabin to rest as if sleep were a bothersome evil which you must treat unkindly so that it does not settle down.

After that she walked around in the living room and wiped her blue apron over every piece carefully, seriously and proudly, more to touch it than to remove the dust. Everything which stood around her, she had bought with her own money, and up in the summer room, "the stage" as the Grafschaft residents say, there was just a table and chairs with bowed legs, a glass cupboard and a clothes' locker with turned top.

Certainly, in the furniture lay the entire eight hundred marks which had remained as her inheritance from the collapse of her father's prosperity. But with complacency, she had spent everything to lead her husband clearly to understand that it would have been easy for her to get someone other than him.

With satisfaction she thought of the loaded up, colourfully beribboned bride's cart load with the butter churn on top which the Lord of the Manor's horses had carefully pulled over the uneven road.

Of everything else which lay further behind her, she did not permit herself to recollect, otherwise it all burst into flood: what she had embedded deep down in herself and which she had sent to sleep for evermore.

The wooden cover of the water pot by the oven rattled.

She started and, astonished, found herself sitting at the table.

She ran hurriedly to the well, fetched water and filled the water pot to the brim.

While she was doing that, a dull droning sounded from the stalls.

"Haha, the cow knows better when it's midday", she said with a glance at the clock, which showed quarter past eleven, "wait, trouble, old one, I'm coming."

Nimbly, she took the beets from the open oven and prepared the feed.

Then she left the room to go to the stalls.

Around one o'clock, she was finished with that. The milk stood emptied in the cellar, the mangers had been filled with fresh hay, and from the stalls rang the gentle rhythmic clinking of chains, which gave the farmer's wife the certainty that the cattle were lying there and ruminating.

Marie sat down and ate her lunch: peeled potatoes, coffee, bread and butter. The washing up and other domestic activities filled out the afternoon.

She had just lit the lamps when her husband stepped into the room.

"Good evening, Marie!" He threw axe, cords and saw in the corner. Then he took his jacket off and shook it so that the drops sprayed around the room.

"Is it raining?" Marie asked.

"Go outside and you'll see. I am almost wet through. It's really soaking!" he answered amidst groans of comfort, stood up on his toes and hung his work jacket on the oven flue. Then he sat down at the table and propped his head in his hands.

"What are the cows doing, are they eating well; is the mottled one milking better?" he asked and directed his face to Marie, who was busy at the oven. Then he stood up clumsily, lit a lantern and went to the stalls.

After a long time, he returned and said radiantly, "They could be dearer, but they are standing there, slick as snails, lively around the horns, like fish to touch. And the pigs, they're as slippery as weasels!" He sounded devoted.

Clear pleasure was still shimmering in his voice when he spoke after dinner, "The forest going isn't nice, believe me."

The Buried God

"Why don't you stay home? You don't need to go", his wife replied.

"But, it brings in extra money from Bohemia. And what would I actually do here, except sitting around on benches and chairs! It brings in twenty marks a week though, if I work myself hard. — It stops in sowing season when I have so much work I don't know where I am. How then were the oats at the Lord of the Manor's place last year?"

Marie thought of her former employer's threatening words, of his contentiousness, and in the attempt to combat the provisioning of the possibility of a maladjustment between him and her husband, she answered eagerly, "Good as gold to start with and like the best grains at harvest time. Absolutely, you won't find anything wrong there. That's a farmer like you find in books."

At that the lame one sprang up and hobbled about the room. Then he stopped and laughed mockingly at her, "That's simply a man like every other is."

"No!"

"Not a hair different from me and the rest. It just goes in the front and out the back, that is. Would he leave a sackful for me then?" he asked after a long silence.

"You'll just have to ask", Marie replied a little testily. After they had been sitting silently next to each other for half an hour, the lame one nodded and they went to bed.

The next morning, before daybreak, he stumbled over the threshold again, the coarse linen bread bag at his side, his work gear over his shoulder, the knobbly stick in his hand.

The same cycle of her days had begun — work, work, work. Thinking of it; serving it with all her strength; speaking of it; from the living room to the stalls; from the well to the house; fetching from the lower field;

sweeping and beating; never sitting, never resting, chasing after dust, worrying about trifles; never seeing past the wall: a narrow, hurried, dreary dance so that her dreams disappeared, her soul foundered, her heart became numb, her eyes only saw what they saw, her ears became dulled to the sounds of things. The sun came up: it did not shine on her — the day expired and was forgotten.

It was happening as she had demanded.

She was falling asleep in the rapture of toil.

And while she was resting, the earth had awoken, awoken to the dream of millennia, to spring. With tepid, gentle rain, it had washed the dirty cracks of snow from its face; moistened its breast with rejuvenating dew until one morning, its beauty was entirely fulfilled. Then the swirl of larks broke away from the reeking furrows to the heavens. A joyfully wondering song jiggled from the young greenery of the trees and led its daughters, the little rivulets, into the valley. They scurried over the stones with pinned-up aprons of foam and sang their eternal wandering song, so devoted, so restrained from deep chests that awoke snowdrops, and primroses and snowflakes watched the hurrying water with sweet faces.

But the first butterflies were swimming in the sunlight so that their colourful wings made the air even stiller.

The lame one and Marie were standing in front of the house one evening in the mild wind and letting their eyes ramble over the fields in order to discuss their cultivation. It was a long, narrow strip, two hundred steps wide and a thousand long, some eight hectares, gently sloping as with all of Steindorf's fields, which lay on hillsides sinking to the small flats in the south-east at whose beginning the scattered houses of Petzdorf were situated.

The Buried God

The lower long and the northern narrow side of the stretched rectangle were bordered by the Lord of the Manor's forest, the other sides were hemmed by a wall of irregular field stones thrown on top of each other — the path lead to a hole in it. The farm buildings stood by the wall on the long western side such that arrivals had it to the left-hand side, and if they were curious, they could creep through the door in front of its entrance comfortably between the stone wall and the back wall of the house to the small bedroom window to peep inside.

The property had previously been scrub which the late Lord of the Manor had sold to Exner's father when pressed for money, on the condition, as the current Wende maintained, that would still make it possible one day to reverse the trade completely. But in truth, the old Wende had only secured for himself and his descendants the right of preemption.

"Jesus Maria, how it looked twenty years ago," the clod began, resting his eyes with pleasure on the green winter grain, "up there we can still see a pair of stones on the meadow by the forest. Like that but worse, it all looked. Rocks like they'd been sown, and here and there a menhir, big as a furnace. In-between lay tufts of grass, small as gobs of spit. No, that wasn't easy work! But we had to work at it, father bestowed hardly anything. In the stones lies sweat and many years' work, and today — there is a wall left too. After, but it was worthwhile. It's a good little field, a little small. Takes the manure which you bring to it well. Just the lower part where I want to sow pasture is a little too flat though and I don't know if I wouldn't be better to dig it up again soon!"

"The ploughing will show it", Marie said.

The next morning, the cultivation of the field began. Manure was carted in and spread, then the plough drew deep furrows into the ground which reeked in the sunlight and spread the scent of fertility and bounty everywhere.

Larks lay high in the air on chiming wings, and behind the blinking plough team, crows were striding with dignity. From the nearby forest, it was singing as though every one of the innumerable needles had become a little trilling beak. In all the expanse, whipping cracks, loud mating calls and joyful singing could be heard.

"It's teeming everywhere, pitchforks are glittering and ploughs sparkling, it's as if they've been harnessed all the way to the Eschberg", Marie said as she followed her husband and raked the manure into the fresh furrows.

"Well, it's high time, it's Florian's Day in eight days", her husband replied morosely, because he could not bear the "dawdling" with the work. He turned the cows, tilted the plough and stepped back carefully again.

The last harrowed strip was soon done, the field "like a carrot", and the sowing of oats began. They were nice, heavy oats, and the clod praised himself for having the agricultural skill of the Lord of the Manor whose father had been just a nail maker. With constant gait, he strode across the field and the seeds flew like pale sunshine from his hand. He had no idea of the deep beauty of his work, but rather thought in ever new ways of a rich harvest and lots of money.

He tilled the other fields with summer grains and potatoes. The clover had come through winter beautifully, the beets were soaking in the barrel. He set about the ploughing the lower part at great leisure ... But, although he had set the plough shallow, he received a rough jolt every instant. After a few steps, the ploughshare always hit rocks again. The cows began to get skittish because of the continual stopping and got ready a few times to bolt: the cows raised their tails, hunched, laid their ears back and roared whinnying.

The lame one had a rest and took them into the barn. Meanwhile Marie was digging up the small garden next to the house with a spade, dividing it carefully into beets and planting them with mignonettes, marjoram, pansies, stock and thyme.

The lame one set in a small strip between the stonewall and the back wall of the house a row of plum and cherry trees.

On each side of the gap to which the path lead, he planted a poplar.

"No, hey, you can spare the poplars", Marie chided and then raised her head towards the village path on which a man and a boy were hauling something behind them. She watched raptly, although she had no interest at all in the affair, because she hoped to soften the effect of that rebuke on her husband by this conspicuous curiosity.

She did not really appear to have calculated wrongly, for the clod laid his iron shovel down and looked up too.

"Can you see who it is?" he asked after peering hard.

"I don't know, they are pulling something on a little wagon. Now the man is going behind and pushing, something heavy ..." Marie answered.

"A coffin perhaps, Franz Tone up the mountain has just died."

"Died? What sort of talk is that! He hung himself, you should know that. He has perished, not died. — No, it can't be that." Marie turned her eyes towards it anew. "They are going to Erlengrund, and the man pushing walks crooked."

"It's all the same", the clod concluded and bent down to his shovel again while Marie went to walk into the house.

"Wait a moment!" he called roughly, straightened up and stuck the shovel into the loose earth. "What was that you said about the poplars before?"

"I meant it wouldn't be necessary", Marie answered with an appeasing smile.

"Yes! Ha, because the Lord of the Manor has them? Just because of that, I'm having them!"

"You know how funny it is when he doesn't take offense either."

"A tree is a tree, where they stand, grow and the rest, the Lord of the Manor didn't decide for me!"

"But, Karl, for my sake ..."

Only the calm words were like oil on the smouldering agitation of her husband, already with the first drops it erupted abruptly. "Karl nothing", he shouted furiously. "What the nail maker's boy can do, I can do even better! Always the Lord of the Manor this and the Lord of the Manor that! Am I a clock then, that he can just wind up?"

Marie made no answer, took a tub which was leaning against the house and disappeared around the corner. The clod said a bit more behind her back and then zealously trod a rain hollow around the young saplings.

Meanwhile the creaking of the light wagon was sounding clearer and clearer. The lame one straightened up. The travellers were already coming jolting down the path: a schoolboy was clumsily pulling the drawbar, Freiwald was walking behind and holding the boards with which the wagon was loaded.

"Well", the old man said in a greeting swallowed by the noise of the wagon, then waved at the boy looking behind to stop and stretched his hand out to the clod.

The latter grasped it and asked with a glance at the load, "the well house?"

Freiwald nodded and told in a long-winded way why the delivery of the work had been delayed so long, and while, after his thorough manner, he deepened the affair into an instructive examination of the new trend of the time, his grey, sparkling eyes were searching Exner's face. "Nobody wants to wait these days", he finished his meditation and started slowly towards the house. "People are making all the same mistakes now: each thinks he is there because of the work, but the work is there because of us."

The clod looked back at the boy in order to give the conversation a different turn, though he did not know yet how.

The well digger soothed him, "He'll come after us", and then continued, "You'd think now that it's all the same, but ..."

"You've done everything, however, that I asked for", the lame one interrupted him.

Freiwald nodded, "the panels are green, the roof battens and crown are red."

The lame one burrowed around checking under the boards.

"Gently, gently," the well digger reminded, "the colour will suffer otherwise. — Don't we get to see your wife?" he asked unexpectedly and fixed his eyes sharply on Exner.

"She will be in the living room", the clod replied indifferently.

Marie appeared just then at he window and reacted to the old man's friendly greeting with a pale face.

"Now Marie, Exner, is the beautiful, the pure mother of God! Already the hands are reaching up to her."

The lame one laughed with an appearance of disregard.

"Yes, yes, I hear it. You will have to acclimatise to the light first."

"But I still have the hair on my head like the shingles on my roof!" the clod answered, irritated to the calm reproach.

"You're right there," the old man responded, "but our life isn't covered just with shingles or with flat rooves or slate. The only roof for the house is a good, very good heart. — Now I'll go and do my work, when I'm finished, I'll call you."

Exner left the realm of those incorruptible eyes, and Freiwald started work with a serious face. Towards the time of vespers, he was finished. The little well house stood like a tidy young girl at the entrance of the yard which it gave a friendly tint to with its lively green and red.

The old man stepped into the living room and found Marie busy with the preparations for vespers' coffee. He plunged his hand in the votive kettle by the door and sprinkled three drops of the holy water on the floor with the wish, "Much happiness and blessing in the house and stalls."

Then he moistened his hand again and crossed Marie on the forehead, "that you think of the good", on the mouth, "speak the truth" and on the breast. Then the old man was overwhelmed and looked for a long time at the young woman's blond parting without being able to say a word. When Marie raised her eyes to him, he finally spoke down to her mildly, "You women bear your cross before you; so enjoy carrying what you must."

At the same moment, a ray from the sinking sun fell through the window and both stood in the light. "See, Marie, how God laughs", the old man said in that deep kindness which only blooms under white hairs, then sat himself down on the bench and looked out the window, because he did not want to display his emotion to the woman.

They were both still silent when the clod entered and looked from one to the other suspiciously.

"Yes, yes, Karl, a young wife shouldn't be left alone by her husband for a moment, for then the white heads will be like flies to the honey."

With this roguishness, he answered the look of the lame one who just grimaced, sat down at the table, drew a cup to himself and invited the well digger to eat, "Well, help yourself here now."

Freiwald adjusted himself, Marie also came nearer, and the old man chatted about the weather. There will be an unusually dry summer this year, the water is already standing deeper in the wells than in other years, all over you see big hairy caterpillars, and the cuckoo has arrived earlier than usual, the wind blows constantly from Poland and the cattle have lost their winter coats early. Exner was of a different opinion and tried to make it probable by all kinds of signs he'd observed. It will be a wet year rather, because the winter had been mild. The evenings and mornings are unusually cold and then so many night snails are found in the fields. With that he looked out the window. "You painted the boards red!" he roared suddenly.

Freiwald smiled and nodded, "The two on the house, indeed. They are in reflection, and red tolerates the shade better than green. Green flakes off in the dampness to quickly."

Then he thanked them for the hospitality and stood up. "Come and see if it isn't spruce", he said, and when he noticed that Marie was of an air to go with them, he added, "The young wife can stay inside, since if she reproves me, I'll feel very ashamed."

With a warm handshake, he said goodbye to Marie, and the clod hobbled behind him.

Outside they walked around the little well house. Exner tapped the boards, pulled on the little roof, stepped back and gauged it with his eyes. Everything was flawless, no split battens, the little roof sat fast, the whole faultlessly plumb.

"And now come a few steps down the path with me", the old man said, having sent the little wagon along with the boy.

Behind the wall, on the Lord of the Manor's estate, Freiwald stopped, looked around clearly and then directed his eyes in solemn gravity at the lame one,

"Now nobody can hear us but the grass and heaven. So I can say what I should and want to say. The boards on the house I painted red deliberately. Red is fury and malice, bluster and blasphemy, and when it's really bad, blows and blood. And that you kept to yourself and hindered with forbearance when the wagon came onto the grass, because of that, I painted two boards like blood."

"How does my life concern you, Freiwald?" the lame one asked quietly and stepped threateningly towards him.

"See how I'm right", the old man spoke fearlessly and smiled. "Karl, would I smote you with stones if I meant well?"

"Don't talk yourself silly!" With these words, accompanied by a discordant laugh, the clod brought the conversation to an end and turned towards the house without taking leave. The old man took a step to go after him, but with a shake of the head desisted from doing so and hurried away mournfully.

Having entered the living room, the lame one walked back and forth a few times, then he stopped close in front of his wife, "What was Freiwald saying to you before I came in?"

"What Freiwald always talks about, of love and goodness", Marie answered openly.

"He's a fairy tale ape!"

Exner left the room and slammed the door behind him.

The young woman mused the entire evening over why her husband had been so angry. She was too proud to ask him about it and the night closed both their eyes before they had been reconciled.

11

After this difficult day, lighter ones followed again, and the unbalanced shadow between the husband and wife seemed never to have existed.

But it had only sunken into them, plunged down into that fathomless region of the soul where our fate grows.

There it bound itself to the old inhumanity of the clod and animated an unacknowledged distrust towards Marie which touched his words before they left his mouth, mixed his thoughts with suspicion and brought a bitter light into his eyes when they saw the beauty of his wife.

Marie became as though touched by a cold breath, and although she could not impute any guilt to herself, she was discontented with herself anyway.

In these opposing feelings, the last work was undertaken and it was possible for Marie to go to church again the following Sunday.

In heightened mood, as though relieved, she left the house towards five o'clock in the morning. The sun was just then climbing over the forests of the distant Schneegebirge. In the valleys below, white mist still lay, full drops of dew hung from bushes and grass, drowsy birdsong stuttered gently from the forest. Her step flushed the first lark from the young shoots, the modest bird climbed silently into the blue and its muted singing only began high in the blue sky, singing that sank down with the sunlight so that you could think that the golden smouldering sparks in the air had suddenly begun chiming by themselves.

This blessed epiphany of nature seized the heart of the churchgoer as agreeably as if an old, dear friend she had long neglected had met her unexpectedly.

As she was walking across the Lord of the Manor's estate, Mrs Wende was just stepping out the yard gate and she greeted Marie immediately with the loud heartiness peculiar to her. "It's beautiful! A good morning on which to meet a young woman. I need not ask first how it's going, we can see that."

"Now, we must thank God." She suddenly felt apprehensive. Her answer came hesitantly and forced.

"Well now, I know that you would have wanted to marry higher. But right, now you are happy and not ruing it?"

"No certainly not, not at all, it's good, quite, quite good, I thank you, for, if I think right, you're responsible for everything."

Marie spoke loudly, hard and bitter in broken sentences, and her eyes were getting moist.

Mrs Wende bent down down and looked her in the face, "But you're crying!" she said appalled.

"Well now, when I consider everything that I've been through then I can't help it at all, it comes over me."

"I can imagine, but open your eyes wide enough that there is place within for you and your whole life, otherwise the shadows will overwhelm you and such a darkness in us is insatiable."

"... and God's tower", Marie added quietly. For in the distance, the Leschkowitz church steeple had emerged from the mist and its giant finger was threatening at the heart of the young, unfortunate woman.

"That too, indeed", Mrs Wende affirmed.

Then they walked next to each other and separated in the church with grave looks.

During the entire mass, Marie sat with downcast eyes, because she could not bear the colourful finery, the play before the altar.

She was numbed by everything, thrown back into her life which she did not understand. So she covered the stars of her eyes and clustered her stammering thoughts and fervent soul by the incomprehensible shadow of God which had become deeper and livelier to her since his priest had committed such an outrage on her.

As she sat there so, her glance fell by accident on the open prayer book and read the words, "If any man will come after me, let him deny himself, and take up his cross, and follow me."

She realised she had treated her husband wrongly from the beginning of the ill-fated relationship, but especially on that Sunday night when he had begged for her love not far from the farmstead in Fuchsloch.

She undertook to be friendly, to want to get the better of herself for love and to avoid everything which could be unpleasant for him.

Thus the quaking undulation of her heart disappeared and that motionlessness which she called peace filled her.

In order to secure still further this intention blessed by God, she waited until all the congregation had left the church and then walked through the Lord of the Manor's forest to her house. The heath in its bareness was turning green, the blueberry bushes hung full of blackish-red bell blossoms, busy beetles stirred in the young, hair-thin wild grass so that the tiny stems quivered.

She was walking entirely lost in her emotions, without thinking, like someone walking with closed eyes through a fairy tale whose cursed beauty nevertheless penetrates their soul intoxicatingly through a thousand mysterious pores.

Then she spotted hidden under shiny leaves a violet. She bent down quickly and plucked it to adorn herself with. As she straightened up and raised her eyes, she spotted through the trees of the forest her house looking out at her with its morose windows. Then she threw the flower down and set her feet firmly into walking onward.

Under the windows, a stranger was sitting in avid conversation on the wooden bench next to her husband. After looking intently, she recognised him with astonishment as the cobbler Klose.

With pounding heart, she had to stop, then she took a few more steps mechanically and stepped behind a large spruce from which she could observe everything unnoticed. The longer she watched, the more incomprehensible the incident became.

Klose was now sitting motionless, sunk down like only broken men sit. He was still wearing his work suit whose trousers were torn at the knees so that dirty skin was visible. Now he raised his head and looked straight ahead for a long time. His face had the colour of pale yellow leather, and the lids of his empty eyes were reddened. His moustache hung mazily over his pale lips.

Clearly he had encountered a great misfortune, because he had given up his self-willed isolation and come here where he had to meet her who had mocked him so. Finally she emerged and headed for him with a friendly greeting.

The Buried God

He tore his right hand out of his trouser pocket and stretched it out to her while he eluded her glance and bent down to the cat which had run over and was stroking its arched back around its mistress's dress. "Well, Guste, how are things looking for you then?" she asked in a dither.

The cobbler stroked his trembling hand over the soft fur of the cat and said with squeaky voice and without looking up, "pussy, pussy, pussy!"

Suddenly he pulled himself up and answered roughly, "As it looks to me, when I never know where!" Then he looked down silently again at the ground.

After a while, he said, "Whoever cares for their parents these days is an absolute ape!" His tinny voice rang scornfully. "But can I help it? I labour and draw the twine through the old leather into the night, just so that my poor mother doesn't have to die hungry. In the meantime, I forget that I'm actually a man too and become a fool everyone makes fun of. Most likely so! What I must, I should enjoy doing, and has anyone heard me complain?"

He broke off and waited for an answer. Only they both remained silent.

Becoming vehement, he began anew, "But, am I an only child? — isn't Paula — dammit! — I — see because of that I have gotten drunk, fallen about in ditches and slept in the bushes."

With blinks and gnawing lips, he fought himself, then he slammed his fist decisively like a stone and lost all moderation, "Then the woman comes! — Then she comes home on Friday, right on Friday as if the week only had one day in it. — I'm sitting on my stool and striking the last nail in the heel of Klenner's boots, am finishing and longing for the tavern. Suddenly the door opens ... I think, strike me dead. — There stands Paula who is in service in Silesia, there she stands in the doorway, not in and not out, cries and laughs, laughs and cries, plonks down her pack, drops on it, holds her hands over her face and cries for pity ... no, cursing. I knew what it was about straightaway, sprung up, went to her, pulled her up and shouted, 'Who did it!' There was a moment's silence, silence as though the trees were at church. After that she retched and retched ... by such a wild stallion, such a fellow who has no parents himself, who just runs around and brings children into the world as if there aren't enough people, as if who knows how nice it would be here on this earth! And now tell me, is there a God?

I earn only so much that my mother can have a piece of bread, potatoes and coffee, and now she comes home, now, where work is everything, where everyone who has healthy feet runs around barefoot. No money and hunger, misery and not knowing from where ..."

He had spoken the last words quietly to himself in despair. Then he let his head fall and moved his lips silently so that you could only see the trembling of his overhanging moustache.

"Now, Guste, don't you know what you have to do there?" Exner took up the conversation, shaking with agitation, "Have you no courage? But you'll know what such a man deserves!"

With a wild laugh, the cobbler threw his head back, "Karl, not know? me? — Look, my hair just flew. Mother screamed and fell off the bench in fright, and I already had the hammer in my hand, raised my hand and thought: eh, to the devil! ... but then it trod silently behind me, I thought to myself, sat mother on the bench, leant her against the wall, put my cap on and went out. On the threshold, I turned around and shouted, 'Well, wanderer, see how you get by!'"

"You belted her, Guste, and the child? Don't you know that you could already be a murderer?" Marie asked with pale face.

The cobbler sat obdurately and then shook his head as though over a curious thought, "The child — haha, what a joke", he said dully to himself, straightened up and held his open hand before Marie's face, "There, Marie, take the ring!" The young woman looked speechless from the empty hand to his tense face and thought, 'He has gone mad.'

"I'm quite rational, you mustn't fear", he said smiling, turning his hand down as though throwing something away, and then stamped his feet on the floor as though crushing an object. After that he broke out into howling laughter, "If it were true, what you said before about the child, then you would also have to find the crushed ring here. Haha! — But even if it were true. You won't bend down for what's mine. It stinks, that I know, it stinks!"

Pale and sorrowful, he looked for a long time at Marie, who could not withstand his rigid gaze. Finally he awoke from his painful befuddlement and spoke full of sorrow, "And if it is, which isn't, oh my God, I believe it, perhaps my head is all at fault, that is, my entire life just deceives me. Well now ... but if such a hidden thing takes from you everything that you see in front of you, the entire ragged hope and nothing remains to you, just the courage to drink ... no, you won't know how that goes."

After pondering a bit, he turned again to Marie and, as though he had offended her and must now console her, his bitterness rang softly trembling and a glow came into his disconsolate eyes which only radiated for her.

"Now tell me what I should do and I will go home at once, shut my mouth and be how I have always been."

The lame one had been sunk in his thoughts and had obviously not been paying attention to the pair's conversation. Now he turned to Klose and asked, "What are you lacking actually?"

"If you're asking me, Karl, the best is missing."

"Now, Guste, when it comes to that, don't tear yourself down. If you want to work, come to me. I want to clear the lower part, you can help me there. You'll get eight bohemians a day and board. If you want to, here's my hand."

But the cobbler did not grasp Exner's proffered right hand, rather he asked, "Yes, should I stay here, go in and out your house, sit at your table? No, all that, it just won't work!"

He jumped up abruptly. "Adieu! and imagine I wasn't here."

His entire body was shaking and his face was chalk white.

The lame one seized his hand and did not let it go, "Guste, wake up! You're being irrational!"

Klose made despairing efforts to break the lame one's iron grip and stuttered in utter confusion, "Should I lie to you, hoodwink you, betray you! — Let me go, let me, I must run, though forests, over water, always past people and houses until I collapse with the last breath in my lungs ..." Exner had sprung up, had seized him around the body and wrestled with the raving man until he lay powerless in his strong arms.

Breathing heavily he finally let go of the cobbler, "Guste, you have strength I didn't see in you. But be reasonable, I don't want to give you presents. And here you'll have a day's wage in advance so those at home aren't without money."

But Klose did not stir. The lame one stuck the coins in the pocket of his jacket and then turned to his wife,

"And you, Marie, go quick and get him a decent jug of milk, some bread and a quarter of a block of butter!"

Marie hurried into the house and after a few moments, she appeared again and held out everything to him with poignant face.

Klose stood like a crucifix and stared appalled at the beautiful, young woman who requested coaxingly, "Guste, do me the pleasure, take it and don't be angry anymore." Blushing, the cobbler finally reached for the gift, stammered something and went away as though in a dream.

They accompanied him as far as the wall and watched him as he strode up the lonely rise to the village. —

Marie had the feeling that a deep, indescribable sorrow had gone from her with the unfortunate man. The expanse of her soul opened up again radiantly.

He who she had bound herself to like a dismal, inescapable destiny had suddenly become a being to whom she was allowed to open up the chambers of her inner being to, because he had mercifully helped the inconsolable. A happy, solemn mood was overcoming her.

In this hour, she had become his wife in her heart.

They were still standing there between the stone walls, which lay inhospitable and bleak like their joint life up to then, and looking out on the morning.

The light flowed over their foreheads and Exner's large, coarse face shimmered like a rock lying in the sun. Then, blushing, Marie embraced her husband, he bent down to her and she kissed him on the mouth.

Then they strode hand in hand to the house, and Marie gladly gave him the sweetness of her inviolate body.

The clod drank her like the hot summer storm slurps the water.

12

Exner awoke in the grey morning as though shaken awake. The first light was falling over the blond hair of his wife, her head resting on the naked arm pushed under it. Her face was turned towards the living room, in deep sleep and shimmering in the languorous beauty of a fertilised flower.

The clod smiled dismissively at her tiredness, hastily dressed and disappeared quite noisily from the bedroom. Every man rises from the meal of life strengthened and grasps more vigorously the spokes of duty.

For the lame one, it had been the lash of a whip and, impatiently like a thoroughbred rushing to the racetrack, he went to work even before the first cock's crow had sounded.

The sky hung mistily over the earth like a feather bed. The grass and bushes were dewless in the quiet, musty warmth. The cuckoo was calling indistinctly as though someone was talking from a distance through a hollowed hand.

Exner took ill-temperedly to a tour around the fields. Here and there, he bent the shoots apart and looked to see if they had lateral runners. Then he shook his head a few times and gazed over the broad expanse, up and down, but he did not become any happier. Every stalk, fine and translucent, carried motionless the small cluster of morbidly green leaves. The fields lay there like yellowing garments.

Walking further, Exner again and again pushed his foot through the short grass and murmured, "No dew again, again not a drop", and did not raise his head for a long time.

When the sawmill began howling from Erlengrund, he entered the house again. In the living room, Marie was standing before the small mirror and pinning up her heavy plaits. When Exner opened the door morosely, she was just finishing, let her arms fall and went to him joyfully, grasped his sagging hand and said, pressing it, "Well good morning, you runaway!"

Misunderstanding his rigid gaze, she blushed deeply, turned abruptly to the oven and said in passing with tender pouting, "I call and call, while he's walking about who knows where."

He turned his head to her and responded harshly, "Yes, about. Would rather get up with you if you didn't act so cheeky. Your laugh would disappear if you saw the oats!"

"Now, Karl, it can't be that bad!" she answered affectionately.

"There you have your Lord of the Manor! It's rubbish, the oats!" He had sat down on the bench. After a raw laugh, he looked half out the window, saw the bloody boards of the well house, recalled the amicable silence in which he had found his wife and Freiwald and the latter's prophecy over the weather. And as though Marie was at fault for the weather through her being too friendly with the old man, he spoke bitterly, "You're always crawling behind my back, to the Lord of the Manor and to Freiwald. You'll see where it leads."

Then he stood up and walked around the room a few times. Marie attempted to dispel his temper through gentle comforting and pleasantry. She did not succeed. He kept walking back and forth and looking at her from the side. In the end, he said, "Say what you want. I followed you once but no longer, take note!" With that he left the room again.

His wife was still looking at the door when it had already closed behind him a long time before and the towel hanging on it was completely still. Finally the deep gravity of her face gave way to a sunny smile.

"Such a man, my soul, is too funny", she said, shaking her head, and briskly worked the oven.

For she thought he had been hooked by her sweet power. Only, even as the lame one hauled the plough to the field with the cows, his demeanour was still irritated, his eyes narrowed. He looked out impatiently for the cobbler and when the draught animals lapsed into a somewhat livelier gait, he struck them over their noses with the whip handle.

Finally the expected man came. Sorrow and woe still lay clearly on his face, but in his moustache you could discern that the despair was not operating so strongly anymore. It did not sprout so mazily over his lip anymore, but was carefully parted in the middle and turned out.

With a quiet greeting, Klose approached and then also spoke indistinctly as if through clenched teeth.

The clod did not hide his anger at all, even if he gave no explanation for it. The cobbler took no notice of it at all. In silence they both began their labour.

The unfriendly mood did not give way for hours. With the exception of short questions, as well as short directives and abrupt exclamations, nothing was said.

If the plough became stuck in the stones, then it was carefully lifted out, the pieces of rock struck out with the pick and pushed to the side with wooden staves.

The frail cobbler, unused to this work, took his jacket off after a short while and wiped off his sweat. Towards the middle of the morning, he had become so powerless that his pick already descended wonkily and often tipped over.

But Exner became even tidier. When he saw the power he had over the stones, he was not so despondent anymore over the bleak outlook for the harvest, the nasty heat, the Lord of the Manor, Freiwald, and his wife's secret understanding with both. They should just come! The bigger the rocks were which he hewed out, the more cheerful he was, "Yes, a pickaxe isn't a leather needle!" he shouted at his friend once as he toiled in vain to strike out a stone.

Klose would normally have been quick with a fitting answer at hand, but now he just puckered his face into a weary smile and remained silent. He paused often in mid-swing and looked away helplessly. On Exner's shout, he started terrified from his stupefaction and struck anywhere with his pick.

Thus the work went on slowly, and the clod said sullenly, "You have to knuckle down a bit more, Guste, else we won't make any headway!"

"Well yes, yes!" the latter replied and ran his hand through his hair self-consciously. "Courage, courage!" he then murmured to himself in encouragement, and his face took on an infinitely painful expression.

After the end of work on the second day, he asked the lame one for an advance of forty pfennigs.

The next morning he appeared singing at the place of work. From a distance, he ripped his cap from his head and shouted, "Now it can kick off, now I want to dig hard!"

From now on, the work strode forward really quick. The cobbler did not just take a hold dauntlessly, no, passionately, but showed himself inexhaustible in coarse jokes and snappy sayings. The clod was infected by his joviality and even revelled in adding some tones in his shapeless bass as accompaniment to the songs which the cobbler gave his best to sing. When the poor man's humour petered out and the morbid fervour began to drain away from his pale, bony face, then he disappeared behind a hedge of thorns, and after a while, he had become boisterous again.

"Now," he said that evening to the clod as he was chatting with him for a moment in the hallway of the house before leaving, "did I not have courage today?"

"No, today you were like you'd broken free from bonds!"

"That must snatch forty again surely!"

With a laugh, the lame one gave him the money and soon the cobbler was on his way whistling.

It now became the rule that he was paid out each day the same amount for a "gristle", as he called the schnaps in jest. Both made fun of it every time the cobbler hid the schnaps bottle from Marie. But once at lunch, as Klose was telling an anecdote and rose to illustrate it, leaning over the table, he came so close to Marie that she smelt his breath.

"Guste," she interrupted him seriously, "have you been drinking schnaps?"

"Oh no, Marie, it smells of peppermint cake, you know, I have it stuck in my teeth."

The two men exchanged glances and laughed riotously. Marie was obviously soothed by the answer, but kept an eye on the cobbler.

In the afternoon, she saw him go tumbling head over heels. She immediately hurried out and put it to him, "Guste, you're drunk!"

"No, just tipsy. Now, and doesn't every bird drink?" he asked with the gauche sedateness of the drunk.

"Why don't you just give the bottle some peace?" The young woman had come closer and was looking at his neglect with sympathy.

"Put the question away again quick, it's an evil pfennig you're spending there." Klose turned away with a laugh and went to walk away.

"No, stay!" Marie persisted, "hey! — it'll be no different with Paula if you don't sober up!"

The cobbler reversed the few steps he had taken in the meantime towards the barn, and asked, stopping close in front of her, "What do you care really! — Is it never enough, should it be even worse?"

He said that to her in fury. But the hate soon gave way in his eyes to an unapprehending stupor. "Paula, haha, you're quite right there! But that was just the axe; someone has struck quite differently, perhaps not the sower of oats and the like!"

"Guste, if you pull yourself together with all your will however ..."

"What do you know of the words which were warm in your mouth! Now listen, I need strength, I must keep a clear head, that's why I drink. Woe betide the day in which I am sober again! And anyway, there is still lots! lots! When it rains, the drops come from all sides."

Marie was getting ready for a new objection, but the cobbler cut it off in advance, "Don't bother! With me the uppers are worn out before the soles burst. Nails are no use anymore then."

He went into the barn and left her standing. Looking out from the living room, she saw him soon afterwards going past laden with a new stave.

Marie had surely heard the accusation in the alcoholic's ambiguous words. The painful feeling of being jointly responsible for the descent of the poor man became so strong through pure sympathy that she asked the clod without hesitation to deny the cobbler further advances. Her husband listened to her attentively, looked at her intently and left the room without giving any reply. In the evening, he gave his friend the money for drink again right before her eyes. After that she repeated her demand more urgently and declared to him that he was becoming jointly responsible by his obstinacy for Klose going to rack and ruin.

On his side, Exner waited calmly until she had exposed all her reasons. He looked at the floor and changed colour. Then, as if he wanted to set off against her, he tore his head up and looked furiously at her, tempered himself, however, and just replied, "No, you don't decide that! I'm still the man."

Only — was it the effect of Marie's words, was it the consequence of the quiet vigilance of her eyes — after days of the cobbler's desolate, industrious drunkenness, a period of strict sobriety followed in which he seemed transformed: taciturn, irritable, his hands dallying intentionally, he struck the blade of the pick industriously into the stones wrecking it, and spoke bitter words about stinginess and not getting enough when the lame one was indignant about it. When he thought he was unobserved, he looked at his friend full of hate.

He encountered the young woman during these days in abject awe, was thankful for every glance, gratified by every good word.

After four weeks, the field was finally broken in. Dotted with large and small stones, it was like a stone mason's deserted workplace.

The dry heat had lasted the entire time. The summer grains were very weak, the winter rye had withered, was short and fine stemmed, the grass in the meadow "crawled into the ground more and more". The hay harvest had to begin, as the grass was already shedding its seed. While the lame one was scything in the early morning hours, he mused over his fate. A old superstition of the Grafschaft's countryfolk said that the first year of a marriage was decisive for a couple's fortunes. Exner found in it an impartial rationale for his misfortune. Why, when it would have meant nothing, why did this poor harvest fall right in the first year of his marriage?

After this epiphany, he began to deny Marie insight into his plans and designs, in order to prevent the possibility of her unlucky influence. This change in his being expressed itself more and more brusquely. It was not a change at all actually. The process portrayed itself as the necessary movement of a feather which, brought out of its place by some external pressure, immediately springs back into it when the influence of this opposing force drops off.

As though after a long, unnecessary digression, he gradually arrived back in the lonely track of his earlier life again. The appearance of mildness and sweet temper melted away from him and he unhurriedly burrowed into the turbid impulsive cloud of his past. In direct connection with that stood a closer alignment to the cobbler.

He finished the harvest as sullenly as he had started it. The three cart loads of dried grass barely filled a third of the hayloft. That's why he made himself busy with Klose in the clearing of the lower piece to at least still grow fodder and thus cover the shortfall a bit. Exner broke up the large stones with an iron hammer, and the cobbler took them in a box cart across a long board to the wall and dumped them out on arriving. On the other side of the clearing's wall, a narrow strip of meadow belonging to the Lord of the Manor stretched out by a field of rye. The lame one did not suffer the stones being dumped on his side, because he would have lost a few feet of field otherwise. Likewise, he did not allow his friend to empty the cart on the back of the stone wall.

"Should it damn me completely? Dump it on the other side!"

"No, the Lord of the Manor won't stand it!" Klose answered, having one of his dry, recusant periods again.

"The Lord of the Manor! What is it with you all and the Lord of the Manor! It's as if he was God. Is there a boundary stone over there?"

"No, but the wall is here."

"Show me the boundary stone!" the clod shouted enraged, threw his hammer down and climbed over to the wall with long strides. "I want to see the boundary stone!" he foamed continually whilst clambering up.

They examined every stone which protruded from the Lord of the Manor's strip of meadow: none bore a cross. The cobbler had a close look again at this one and that one. They were really no different, no boundary stone was present, and even on Exner's side they were missing.

"When I say there isn't one, there isn't one. Take note. And the Lord of the Manor should just come to me, I'll throw plough and harrow at the nail maker."

Nevertheless Klose firmly refused to fulfill the wrongful work. They exchanged activities. The cobbler smashed up the stones, and the lame one took them away.

Now the pieces of rock were tumbling wildly down the wall into the grass of the Lord of the Manor's meadow, and the lame one was giving the cart a rough shove every time so that large freestones rolled down almost to the field of rye. With that he laughed wantonly and shouted at them, "Give my greetings to the Lord of the Manor!"

The heat of excitement only dwindled a little when the last cart had poured its contents over the ground on the other side.

Then he went home with the agreeable feeling in his breast of having performed some very good thing.

The next morning, he drove his draught cows with the harrow over the field at an early hour. He lashed the whip without a break and shouted loudly at the animals over every trifle from pure wantonness. Now and then, he laughed out loud, "Haha, Wende, get up!"

And there he was standing already on the wall and had heard the mocking cry of the man striding towards him, and his paper-white face hid itself even more in his bristly beard with fury.

"Good morning, Exner!"

He acted as if he heard nothing, began to scream loud and prolonged at his cows and adopted a slow, ambling gait. Finally he had arrived at the end of the field, turned the cows and acted astonished, as if he only just then noticed Wende, "Oh, is it you, lord? I thought it was just the bullocks mooing."

The target of his mocking seemed not to have heard the offense and shouted down in an imperious tone, "Who gave you permission to dump stones on my land?"

"Who gave you permission to ask such a thing?"

"Who? Don't you know that that is my meadow?"

"No, is that so! — Where are the boundary stones then?"

"The boundary stones! Here's the wall, here's the boundary."

"Yes! I thought you had them in your pocket and wanted to show them to me. — They are under the wall! No, that sort of Lord of the Manor isn't clever!"

Then it was over with the estate owners self-control.

"I'm giving you eight days respite to start on it. If the stones are not gone then and I don't have compensation for the trampled grass then we will be speaking some-where else."

The last words were spoken in great fury, they came out his mouth hissing and seething like boiling water.

But now the clod also flew into fury, threw down the reins, turned his whip and struck out with the most horrid curse to make contact with the Lord of the

Manor. Without waiting for evidence of his fury, the bearded man set off into a walk which broke into a proper flight and only came to half-calm steps at the path.

The lame one was still grumbling when Wende was already long out of sight. He unharnessed the cows and tied them to a tree. On his entrance, Marie came to him pale with fear. He thought she wanted to reproach him, and threatening to murder her, he stormed into the living room, thumbed the table and screamed constantly as though possessed,

"I'll show him, I'll show him! But it all comes to that when your wife doesn't pull together with you. I want my rights, my rights, and even if it costs me my business, my life."

Then he plunged out the door again and gave himself to his work.

The next morning, the cobbler stepped into the living room and was sober like he had not been for days. "What are the poplars doing?" he asked with a terrible smile.

"What they do, sheep, they're standing!"

"Do you think so, Karl? Well, come out and look at them."

They went out to them. Both saplings had been cut in half by a criminal act and their crowns lay on the path.

"Aha? — that's the answer for the stones! Don't you think?"

Klose shrugged his shoulders indifferently and bowed, lifted up a crown and examined the cut which had been done with a very sharp knife, smooth and sure through the small trunk which had the thickness of a child's arm.

"He could have", he then said, went to the sapling on the right and held the cut off part on the stump. It fitted exactly. The pernicious cut to the other tree showed two attempts. The criminal must have felled the righthand poplar first and then, already weakened and worried, had a go at the other.

The cobbler deciphered that, and the lame one agreed with him after some thought.

"Certainly, where would he have gathered the strength from."

With that the cobbler examined the distance of the cut from the ground and checked it against the height of the lame one. It was easy to see that the nocturnal vandal had been of medium build and must have driven the cut from below.

"He was your height!"

The lame one measured his friend with his eyes, and Klose laughed at it with his mouth shut.

"And he stood down here with his back to the house, as the cut is towards the well", the cobbler continued his investigation and was obviously enjoying his ingenuity.

"He must have been damned confident", he took up the thread of speculation again after a pause and took evident pleasure in the bewilderment of the clod, who stood up and, after a heavy breath, yielded nothing but a beseeching, agonising word, "Cobbler!"

"I can't help you, it is absolutely no different."

"Then you are really of the opinion it was another. Guste, consider carefully!"

"I know who you have had an argument with. It was an enemy of yours or one who you mocked or wanted to play a prank on you, et cetera. That is your affair!"

He said all that with a pitiless objectivity. His features had wrinkled deeply.

The clod stared helplessly at him.

"Look at it, convince yourself, Karl, and he even came from below. For here and there, around the rain hollow, the grass is trampled to the wall. Are you so brainless to think, he came down the path and then turned around after a while so that you could have easily collared him from behind. Look!"

Exner bent down and saw footprints in the dewy grass, half covered by erected stems. His large, brown hands trembled as they moved through the green. Then he burrowed in the fallen leaves absentmindedly. Suddenly something crinkled, and when he looked, his fingers mechanically crushed a white slip of paper. He stood up and stared at the paper, but the letters were dancing before his eyes.

"What is that!" Klose asked tensely.

"Read it out", the lame one answered with arduous self-control. With disguised handwriting, in large capital letters stood the following,

"To Lord of the Manor Exner."

"Read it once more", the ridiculed man requested haltingly, and his face collapsed in horror.

"It agrees with everything, everything, too well, it agrees too well ..." he then murmured.

"What then?" Klose asked.

Exner remained silent, took the note off him, pondered for a few moments, then tore it up and turned to go. He often stumbled with his clubfoot on the stones of the path. His head bent slightly to one side, he limped to the barn.

Klose made to go into the house.

"Where are you going?" the lame one asked looking back.

"I want to tell your woman."

"My woman — my woman? — I thought mine already knew."

All of the blood had drained from his face. He attempted to smile, but did not succeed.

In the barn, he walked around numbly, moved a potato hoe around ten times, struck the walls drumming with a piece of wood and then began rearranging a heap of wooden staves. He did it all hastily as though he was being goaded. Finally his soul disgorged itself. He contemptuously tossed away the piece of wood he was holding. It flew down safely before his eyes. Marie had spoken from the start against the enlargement of his holdings, never straight to him, to her husband, but always to another, especially to the Lord of the Manor. She had not even shied away from their first quarrel in order to prevent the planting of the poplars out of consideration for Wende.

The cobbler, before whose impartial eyes the explanation of the crime was fulfilled so casually, had, despite his sympathy with Marie, unknowingly encumbered nobody but her with the suspicion of being the perpetrator. Carefully and slowly, the clod rebuilt the strewn woodpile and went into the living room. Mealtime had arrived. He realised that he had spent four hours in the barn, and he observed Marie without attracting her attention as she went back and forth, with uncertain haste, paler than usual, and avoiding meeting her husband's gaze which she felt resting on herself.

"It is right of you, pound your legs for my sake", the lame one pondered, noticing her uncertainty, and was reaching for the spoon as the cobbler entered.

"Now come", he said to the new arrival, "sit yourself down and eat. We have deserved it, we stick together."

Despite all the cheerfulness in his compliance, he noticed a frostiness in his friend too, a dejectedness. It was incomprehensible to him, and after he had thoughtfully slurped a few spoonfuls of soup, he spoke to the rhythmic clatter of the metal spoon,

"Guste, what is it then? You are acting just as though you had drawn your knife through the poplar last night!"

The cobbler's eyes adhered to the bowl, he remained silent and then distorted his face into a smile.

In order to lead the conversation to a calmer place, Klose began telling the ancient smugglers' story of the crooked councillor Bene of the mountain. The lame one listened with half an ear, looked around the room and then looked out the window. He saw the bloody boards of the well house, threw his spoon onto the table and screamed mindlessly at the cobbler's tale in turbid rage:

"You wouldn't be mild and gentle if such a thing happened in your house!"

Marie turned red and pale, the spoon in her hand trembled. She opened her mouth to speak, but no word passed over her lips.

Klose tapped him with his foot and made a sign with his eyes that he should moderate himself.

"Karl," Marie finally began, "Guste told me what it's about ..."

She was interrupted by the entrance of the postman, who laid a letter before the lame one and hurriedly disappeared.

Exner disgorged the letter, looked at it for a while, and as he was not certain of the reading, he handed the paper to the cobbler. The latter made to give it to Marie.

"You read it!" Exner called with a vigour that Klose had to yield to.

The cobbler read,

"Steindorf, 17 June 1893.

I hereby notify the Lord of the Garden, Mr Karl Exner, that the stones must be cleared away from my meadow by him or his people within eight days, otherwise I will take legal steps against him. In the same period, ten marks are to be paid to me by the above named as compensation for damaged grass on that very field.

Joseph Wende, Lord of the Manor."

The lame one sat for a while as though frozen, then tore the letter from Klose's hand with a raw laugh and pocketed it.

"Now, Marie, are you finally content?" he asked and looked at her with restrained fury.

The tears were falling from the eyes of the young woman. She stood up and staggered out.

The lame one shoved the table from himself and began hobbling excitedly back and forth in the room.

The cobbler had become ashen and stared motionless at his hands which he laid in front of himself on the table while he chewed on his moustache.

Suddenly, as though by an unexpected push, he sprang up, grabbed his hat and ran away as though chased.

13

After this incident, the cobbler Klose was never sober again. He did not enter his mother's house anymore and also avoided the lame one's farmstead. He acted as though possessed by an evil spirit.

He behaved timidly indoors, as though in a prison. He had a horror of anyone with a settled way of life, as if they were addicted to secret vices. He always walked with bowed head, murmured incomprehensible things to his feet, often paused and began an invisible argument with passionate gestures, which he ended with rueful slaps to his chest just like the christian closes his silent devotion.

He had the half-extinguished eyes of an active ferocity, and his face shook despite his neglect, for it had become quite gaunt, earth-coloured and deeply wrinkled, like the countenance of a fanatical penitent.

As soon as he was drunk, he lapsed into a paroxysm of self-torment, struck himself with his fists, tore his hair, ran through hedges of thorns and then sat a long way from human dwellings in a remote field, crying, lamenting and praying to God for mercy with far-reaching, beseeching voice, to then suddenly spring up, run through the lanes of the village and ask to be sworn at, stoned and spat on by the horde of onlookers.

On a clouded, moonlit night, the old forester Knölle saw how he crept in wide arcs conducting his nasal monologue around the homestead of the lame one.

Everyone held him to be mad, and a few thought the constant, extraordinary heat was much to blame for this sudden confusion in his soul.

For day after day, the forested mountains of the Grafschaft swam in trembling fervour. They looked like giant pack animals who, half buried by grey sand, were striding far off through an endless desert. Always moving, always held in place; no breath of wind to cool them; the sky ashen, a withered blue. The sun looked on the earth as if through a dead, destroyed infinity. Only now and again, a searing wind from the east lifted its wings and flew through the windings of the Wartha pass with a subtle swishing which sounded like the whistling of cutting scythes. Then the few clouds fell as though mown down and melted away to a seething fervour in the sky.

The unripe fruit fell from the fruit trees wilted and yellow onto the burnt grass.

The forest howled in the night wind like a pining lion.

Dust lay in the small rivulets, the amplest wells gave water in drops.

The heat went crackling through the ripening grain. The towers chimed for rain. In the churches, piles of humanity knelt at all hours and cried endless litanies in timorous faith. The crucifixes and chapels in the fields and at crossroads were hung with wreaths, women crouched on stones before them and raised their hands, the men walked past and crossed themselves. The clergymen carried the shrines into the meadows, sprinkled holy water and spoke the ancient weather blessings to the rustling of the colourful church standards: it was all in vain.

The earth gaped with broad cracks as if screaming to heaven for help. The wizened leaves fell thicker, the forest lay grey in the heights and groaned from time to time as if it was on its last legs. The seedless heads of the oats flackered like tiny beggars' sacks. The hopelessness lay on the paths. Despair wove into the houses, and they went timidly to the crops as though they were not obtaining blessing, but rather reaping curses and piling it up on the ground so that it became the food of life.

In this period the action began that the Lord of the Manor had brought against the lame one, because his letter had remained unanswered.

Exner laughed his head off over the first judicial servings and signed the postman's receipt as though it was a pretentious child's prank. He saw the "nail maker" similarly. He wanted to scare him with such scraps of paper, him, whose arm had set the heaviest logs in the forest rolling!

In good mettle, he jogged to the first appointment and thought on the way of his short victorious fight with the greycoat. That lifted his confidence still more. As if to a cheerful fistfight whose smooth outcome could not be doubted, he climbed the broad steps to the local court.

But after half an hour in the bleak courtroom, his bristling, fervent pretension was badly upset. The clerk's pen pricked it, it was rolled thin by endless talking, soiled by devious ruses. It was not much use that he defiantly reestablished it again and again. The judge finally reproached him for his improper behaviour and threatened him with imprisonment if he injured the dignity of the hearing further by his offensive sallies. Then the confusing questions and addresses progressed. In the end, his pretension had become a shadow, and only the shrewdness of his lawyer had rescued him from a thorough defeat.

For the first time in his life, a strange hand inconsiderately took hold of the compass of his desire. He had to resign himself to the verdict of a third party who looked after him as much as after anyone else. And when he recalled on the way home the details of the hearing, he found that everything abounded so much with arbitrariness and contortions. Then he became truly intoxicated with fury and revenge, an intoxication which subsided days later into a sultriness that spread over his entire feeling and thought and was very similar to that fervent heat which had been drying up the earth for weeks. It was a hidden fever, a secret illness of his violent spirit. He strode around the house and fields with eyes smouldering from constant lurking, with a forehead that never lost the wrinkles caused by its furious mental work. The thin lips of his unlovely mouth shook constantly from withheld curses, his hair was turbid, his entire attitude crumpled in sullenness: he was thus pursued restlessly in his fields by the dammed up fury.

His search for revenge mixed with the hope of rain, and it inculcated the belief in him that his outer and inner misfortune was insolubly connected.

"If only it'll rain", he often said to himself when he leant out the window and looked at the sky for clouds. But the discharge of his soul came unexpectedly.

One evening the lame one was standing in the middle of the room and listening attentively to the sound of the wind. It was a deep, restful rustling in which the trees' weary branches swayed as though they were hearing consoling words of comfort. Sometimes the wind drove against the panes so that it tingled as if was raining.

Marie was sitting at the table bent over her sewing before a small, open kerosene lamp.

"Wasn't it as if it was raining?" Exner asked dully.

The young woman raised her head and listened,

"No, it's sand driving against the panes", she answered and continued sewing assiduously.

"There you sit and needle about in the scraps!" he said reproachfully.

Then a lifeless mood took command in the room. The cat cowered on the bench by the oven, and its green iridescent eyes stared unmoving at the small circle of light, the clock quivered in hard, fitful blows.

"A lucky year, you have to say that, I can be happy. Don't you think?" the lame one asked in need of a quarrel.

Opposite her husband, Marie had come upon the invariant, dry patience with which strong natures take on a blameless fate.

She remained silent for a while, as if pondering, and then answered with the calm counter-question,

"Does it only cook over our fields?"

"As if we would have more when others have nothing!"

The lame one laughed irritably.

"Don't talk so that God besets us even worse. Rather think of what the poor should do!"

"The poor! Them! Whoever has nothing, can lose nothing. You are a neat wife for me!"

"Do I do too little? Here, look at my hands!"

The young woman held out to him her palms which were raw and cracked like the bark of a tree.

The clod laughed roughly, turned around and disappeared cursing into the bedroom.

With impassioned zeal, he primly abandoned the matter, threw himself on his bed, turned his face to the wall and for a long time, the darkness before his eyes was completely red with his soul's fury. The images of his dealings with the Lord of the Manor ran back and forth before him, and he spoke to them about the com-mission which would arrive in the next few days and investigate the boundaries. He spoke heated words to them, furious, hate-filled sounds. A swaying gradually came over him, from whose swings shadows streamed, slowly shrouding everything. In that way, he fell asleep. It seemed to him as if the full rustling which preceded rain was approaching from a distance, and it came nearer and sounded as if it was the clapping of drops falling. He opened up the ears of his dream completely wide and convinced himself that he was not deceiving himself. The rustling was trickling quite clearly over his roof, and the drops were falling through the dry leaves, single ones at first, then quicker and more often until they created that humming with which a well-ordered country rain pelted down. And as he doubted blissfully in order to be able to hear it again, he heard prolonged wailing, like that which pours out the mouth of a child who is already tired of crying. It was moving up and down on the other side of the wall, sometimes engulfed by the blasts of the heaving wind, sometimes clearly audible if not even louder.

Instinctive fear tore the half-awake man from his sleep and sat him upright in bed. Tense, a half-dazed foreboding in his soul, he listened.

Everything was completely still. No humming rain, no falling drops, no rustling over the ridge of the roof. It had all been an illusion.

Exner shook his head in astonishment that a man could dream so clearly, and was even about to lie back down on his pillow when this peculiar wailing began again: as though pining, lost in the trembling of a great fear, then sobbing like a drowning man slurping water, and then seething in the confused sounds of despair. Truly ... now it stood right under his window, and the strange tones were striving up at the panes like the quavering pale fingers of a ghost.

Then it went away.

Now it was whining in the living room, then on the stairs to the summer room, then above him in the loft. There it was as though soft-soled shoes were shuffling back and forth. The lame one's heart was pounding. He sank down, buried his head in the pillow, pressed his dying fists against his temples and murmured in cold fear, "It's the wailing mother. It's the wailing mother. What, will it just have everything in my house too."

The grey, mysterious spirit, in whose existence so many Grafschaft residents still believe, had moved in with him. Its whining announced loss, sickness, death, every misery. Attired in long vestments, its face shrouded, it shuffled back and forth. In the heights from which it climbed, it floated away like a shadow which came and went, and left nothing behind but invisible tracks from which the ostracised human life lapsed irretrievably into torment.

For a long time, the lame one lay in an icy numbness, horror was running through his body.

A soft sound coming through from the living room brought him to his senses. Without getting dressed, he sprang up and tore the door open. The kerosene lamp had been extinguished, instead the little light before the image of the Virgin Mary in the corner was burning. Its reddish light flowed down and was spreading like the first glow of morning over his wife, who lay on her knees before it and had raised her hands in prayer.

She turned her pale face to him and looked at him questioningly with glimmering eyes.

The clod proffered a wild sight: his hair hung mazily over his face, still deformed from the fright; his eyes blazed. Marie could not bear the sight and turned her face away.

"Did you hear it?" he asked shaking.

"Hear what?"

"You still want to argue!"

"I don't know what you mean. I was praying, as you can see."

"You — you — first you get in close with the Lord of the Manor, then —"

"Me!"

"Yes, you! What do you need to fear from the Lord of the Manor, because of the poplars and the note you wrote!"

"Me, writing a note!"

"You wrote the note: 'to Lord of the Manor Exner', you and no one else."

Then the young woman sprang up and stood before him.

"You are my husband, and I would make things bad for you?"

"Your husband? I am the clod who you've always made fun of. I'm not a fence post, when you cut me, I bleed."

Now he was giving the reason for his suspicion toward Marie. She lowered her eyes ridden with guilt.

The silent confession incited the furious man still more.

"You did all that!" he screamed. "And now you kneel and pray the wailing mother onto my neck! Down with the puppets from the shelf, down with it, now you'll clear it all out!"

"It stays, it's my God!"

Marie confronted the furious man firmly and spread her arms out protectively.

"It's your devil!"

He pushed her to the side so that she staggered against the oven.

"I'm a mother, Karl!" she screamed and got back on her feet again after the fall.

But the lame one did not let it hinder him. He grasp-ed his stick, sprang into the corner and with a single blow, he belted the corner shelf, Virgin Mary, angel and little lamp under the table.

After he had beaten to bits the powers his wife was quietly in league with against him, he said to the soft sobbing in the night, "And that's so I won't see it again in my room!" and returned to the bedroom.

Marie did not stir from the bench by the oven where she had sunk down.

She had pressed her hands to her face so as not to watch, and fervent tears were streaming out between her fingers. Despite a swirling stupefaction lying over her, she saw motionless in the darkness before her an ugly, threatening male figure with long, thin legs, arms hanging far below his hips, an unshapely head in whose wrinkled face, blinking eyes crouched like poisonous toads. Long sparse hair hung over bulging temples.

She struggled against the image of the lame one which her mistreated nerves arranged distortedly before her, but it doggedly created the fancy anew whenever her will had barely suppressed it.

Then she slid to the floor on her knees and prayed,

"Oh my heavenly God, you lie shattered in the dust, but my heart carries you like a soft cloth. You punish me strictly. I want happiness and money and a good life, but I know well, happiness only comes through misery. Break me like a shell, just take pity on my child." —

Then she slipped under the table and collected the figures of the Virgin Mary and the angels into her apron. She kissed each piece. After that she groped her way cautiously out the door, up the stairs into the loft and buried them in the hay.

But the distorted male figure did not disappear from the darkness before her. As she fought against it, standing in the spell of its ugliness, her spirit stared at it always, and this mysterious mark of life in which everything originated impressed the delusion's form on her torment.

The aromatic scent of the hay finally numbed her senses so that she fell asleep.

14

Exner walked around for a few days as though shattered under the influence exerted by the wailing mother's appearance to him. If he was walking to his work then he told himself it was no use, all was lost. Then every movement seemed difficult to him, as if the load he had to lift was invisibly topped by an even greater one.

But this deep despondency did not last long with him. It soon left him, for despite the bleak foreboding, everything was turning for the better.

The rain on which everyone was waiting despairingly was priming itself. Clouds were rolling over the ridges, cool air was climbing from the hollows. The sun lay high after the long blaze as though weary. The chaffinches emitted long, mourning calls. The swallows skipped thickly over the ground, and when it finally rained, it sounded to everyone like joyful giggles.

Then the weather became milder again.

Even the progress of the action agreed with the lame one more and more. The local appointment had passed inconclusively; no boundary stones had been found. Even at the land registry, there was no information because at that time the separation of Exner's parcel from the Lord of the Manor's estate had not been noted down on the cadastral map.

The court suggested an amicable arrangement to the parties in the dispute, by which Exner would clear up the stones onto the wall and Wende would relinquish the claim for compensation. The costs arising were to be borne by both in equal measure.

That suited the hard-headed men nicely. Wende just laughed hoarsely, the clod grouched about it: not yielding a finger's width; making an end forever; not giving a damn, and left the meeting.

After some time, he received a letter from the court in which he was asked to take away the entire stonewall, since the presence of boundary markers under the wall was affirmed by the testimony of independent parties.

An appointment would take place again. The testimony of both old men who knew of the existence of the boundary stones was contested by Exner's lawyer as biased because they were temporary workers of the Lord of the Manor. After some to and fro, the Lord of the Manor finally assumed the clearance of the wall with the explicit condition that Exner should bear the cost of this work if boundary stones were found under the wall.

The lame one was very happy to agree, as he was certain that no evidence of former boundary setting would be found and already hoped to then be able to quietly take possession of the narrow strip of meadow too.

His wife suffered the most from the dispute. Even after he had robbed her of her God, he did not become gentler. All the fury which he felt climbing in himself with any unpleasant turn of the proceedings and which he yet must not pour out in them, all the fury which it called forth, he vented on his wife. She had to get up in the night to sweep the hall and living room. He threw plates and bowls onto the floor when his dinner did not taste right to him. Now she came to him too quick, now too feebly, now she should laugh, now she should not act so sullen. Sometimes she wore her hair too fancily, other times she was too pale. Every look, every step which turned out differently than he thought, he experienced as an expression of recalcitrance which she really had no right to because of her machinations against him.

The people from whom Marie's fate was not hidden shook their heads over how this young thing's harsh pride had turned so suddenly into the opposite.

She did not let herself be seen anywhere, she did not seek to speak to anyone. She even avoided Joseph and Kath, those two eternally good people, as though not to offer her husband cause for new oppressiveness. She came after the beginning of church service, prayed without raising her head, and left the church either before the completion of the holy acts or behind the last believer so that no one would talk to her. If someone called to her then she visibly started in fright. But then she would look up with her blue eyes, which had become even larger and bore a morbid lustre. She looked like someone from another world. No lament ever passed over her lips, she obstinately steered every conversation away from momentous things and spoke about everyday things with a serious, almost wavering voice, and although her words sounded firm and certain, you could feel a trembling in them like the movement of dry blades of grass.

But wherever she walked and stood, her soul rattled at her life's fate. "Why did you drive me to him? Do you want me to suffer so?" she asked God in her heart.

The incomprehensible one answered with new torments by her husband. Then she cried out, that emotional cry in which the heart falters as though pierced and the thoughts whirl as though in madness. But no one heard her despairing. It just became dark before her eyes, she did not eat, she did not sleep and she worked as though in a fury. At the same time, she smiled constantly. That was her cry.

When she came to herself again, God's countenance had changed. Out of the confident man of her childhood confessions had come an incomprehensible, immeasurable power, an ocean on which her life roved about like a detached leaf. Then she looked seriously about herself and noticed how the lives of others glided along chained to immovable tethers. "Why do I have this unendless hardship by your command, eternal one?" And the longer she looked at her fate, at this necessary knotting of confused threads, the more an inconceivable certainty opened up in her, a fear which was at its base a sweetness. She glided into the blossoming twilight of a mystical closeness to God, which from every doubt gave birth to a new ardency, from every catharsis a firmer connection; every hardship became the promise of a joy. Thus the certainty grew in her, separated from the thinkable as though by a dark, bottomless water in which every outline was extinguished, every colour dissolved. Sometimes it seemed as if a face emerged from the depths in her. But if her soul bent down to interpret it, it melted away and she went along again, doubly oppressed by the misery of her life and the turbid gloom of pregnancy.

Then she felt more than just every inner comfort and saw in it the just punishment for not having struggled with her whole life against her husband's crime in that wild night of God's eviction. With the shadow of this hour, the grotesque delusion which had so tormented her in that night arose in her memory. It did not stand clearly before her. All the ways of her soul were in fact tainted with its distortedness, shimmering in the inept light of her eyes and reverberating with the inert, hard sounds of its unlovely mouth as though it was not an affliction from without anymore, as though it was contaminating the cradle of her existence.

In this time of being trampled down, she also often became the prey of bestial carnality. Every higher thought was extinguished. As if she had never known shame, it drove her with disregard for her personal dignity in pursuit of pleasure as far as disgust.

In the end, however, the sweetness of her mystical connection with God blossomed again and again from the frightening causes, at first timid and trembling, then in ardent triumph.

In order to be able once to relish this inner joy completely undisturbed, she knew to bring about with inconspicuous slyness that she was permitted to carry the breadstuffs to the mill herself.

The mill lay in the next village. Of the two paths that led there, she chose the longer footpath through the Lord of the Manor's forest, past the stone walls and across the secluded fields. The beautiful days seemed to be tethered to the earth, the sunshine played raptly around the colourful bushes, the white clouds lay motionless so that they looked like distant mountains, and a leaf fell so that it danced blissfully through the golden air as if blown from the bush by the mouth of a hidden child.

Marie was walking with her head inclined to one side, and when a leaf tumbled down once more, her desire's face and her little child appeared to her left, the pretty girl, blond haired and blue eyed, smiled and skipped next to her without touching the ground.

"Is it you, are you my child, mine, my little angel, mine alone? Come, come on! I know well from whom you come: such a look like only our Father in heaven", the young woman whispered in the intoxication of great joy.

No, it was not his child, God had gifted it to her as reward for her faithful execution of his command. Her husband had been only a tool in God's hand, the hand which also brought the flowers up out of the stones. That was definite, his hand would not destroy the magic of her hopes. With him, but to one side, she wanted to build a world with her child where her degraded life would become safe, free and happy.

Sudden weariness, stabbing prickling which made her legs rigid, drove her to seek a place to sit. Because the Petzdorf sanctuary was not far from her, she did not sit down by the side of the path, but trudged all the way to the two decapitated lime trees before which a slat bench had been placed. She arrived breathing heavily, let her burden slide to the ground, sat down and lowered her head to keep the broken off train of thought spinning on.

Then she remembered she was before a sanctuary, turned around and sank to her knees before the image. It was painted on canvas and wedged in a black frame which was held to the trunk of a lime tree by two iron hooks. The scene depicted was very simple. In a landscape only given in outline, and over which the ultramarine sky lay, a farmer was kneeling with his hands raised in prayer. His long-tailed coat was black, his face pale. The unknown painter had succeeded in placing some of the dull soul of a farmer in his traits. The man's eyes were directed rapturously at the Virgin Mary, who floated in the sky up to the left. Not far from her, at the same height as the divine apparition, a bird hung in the air, which you would have thought to be a hen with a plucked out tail if it were not for its talons. In these it carried something black from which a number of ochre-yellow coins were falling, the first of which had arrived close above the praying farmer's nose.

Underneath was the explanation:

"In the time of the Swedish war, a farmer, Georg Tiffe, lived who buried his wealth, a few ducats, in a hollow tree. When he wanted to fetch his money, it was all gone. What did he do? In fear he fell to his knees, vowing to the sad Virgin Mary to erect her effigy where he found his money. As he was praying, a raven came flying, bringing the money in its beak and letting it fall by the man. The man fetched the money and the next day brought a ducat to the pastor, Reverend Wendelin Kasper in Alt-Walsdorf, to fund this image. Alt-Walsdorf, 2 March 1645. Do not, oh Christian, walk past this image! Pray, Mary has helped and will help you too in every hardship."

Completely occupied by her maternal joy, she could not arrive at any prayer. As a substitute, she contemplated the familiar picture more closely than usual and read the explanation slowly, word for word. She spoke the call at the end in a low voice and added from her own heart a quick little prayer, "Oh, my God in heaven, merciful Mother ..."

Dry laughter, quite close by, made her break off and look up startled.

Across behind the bench, a man was sitting on a stone, hidden by the shrubbery. Now that she was silent, he bent forward and looked at her. "Klose?" she spoke into his wild face and felt her heart clench with pity.

The cobbler moved his head in affirmation and did not stir his blurred alcoholic eyes from her.

"We don't see you at all anymore, do we, Guste?" she asked, sitting on the end of the slat bench and picking up her burden.

He withdrew behind the bush again and let out that dry mocking laugh again.

"You!" she rattled in answer.

"I am always home", he finally replied indifferently.

"Oh no, I don't think you let your mother see you anymore."

"For that reason alone, I'm always home."

"Cobbler, really, what are you saying!"

He rose, stepped across into her view and then said,

"Well, here I'm home where I am."

His coat was torn. A rumpled hat sat on the dust-grey hair which hung down over his collar.

When he now felt Marie's eyes on him, he became uncertain and arranged his neck tie, a colourful handkerchief, and laughed again.

"Why did you laugh before?" Marie asked, because nothing but pity occurred to her.

Klose stepped forward, lifted the burden onto the bench, laid it between the young woman and himself and sat down at the other end with the words,

"If you don't mind and you aren't angry then I will sit a while."

"Why, yes, yes, sit yourself down, but what I want to ask is why you don't set your pack down?"

The alcoholic stared at the ground for a long time and then said, "Blessed girl — blessed girl", he looked at her, lowered his head again and repeated once more "blessed girl".

After that he straightened up and answered,

"Small is big and big small. A good heart has no head, but it thrusts in your eye anyway! Yes, yes! — It's not something to laugh about! When we suppose, it rains or the wind rises or a fire comes over the house, in a bush, et cetera.

Isn't it so? — Good. You kneel and raise your hands up high. For? Hahaha!"

He looked at her reflectively, stood up, trod back and forth and finally sat down again. With a dismissive gesture, he began anew,

"Hahaha! When we've done everything, still more! Like the to-do in the middle of it: singing, pushing, freezing, hungering until the hair knows as much as the head, hahaha! but not going limp, always on, always on, into the middle ..."

Shaking his head, he broke off and intertwined his scrawny fingers despairingly, concluding dully,

"It keeps raining ... it keeps raining ... that's probably why it's said: the devil is sometimes a billy goat! The more you defend yourself, the more it pushes. Leave me alone!"

He spat, supported himself on his knees and stared at the ground as if he was completely alone.

"But Guste, the Lord God, just imagine! ..."

Klose did not stir. He looked as if he had shrunk into a ball. His arms hanging down, hands entwined, clenched between his knees. His head pressed into his shoulders. His back bowed like a morbid hunchback. For a long time, Marie did not hear anything but the wheezy breath which is inherent in being misshapen.

Then the words came, weakly as if a thin rod was stirring the emptiness.

He seemed to have completely forgotten her again and only to be talking with his destiny. He pulled himself apart with reluctant sounds, sat rigidly for a while and then began to talk dully to his toes as he wiggled them up and down,

"But it still isn't right ... no, no! I feel it ... it isn't getting easier ..."

Sorrowfully he raised his eyes to heaven and addressed God himself,

"He is a miller! not before the last dust is ground, does he let up. Do you see who I really am?"

With this question, he suddenly turned to Marie again.

The tears were entering the young woman's eyes as she looked in this tortured earthly-pale face, and she uttered not a single word.

"Marie! Don't you see?"

His voice was trembling in fear.

"You are a good man ..." she answered pitifully.

A deep agitation came over the alcoholic, he stood up and breathed as though he was about to choke, got ready to run away, looked at her haggardly, came back and sank down on the bench groaning.

The young woman thought Klose had suddenly gone mad, but did not dare to move, because she was frightened that he would then attack her and do her harm.

"Right isn't it, he pushes you so that you fall?" the unfortunate stuttered softly to himself.

But Marie sensed that he was asking her.

"He drives you from bed at night, throws food at you?"

Marie winced without a whimper.

"I know everything, everything!" the cobbler finished when he had looked up and perceived no agreement in Marie's face.

"Haha, and you want to say that I'm a good man! Blessed girl ... but, let it be, it will go on as long as it goes on, once it comes over me entirely, entirely, and I have a strong hand and extinguish everything ..."

His voice had become full, a singing, young, avid wavering. He had intertwined his hands and was nodding softly to himself.

Marie recognised that he was reflecting again, rose noiselessly and took her burden up on her back.

"God protect you," she said, "and if you don't know where, our house is behind the forest", and went away from there.

The cobbler did not stir. Only when she was already far in the distance did he raise his eyes and look towards her, pondering for a long time.

The still light of autumn ran across his face, and it seemed as if he was laughing in blissful certainty.

15

Six weeks had passed, the parish fair of Alt-Walsdorf was over. It was the last third of October. The lame one had his good days once again: already early in the morning, he was leaning idly against the well house, gnawing his upper lip and scraping the paint on the boards with his clubfoot. It was probably about half past seven in the morning, for the sound of the children going along the path to school was losing itself towards Erlengrund. From the forest, mist was rising and stretching itself in quivering strips towards the sky whose heavy, uniform cloud sank more and more until only a thin streak of yellow light lay over the black mass of the forest. Soon this sparse consolation of the October day had also disappeared, and the cloud ran to the ground like bleary dishwater. The trees in the field disappeared and the hidden sun, last seen over the Hedwigstein as if someone was going to the mountain with a lantern, spread a pale brightness like the pitiful light of a patient's room. The lame one saw his house becoming indistinct, it seemed as if weak smoke was coming out all the pores of its walls. In front of him and to the right was the Lord of the Manor's forest: blurred, dark walls.

If it were barns, Exner pondered, and stalls and sheds, what a farm it would have to be! Oh, that would be something!

After a while, it occurred to him that he was pilfering the day, standing there and watching, and he slowly set himself in motion. He went past the house to split wood in the shed. Then the cobbler was suddenly standing before him as if he had emerged out of thin air.

"Well, you let us see you once more! Where have you come from?" the lame one asked in astonishment.

Klose lowered his sleepy face in embarrassment, stuttered something and then walked past. Exner watched him, laughing scornfully, and because Marie appeared on the threshold in the same moment, he called mockingly, "Look up, we've got a visitor."

The drunkard smiled at the young woman, stepped to the well, pumped water into his cupped hand and began to wash himself, sputtering and gasping mightily. Exner had stepped up to his wife and asked her,

"What does the rogue want here?"

"I don't know."

"Such brothers all have something on them: scabies, louse or something like that."

Marie shrugged her shoulders.

"Where did he probably sleep then?" the lame one continued talking. "That he keeps out of my house. I need one just like him for winter ..."

He could not finish, for a many-voiced clamour sounded out of the mist from the lower field,

"Won ... there it is ... haha! Franz, hurrah, hurrah!"

No more could be understood. Hands clapped a few times in conclusion.

With the noise's beginning, the cobbler had lifted his cap from the ground and quickly dried his face. His mazy, wet hair stood up in strands. He stood there thus and listened. When everything was still, he looked back at the couple questioningly.

Exner shouted at him,

"Go and see what sort of carry-on it is! But act like you know nothing. I didn't send you."

The cobbler obeyed wordlessly.

Marie took the bucket which she had put down and went into the stalls.

A tremor played around the corner of the lame one's mouth, and he listened tensely.

Then he heard exuberant laughter, from which he gathered that the cobbler had arrived at the labourers.

For a moment, he thought they were making fun of him. "I'll mark them!" he said and rushed forward a few steps.

But at the well house, he stopped and listened again full of agitation.

All at once, the mist retreated and the field lay there clearly. The cobbler stood with lowered head in front of three labourers who were eagerly trying to convince him. Then they raised their heads and looked over. They must have caught sight of him, for as though by command, they all cried,

"Haha, found! Hurrah!"

Exner cursed gritting his teeth and did not stir.

When he dared to bend his head forwards again, he did not see anything anymore, as the mist had covered everything.

Then stumbling steps approached.

The cobbler stood before him and said,

"Now, they will drink straightaway, schnaps, two litres. The fellows made a bet! And Franz, the pixie, won it out. He couldn't believe it, but they are there, I saw them."

"What's there?"

"Stones."

"Stones?"

The lame one repeated it with breathless voice.

But he quickly though again and laughed mockingly,

"Stones! haha! Well now, stones! They wouldn't need two moons for that. There are enough down there."

"Ah no, Karl, what I'm saying to you is boundary stones!" Klose responded. "I can recognise boundary stones. It has a cross on it, a proper cross."

Exner moved up to the drunkard and looked down threateningly at him.

"Guste, go into the house, eat, drink and warm yourself. But I advise you this, I advise you this, understand? They did not find anything."

With that he left him and went into the house.

The cobbler stayed behind and, after pondering a long time, said to himself,

"Well, yes, yes. But that may be. Though he actually found it."

All around the sound of bells began. The confusion of children's voices ran past not so far away.

"It's Wednesday, the children are coming from the school", he then murmured, shook with an inner chill and hesitantly walked after the lame one. He found him behind the large, white corner table sitting before a steaming bowl and rattling the spoon.

"Come and sit down", Exner said and continued in his occupation.

"Snow will come from the mist." With these timid words, Klose took his place.

The lame one raised his head. But the look in his eyes was extinguished, his face pale and suffering, a furious resolve came into them from time to time and made his coarse features angular.

"Have you really bought the tavern of Rathmann-Rappen?" he asked and stared down in front of himself.

"I don't know", the alcoholic answered and stroked his moustache. The lame one burst out into laughter meanly.

Finally he raised the spoon and began supping eagerly.

"Eat, cobbler! Franz has been an ass all his life", he said between swallows to Klose, who sat there with face averted and now slowly and grudgingly also helped himself.

But the lame one threw down the spoon again, clasped his hands between his knees and lapsed into musings.

The following dish, boiled dumplings in some sort of sauce, did not stir him.

When his wife timidly asked him to just taste it, he straightened up, looked past her and said roughly to the cobbler, "Guste, eat your fill, as much as you can. After that go to the shed and cut the wood up small."

The cobbler nodded silently, gulped down quickly all the food proffered, thanked them barely audibly and went off. At the door, he turned around and asked,

"But, Marie, if I could do something for you, then you only need to say."

"No, cobbler, no, go."

After a while, idle blows resounded from the shed.

The lame one stood up, walked agitatedly about the room and threw furtive looks at Marie.

When she had left the room with the milking gear, he stopped and listened. Now the latch of the stall door fell into the hasp. He waited a while yet, then crept quietly out the door, along the wall, into the shed.

There he sat down on a wooden block.

The cobbler turned around, struck the axe into the wood and stuck his hands in his pockets. "Do you want to help me?" he asked and lowered himself onto another wooden block.

Exner breathed deeply.

"It'll be a cold winter, cobbler", he said after pondering a while and looked out the little door.

"Yes, yes, it could be, a dry one, for it isn't sinking like mist."

"Will you be going home?"

"What would I do there!"

"Eat and sleep."

"Well yes, eat my fill, have a warm room, be at home ... you see, that still isn't for me right now. It's not time for me yet. I have other things to do."

Then a long silence occurred. Klose looked sadly at the ground before him.

The lame one's face was working. Then he began with a soft voice,

"Would you like to buy another coat. Your trousers are ragged too. I can see straw coming out your boots."

"Yes, taking whatever and not stealing."

"Eh, who's talking of stealing."

"Or robbery, murder."

"None of that."

Again a pause occurred. Then the lame one began again mutedly,

"It has gored you, poor fellow. But I'm your friend."

Suddenly he became agitated.

"If I was a bad fellow, I wouldn't pay my taxes, I'd let my wife starve, I wouldn't have well-fed cows ... cobbler, am I not fair, keen and just?!"

He had become involuntarily loud.

The stall door creaked. Then steps could be heard in the yard.

"Cobbler, chop, strike, hew at it!" he strove.

The cobbler slowly grasped the handle.

But the steps lost themselves in the house.

Both of them took their previous places again.

"Karl," the cobbler asked the lame one when everything was quiet again, "isn't your wife like a cat?"

"You're right, like a cat!" Exner confirmed, and the creases of a bitter fury burrowed into his face.

"I mean, we must act nicely to her if she is to make us happy", Klose rebuked him, but at the same time lowered his eyes embarrassed before the lame one's piercing glance.

"What are you trying to say then, hey?" the clod asked, and his voice shook with fury. "Should I look after your rags or should your sister, the stubble stallion's Paula?"

Then the clumsy fellow sat motionless for a long time and his eyes looked broodingly at nothing.

The cobbler crouched where he was as though chastised.

Finally he looked subserviently at the lame one.

With this look, the silence between the two of them became easier, and the lame one took up the conversation again, whispering,

"Look, Guste, I'm your friend, a good fellow — is that not so? I don't have to be done in with such a witness, no! Look, there is room here, I won't cast you out even if you stay the whole winter. You get to eat, to drink, I have a good coat, there's also trousers and boots ... You don't have to work hard ..."

The cobbler turned paler, the creases of his repentant face furrowed deeper for a moment, then it took on the shimmer of a soul which had cast off its deepest worries.

"Karl," he stuttered, "if there is a God in heaven, you are worthy of him. Perhaps when it's spring, I'll be gone again and let the rope fly."

"Well, be sensible though and don't trust your horns like a goat. If you understand all that I said, stay. Guste, were they boundary stones that the Lord of the Manor's labourers found, were they boundary stones? If you keep irritating me then I don't know what I'll do, I'll strangle you."

Exner's voice shook. He had stood up and had approached the cobbler slowly. Now he was shaking his big fist in the drunkard's face and his countenance deformed into a deadly desperation.

Horrified, the boozer backed away. His thoughts were whirling in fear. Without wanting to, he had already answered,

"No, Karl, no! No boundary stones, stones like all the others which the Lord lets grow."

"Now you see, I knew that, you fool! Is it a sort of sin if I swap an old coal here or there for a stone, is a stone not a stone? Couldn't other ones stand there for the clods? Haha! — it's night — there's a mist — the hoe works quietly — people walk behind the wall, but nobody sees anything — out with the rock, out! — into a well — the water gurgles, thirty metres deep — you don't hear anything fall — in such a deep hole, the best glasses see nothing. The pickaxe is leaning behind the well house where the blood-coloured boards are. When the rooster crows, it's all over."

The lame one spoke quickly. In his eyes, a persistent fury lay, so cold, so determined that the soul of the reprobate was numbed by it. The cobbler saw nothing before himself, it lay in his inner being like a humming mist. A turbid outrage was fermenting in him, but his will had run off in all directions. In its place, a strange urge was taking effect, inexorable, inflexible.

Heavily, as though lost in the force of an oppressive dream, he let his hand sink into the right hand offered by the lame one.

When he looked around, he was alone.

He rose hastily to flee, turned around by the door, went back, sat down, stood up, pulled the axe from the block, raised it to strike, threw it down and stared at the wooden block for a long time. "... it's night," he murmured indecisively, "there's a mist — the hoe works quietly — out with the rock — the board is loose — the well is deep — you don't hear anything fall ..." He shook, his heart froze, but his consciousness turned as if he was sitting on a carousel, and as he sent the eyes of his helpless soul over these dancing grey shapes, a shining light emerged from the disconsolate expanse within him, knelt down, raised its hands in prayer and watched him fearfully with large eyes. It was the same image before which his poor solitude had so often lain stammering in repentant torment, in torturous ardency.

Once more he looked within himself. Then he knew that what he should do, was that which was wanted.

He sat poised on the block of wood, propped his head in his hands and waited. — — —

The forest started rustling. Mist flowed under the door: it was darkening.

He raised his head, looked out, checking, and then let it sink again: it was still too light.

By him in the stalls, the cows began stamping, the pigs ran squealing at the boards of the sty. Then a soft voice spoke affectionately. At the same time, he heard the milk whining regularly into the tin pail. The doors swung a few more times. The lame one hobbled into the yard and returned shortly to the house again. Then everything was soundless.

Only a soft trickling in the dead, deep night and a burrowing sound from the forest, as though a sleeper was stirring in his bed.

The cobbler stood up, ran his hand through his hair with a deep breath and then crept cautiously out of the barn.

16

The lame one had a night full of torment. What — if the cobbler went to work too soon and woke his wife! If, in this pitch-black night, someone came across the cobbler and caught the unsuspecting boozer on his tortuous path by chance! What then? He was getting hot, and he carefully slipped the bedcover down, raised his head a hand's breadth above the pillow and listened tensely. But nothing stirred. A slipping noise came through the plum trees outside the windows. The clock in the living room struck eleven. Or, if the cobbler slept instead of saving him, if he, the sufferer, on to every dodge, had sought the open spaces and then walked around and told all who wanted to hear of his attempt.

— — —

With this thought, his soul was blinded with fury.

But no! Now shuffling steps became audible, stopping a few times and losing themselves in the distance.

Now he is gone.

To Exner it seemed as if the darkness around him had begun to seethe. But he did not stir.

After a long, long time, the steps drew near again. But now they were slower and heavier, as though burdened. They stopped in front of the house. After a while, they went away again.

The lame one pondered: the stone cannot be light, he is not carrying them both at once. Certainly not, he is emaciated from drinking.

Now the steps were creeping back again, heavy, hesitant — just like before.

Exner breathed out. Thank God, now it would soon be over! Then if someone should appear! he had been right, now it was clear as day that ... Suddenly! The

crashing of low-lying boards. A frightened scream — —
He jumped up, forgetting everything, and cried, "The
hound!"

His wife awoke,

"Karl, what is it!"

Full of horror, he sank back softly and began snoring
loudly and ever louder.

Marie rolled back and forth a few times, then her
regular, deep breaths sounded again: she was asleep.

It shot through the listener's head: perhaps the stone
slid from his hand and fell on the boards. Yes, it
couldn't be anything else. But the scream! It was a
scream ... and then: no door had stirred afterwards.
Klose had to sleep under the roof, he could not spend
the night in the open!

This and other doubts assailed him.

Finally he dispelled them,

"To the devil with you, ass! Sleep underground for all
I care! It would be for the best. You have not deserved
anything more, and I'll be rid of you."

He turned to the wall, shut his eyes defiantly and
went to sleep.

Soon terrible dreams were chasing through his sleep.
He was continually perishing. He fell from one death to
the next. First he was being thrust from a train and
being mangled by the wheels, then his house was
sinking into an abyss from which flames were leaping
and he was incinerated, then he was fleeing in front of a
pale, terrible giant who ran behind him with a rope for
catching him. For he had been a hail and had devastated
the entire land, a plague which killed thousands, a
famine, a terrible drought. For that he would die. Every
tree to which he was chased stretched a blood-red
tongue out to him and reached for him with its
branches. In danger of death, he flew to the mountains,
clambered to the stars, perched on the storm, crept into

caves. But the giant caught him, threw the rope around his neck and dragged him along behind. But he did not die. When the stones of the path were already all red with his blood, he pulled himself together, threw himself despairingly at the abomination and fought with him. The sweat ran swishing from his body, his eyes bulged from their sockets. At last he was victorious and trampled the monster underfoot. Then he was growing, growing as a tree, as stone. He looked around, found himself in a hut in the forest and said dully to himself,

"I am in hell."

Then he awoke, stroked the beading sweat from his forehead and shook the savage images from himself. But hardly had his soul been transformed and had lit up its inner courtyard, his temporal consciousness, again, than he also saw the necessity of his situation.

He carefully gathered the clothes from the chair by his bed, bent over his wife to see if she was sleeping, slipped into his shirt in the living room and dressed himself there. Then he stepped out of the house.

The moon hung in the west. Its red light was dimmed by a white layer of haze that lay spread across the entire sky. It looked as if an extinguished fire was glowing through clear ashes. The trees of the forest were coated by a thick frost which glittered in the bleary light. Soft, dissolving shadows ran from every object, transforming their substantiveness into spectres.

In this light, Exner felt his way to the well house and saw to his astonishment that the well lay open and the pick was lying next to it. Noiselessly he put the elevated board back and in its place and hid the pick in the barn.

Then he set out on the way to see if the boundary stones had really disappeared.

Klose had seen to everything. There were stones there like every other that God had created.

Soothed he went back into the house, for the light in the east had increased. Steps sounded on the way to Erlengrund and he saw a man's head dipping up and down behind the wall in step with his gait. In the interests of safety, he crouched in the ditch. The steps also skipped for a moment, then strode on steadily and were lost in the swishing of the spring wind which had picked up quite gently as if it was wandering there drowsily from a great distance. A light was burning in the living room, so his wife was already awake too. He peeped in and found the room empty.

"Where else would she be than with the puppets!" he murmured, and by that he meant his wife was secretly seeking out her God again. But where could the cobbler be?

Exner searched the barn, the shed, the stalls and, when he heard his wife busying herself again in the house, the hayloft too. Not a trace of him anywhere. Again and again he combed every nook and cranny. The thought that Klose had deliberately hid himself to scare him led him to search for the missing man, not as though he was a man, but rather as though he was a nail, a stick or a feather. In the barn, he raised a chaff basket and thrust with a stick under the thresher. In the shed, he began clearing away the bundles of brushwood, although between them and the wall, there was hardly a hand's width. He called to the cobbler in all the shadows: joking, threatening, indifferent. The corners remained silent, no stifled breath wheezed from the darkness.

Then a terrible thought came to him.

He threw down the bundle of brushwood he was holding, hurried to the well and stared at the boards.

No, that was just pure madness.

If you raised one of them up then it created a gap one and a half feet wide. Yes, but ... if you stepped on the loose board, then tilted it perhaps ... trembling, he stepped back, went into the house, sat down at the table, clenched his hands between his knees and, bowing his head deeply, began thinking. But it was a burrowing in an amorphous mass.

Finally he restored some comfort to himself, "If he is gone then it is the best for me. I'm my own witness and the money remains with me, the trousers and coat too."

"What have you done with the coat?" his wife asked from by the oven.

In order to lead Marie astray, he narrowed his eyes, looked up with a smooth smile and asked,

"Now tell me, what sort of coat!"

"Yes, that I don't know!"

"No, no, Marie, you can't talk riddles, you're not bright enough for that."

With that he laughed mordantly.

After he had averted this unexpected danger, he stood up and left the room, dealing his wife a derisive blow on her back. A sort of faith had come over him and it became easier for him to believe what he prescribed himself: the cobbler had run away from fear of his crime being discovered, would keep himself hidden until the boundary affair's happy end and then be standing in the yard again as if he had appeared out of thin air. But the unease did not go away from the lame one. Cast out by his will, it burrowed into the depths of his being.

In the walls of wooden houses, the woodworm grinds away, quietly and slowly. In the noise of work and the day, you don't hear its burrowing. But in the peace of the night, its low ticking resounds. When people hear it, they are frightened and say, "Death's clock is ticking."

Marie did not notice any change in her husband, for her heart hung in the blossoming branches of her dreams and was singing children's ballads and lullabies.

In the night which followed this restive day, the sky became overcast with heavy vaulted clouds: snow fell. In the morning cold, the snow abated, and when it had become completely light, a sparse rain of fine hail came down, tingling against the windows. When Exner saw that, he was very cheerful and went straight into the yard after getting dressed. Everything was white, every track covered up. He strolled to the corner of the house, looked to the road which led to Erlengrund, and whistled like he usually tended to do.

Then he returned and called to his wife to fetch the water. Marie stepped out obediently.

"Always go and step on the boards!" he shouted to her, and when she looked at him, perplexed by these unnecessary words, he added laughing, "No, no, they are firm. Have no fear, no one's fallen in."

Marie's steps rumbled on the covers, the water streamed from the tap, clear and lively, and filled both vessels.

"Well, you childish ditz!" he called cheerfully when he had seen all that.

For a long time, he then stood and looked at the well house, as if something unexpected could happen with it. But it stood motionless as ever there and the red ball kept brave watch from the little roof as always.

Then he shook his head laughing and murmured, "What more do I want! Haven't I seen it? Sometimes it's like I'm riveted with a hammer."

The cobbler must come — from the forest, the ditch, the tavern, the barn, from somewhere. There was not a man in Steindorf and the entire area who expected anything else. He breathed out in relief when this occurred to him. His heavy worries slipped into the spotless expectation of others who knew nothing of the ill-favoured night and the foreboding which had climbed from it into his soul like a heavy cloud. And suddenly it seemed to him that his hidden, strange fancies were to blame for everything and that some of the unpleasantness of his life would still have remained undone if he "had not pushed such crazy stuff into silence".

Hence he did what every small farmer does so early on a winter's day, went into the barn, threw sheaves on the barn floor and spread them out, the ears towards the middle, in two rows.

Distant steps on the half-frozen earth made themselves audible. He quickly threw down his work, grasped a rope so that it looked as if he was deeply engaged, and went across the yard to the corner of the house. There he saw, in accordance with his surmise, the Lord of the Manor coming into view and striding to the place where the wall had been. Now he turned off and hurried across the field in order to shorten the way.

The lame one lifted his cap and called, "Good morning, lord!"

The man with the brown beard and paper-white face gave no answer and hurried to the place where the boundary stones must have been which the labourers had laid bare. He scraped the snow away with his boots, stooped down and shook his head.

When Exner saw that, he called over,

"It's cold, a quite pretty snow. But it'll go away. The Eschberg is worse off, over there Hannig Seffe has certainly got his winter cap on."

The Lord of the Manor probably did not understand a word, but must have thought the clod was mocking him. He straightened up and threatened with his fist,

"I'll get you, my little friend!"

Exner smiled genially as though the Lord of the Manor had enquired after his health and doffed his hat again, as the estate owner was preparing to make his way back.

Most of all, he would have liked to have run after him to ask him where the cobbler was staying. He pondered irresolutely if he should go or not, until this thought was lost in shapeless brooding. He had to get clarity over something and could not figure out what.

His wife's voice released him from this fruitless exertion. She was asking him to taste the water she had pumped from the well. Without thinking he took the can from her, took a deep swallow from it, wiped his mouth with the back of his hand and said calmly,

"Like watercress and as fresh and sweet as almonds. What's the issue?"

"What's the issue! Well, I hear sometimes, something falls into a well, and ..."

"Yes, yes!" he mocked, "no, ha, what a clever woman you are. What would fall in, into the well?"

"Well a cat or something?"

"Or a cow, eh? or a man, eh? Perhaps the cobbler, you think because he's gone since yesterday. Right up and through the boards, eh?"

"Why are you turning pale?"

"Because I'm laughing."

"And you don't need to sink your eyes like that!"

Exner measured his wife with a smouldering look, his breath began to whistle with fury, then rage tore off the mask of his cautious moderation. Fitfully, grumbling, louder and louder, he shouted,

"Sinking my eyes. My hand is loosening and if you don't go straightaway then it'll lie against your face. You! What do you want from me? You have ill-treated me enough already. Now I should be able to make well water! Then you'd better go and ask your puppets. They're clever enough."

Marie went away despondently.

But the lame one had not shelved this eruption either.

He lapsed into a ravenous zest for work, chopped wood, threshed alone in the barn so that everything shook, dug drainage ditches in the frozen fields, split stones. Yes, he did everything aimlessly. Thus he shoved the snow from the roof with long poles and cleared the path although the snow already lay foot deep, just to fight against his fate. It was not a spiritual battle, an emotional argument, for him. He thought he could saw off his misdeed, shatter it with the hammer, kill it with the axe.

But the images of his fear did not go away from him, and at the end of the week, he felt more lost than at the beginning.

17

While the lame one battled against his fate on his narrow field, a net of suspicion was being spun in Steindorf and bit by bit in the surrounding area.

The disappearance of the cobbler, Klose, excited the people's curiosity most of all, the people who, penned together by the cold in narrow residences, could work jointly at unravelling the puzzle.

The most various, contradictory rumours arose: he had frozen to death in the forest, he was sitting in prison for being a vagrant. These opinions emerged at the beginning and were simple and natural. But they could not hold people's interest for long, and since nothing new wanted to occur, people began to explain the event in a more and more intricate way. In some village, something was stolen from someone without any trace being found of the thief. Someone associated the cobbler with it and thought he had set off over the mountains with the booty never to be seen again. Soon people were tired of this explanation and fashioned a dramatic rumour. Quietly, so nobody found out, everyone put it about that the lame one was holding the cobbler locked up after beating him half to death, as he had been caught by him digging up the boundary stones. A man from the Eschberg seemed, as he was going to his distant workplace, to have seen how Klose had been hauled by the neck across the field by the lame one. Standing behind the wall, he had seen everything clearly, but had hurried away out of fear of the clod.

This version's adventurousness drew everyone in and each found opportunity to bring the one or the other variant into widespread fashion. When the rumour had made the rounds through every house a few times, it had grown into a novel which nobody dared to doubt anymore.

Everyone suddenly remembered the lame one's incivility and crudeness. Everyone felt threatened and troubled, their ill-treated sense of right and wrong demanded clearing up.

Thus, fourteen days after Klose's disappearance, his sister Pauline, called Paula, entered the little yard at Freibusch to ask after her brother. She met Marie alone in the living room.

The cold had afflicted the girl extremely and her body shook under her scanty clothing. The delicate mission, which she had undertaken in order to atone for what she had brought on her brother by her lapse, reinforced the shiver which shook her body from time to time. Just the haggard face, which in early youth would probably not have been lacking in beauty, had reddened a little.

She entered hesitantly, made her greeting and lowered her gaze.

Marie coerced her into taking a seat on the bench and sat down on a chair opposite her.

Since the visitor, who was completely unknown to Marie, made no move to speak but rather let her large eyes wander curiously and fearfully through the room, the young woman asked,

"Well, what brings you then, pretty girl?"

Paula became confused, lowered her eyes and then answered hostilely,

"You could probably tell me, but you act naturally as if it wasn't true."

"And what wouldn't be true then?"

"I'm Paula."

"Yes, why wouldn't that be true then? If you say it, then it'll be so."

"Oh, you misunderstand me. My brother, where ..." She broke off and looked attentively at Marie.

"Your brother ..., who's that?"

"Then I see it's all true! You don't know my brother, Gustav, a cobbler who's gone in and out here? — I see. But trust me, I'm not going until I've seen!"

She took up her blue apron and held the corner to her mouth.

"Yes, of course! ... Your brother is the cobbler, Klose ... hmhm ..."

Marie did not know how it came to be that she became unsure. The large eyes before her, which had still been wet and now began to shine so determinedly since she had broken off stuttering, expressed the firm will to solve a puzzle which she too had now obsessed over for days. The cobbler's disappearance suddenly seemed mysterious to her too, so that she wondered over how she could have remained so indifferent before.

That went on in her while she was hesitating for a few seconds. Then she adroitly continued her reply,

"My God, who'd be greatly surprised if your brother has gone! He is sometimes here, sometimes there. He was here with us around the twentieth of last month, ate lunch with us, went out and then I haven't seen anymore of him."

Paula sprang up, and while she stepped to the table, she cast with shaking voice into Marie's face the suspicion that Steindorf and the entire surrounds were entertaining.

"Humph," she concluded, "Everyone is blaming your man! To him it's all the same whether he strikes a cat half-dead or a man."

Then the clearing of a man's raw throat was heard.

Terrified, the women turned around.

The lame one stood in the door. A spasm went through his body. His arms hung down tautly by his sides as though he was carrying a heavy weight in his tightly closed fists whose knuckles shimmered white. His face was ashen, his eyes lay deep in their sockets, around his thin lips lay an unmoving smile, more a rigid distortion.

Quietly and thoughtfully, he closed the door. Quietly and slowly, his head inclined slightly to the side, he came nearer.

Marie's heart was pounding before this terrible sight. She knew that he would rush at the girl in a moment.

But it did not happen.

Some two steps before her, he stopped and looked at her for a long time silently with his cold, piercing eyes. Then he smiled distortedly and silently.

Paula opened her mouth to speak, only she was so afraid that no words could come forth. With open lips, she stared at him and tears came into her eyes.

The lame one browsed for a while at her fright. Then he spoke, with a deep voice to begin with, whose wavering conferred a soft sound to it,

"I heard everything. That's okay. But — don't say it a second time. Sit down, Paula, don't say anything else! Look at my hands. Don't say anything else!"

The threats became more and more furious. But he accompanied them with a friendly aspect in his face, which you would not think it capable of.

Then he asked, "Isn't Guste my comrade from my schooldays?"

Nobody answered.

"Who threw him among the poor when you, Paula, came home in spring in disgrace? In disgrace, without a Bohemian's money, to your poor mother in disgrace! Well?"

The tears were streaming over the girl's tormented face and she had to clench her teeth to not sob out loud.

"Yes, well, that I should strike your brother! Why would I then?"

Exner laughed shrilly after this exclamation, shook his raised arms to the side and became even paler.

Now Paula dared to answer,

"That'd be because he was watching, because you ..."

It was beyond her powers to make the accusation direct to the lame one's face, and she bent down to her feet as if there was something to arrange there.

Exner laughed again, but it was as if his neck sat in a vice. The sweat broke out on his forehead and he dried it with a trembling hand.

"Now," he then answered, "I know all about the maggots that the people in Steindorf fill their heads with. Haha, them, them! Utter asses they all are, nothing else. When Guste comes back then he will tell you if I moved a stone. Would I have myself thrown in prison because of such a little bit of a field? I'd have to have horns and moo loudly! — Where would he be hiding then? You must know if he has cooked it up! Come on, Paula, for fun I'll lead you to where you want to go: in the cellar, in the stalls, to the loft. You can blow the dust from the drawers if you want! — Should I rip up the floor? Haha. — Or — or do you want to climb into the well?"

He had to say it. An irresistible force had driven him to it as though the accursed was far from him when he spoke it. But now that his voice, strange and certain like that of an accuser who stood next to him and knew everything, had sounded in his ear, he felt a pressure in his head which was increasing and becoming so strong that it seemed as if his head was shrinking.

Before his eyes, an ever darkening cloud was setting in. He had to seize the shelf behind his back, clenching it with his hands. All the objects in the room were disappearing as if they were disposed to hover in the air.

Finally the faintness was over, and Exner again saw quite clearly the colourful goldfinch springing around in its cage. That gave him such a great joy that he laughed and laughed until the tears came into his eyes.

In the end, he forced himself to be serious and spoke drily,

"Now, Paula, come, we'll go look."

The girl rose and followed him into the house. There she pressed past the clod, sprang fleeing out the door and called in,

"Adieu, Exner! You're not catching me!"

The lame one watched her and laughed again, but now it sounded like a roosting hen fluttering to the ground. He broke off abruptly, looked around startled and went with serious, pale face into the barn again. Marie sat motionless in the living room and stared with wide-open eyes at the floor, as if an invisible script lay there which she could read quite accurately, but whose content was so horrific that she was seized by a frenzy.

Why had her husband not flared up? Why had he, against his custom, engaged in a long conversation? Why had he laughed so grimly?

The answer lay there on the floor between the rows of black nailheads.

A veil lay over the happiness that she carried within. A veil which shrouded and silently abducted the beautiful images of her hope. Her soul was like a harvested field, and behind the trembling greyness which was clearing her dreams, a desolate, empty area remained behind like the ploughed up field of stubble looking like a graveyard with countless, freshly thrown-up mounds.

"All my future is dead," she thought, "buried and beginning to rot." Yes, and suddenly she really noticed that sickly, oppressive smell which originates from corpses. Hastily she held her breath, but it was not restrained. Now she was tasting it too.

Springing up in fear, tearing the door open and breathing in the house was one thing. The smell lay there too.

She held her breath with tight chest and her heart in mid-beat, stepped to the door and opened her mouth to dispose of this nervous illusion outside in the fresh winter air. But the cold current hardly touched her tongue, as she called out with screeching voice, "Karl! — Karl!"

His large head came hesitantly out of the low barn door. Desperate anticipation was painted over his face. When he saw nobody but his wife, he wanted to back away again quietly.

Only Marie called in extreme agitation,

"Karl, come out and smell!"

He considered for a moment, then forced a smile onto his face, stepped out and smelt the air. He wanted to joke. But the words remained on the tip of his tongue. With effort, he finally wrenched out the question,

"What should it smell of then?"

"Now, don't you smell it? It smells of death!"

To the lame one, it seemed as if he would fall over. Yet in nameless exertion, he continued smiling, the sweat appeared on his forehead and his extinguished eyes rested helplessly on Marie. His teeth clenched together and breathing as if speaking to his soul without making use of his speech organs, the words passed over his lips,

"The cobbler is rotting."

Nobody had heard it, not even his own ears. But in his heart, the confession had not passed without trace. And strangely, this self-confession became a deliverance. The whirl collapsed in him, the shock vanished, no pounding on his nerves, his eyes cold and still.

He threw a dismissive look at his wife and returned to the barn without speaking another word.

There he lay on the straw and enjoyed the change in his nature. The feeling of unrestrained certainty came over him stronger and stronger. He stood out of reach above all men. If his soul had just an indistinct and very eccentric notion of good and evil before, then this difference had now been obliterated. Not as though the lame one would have known that. It showed only when he pondered over how to evade the pursuers who were surrounding him and whose number must be growing daily. Without the least timidity, he now began to ponder over his situation.

He had, even without stirring a hand, driven the boozer into the well. Instead of reproaching himself over that, he worked himself into a fury over the idiot who had brought him into such a fix by his clumsiness.

What must happen first? How would it be if he fetched the body out and buried it somewhere in the forest! — That would not work. He could hardly keep it secret from his wife if he climbed down in the night, and then the danger for him too. A stranger? No, that would be putting his head in the noose.

Best would be to take his chances. He pushed all objections from his head. What did he have to be frightened of! Nobody could prove that he was to blame for the cobbler's death or killed the man or removed the boundary stones. But while he pondered that, he hit a consideration which dealt with it! —

The boundary stones! — If by some accident, Klose was found in the well then the boundary stones would also be discovered at the same time.

That was really the only way in which his ruin would come about.

He burrowed deeper into the straw, took a straw between his teeth and mused over how he could escape this danger.

To start with, it cost him effort to ponder the possibilities keenly and keep them apart, because he was not used to mental labour at all. Only the constant torment of the previous twelve days had pulled his spirit together to a point and sharpened it. It proved that he was not at all the limited clod which people held him to be. Hindered by his early misfortune on an outing, atrophied in a monotonous environment and by his defiant attitude, he had fallen behind mentally. At the same time, his will had become all-powerful. With this unrelenting obstinacy, he was emphatic about his salvation. After long hours, the plan for it was ready.

He wanted to fetch stones and dump them in the well. Under two cartloads, there would have to be one or two weathered boundary stones intermingled which he had lifted out of an unfamiliar, distant field or the royal forest during the night and carried home in his sack unseen. As a result, the discovery of the cobbler's corpse would be thwarted, if he could bring his wife to keep things secret. If the police, who with all the surrounding agitation must look into the cobbler's disappearance, nevertheless climbed into the well, now then they would find the dead man and he could calmly swear a hundred oaths that he was not to blame for his misfortune. At the same time, the presence of so many boundary stones would have to totally confuse the iniquity of the boundary incident. And if he did not surrender too foolishly, he could hope, if not unplucked, to come out again from the whole entanglement. Satisfied, Exner straightened up. Certainly his wife would be surprised by all the stone transporting and, mistrustful as she was again, would torment him with all kinds of suspicions. Then he would tell her that the partial filling of the well with big and small stones was necessary to push the water from the slimy, rotten bottom up higher between the stones so that its earthy impurities would settle in this way and lose the bad taste.

He could also use this explanation with the police.

After he had thus ironed things out with himself, he laughed satisfied, rubbed his hands, drew his head between his massive shoulders and stepped through the little door into the yard. The sky was glowing in a shimmering turquoise and long, tattered, burning red stripes lay in it.

"Dammit, it's evening!"

He had not eaten anything since breakfast.

He acted as though he had been sleeping. Rubbing his eyes, he stepped into the living room and, yawning, asked to eat.

His wife was sitting at the table, her face turned towards the twilit room. In her voice, it could be recognised that she was crying. It seemed like the words were sticking to one another.

"Yes, you want to eat?" she asked in painful surprise.

The lame one let himself fall heavily onto the bench and answered good-humouredly,

"Now, I don't have a wooden stomach. When I sleep, the hunger comes."

"You have slept, have you?"

"Now, aren't I allowed to?"

"Oh, you may, but to be able to!"

"To be able to, I'd think I am", and the clod began snoring loudly.

"Karl, if I'm not to go crazy on the spot, stop snoring!" she called despairingly and began sobbing.

"You women can't do anything but cry and have children."

"Should I dance a bit too? Out in the well lies the cobbler. And I don't know, strike me dead on the spot, if you are guilty."

The lame one sat there for a while silently, one of his elbows propped on the table, and looked straight ahead. Then he laughed contemptuously.

"Haha, you must be crazy then, if the Steindorf people come to a mind, absolutely all together?"

She shook her head and continued crying softly.

"If the cobbler fell into it then he must have been standing on the well", Exner continued talking. It sounded like he was ridding himself of an idle inconvenience. "Because he couldn't fall through the boards again. And why in all the world would I have tossed the cobbler, who'd done nothing to me, in the well! Gossip, nothing but women's gossip!"

Marie shook her head again.

"But Karl, the smell, the corpse smell!"

"That is the bad, rotten water which is coming off the mountain now and the clay in it. You should've tasted it when the well was barely finished and Freiwald brought up the first bottle, just like liquid manure. Good old Freiwald! Now it has the same taste. I'll soon have to drop a few stones in it so it rises above the sludge. And straightaway, before it freezes hard and fast in the middle. Right? Don't think about it Marie, that'd be best."

Marie remained silent. She had lowered her head and seemed to be considering something.

Then she started, lit a candle from the oven and walked right up to Exner so that his face was brightly lit. —

"Look at me, straight, open your eyes wide!" she said with a deeply serious, wavering voice.

The lame one blinked in the light and then again at his wife, but he could not withstand the look of those deep blue, desperate eyes.

When the young woman perceived that, her arm began to shake so that she had to place the candlestick on the table.

"Stand up in front of the bench — and step over to me — in front of the light."

Her voice was soft, but had a strange depth to it.

Exner was becoming uncomfortable, but he obeyed her, laughing.

"Swear to me by the light and by the sun that you aren't guilty if the cobbler is lying in the well, swear to me by heaven and all the saints ..."

"With all six, if you want."

He interrupted her and raised his hand willingly.

But she pulled his arm down and continued,

"And that the Lord strike us all if it isn't true and curse, tear up and drive to all the winds us and the house, the wood together with the stones!"

She said the last with a chanting voice, seriously borne. Then she quit with a deep breath and looked inquiringly into his face.

Not a single muscle stirred in it. It was as sullen as a gnarled branch.

"Well, can I now?" he finally asked.

Marie did not stir. She stared into the light, and tears ran slowly over her pale cheeks.

Then she said mutely,

"Let — let it be — no, no — rather not —" and she did not turn her gaze from the flame.

The lame one sat down, remaining silent, and she also returned to her place by the window, where she crouched as though compressed, with the same gaze into emptiness. Suddenly she rose quietly and quite slowly, just like dreamers sit up in bed in a frightened, fearful midnight hour, and with searching steps, as if she was walking through a dense gloom, she headed for her husband, stopped in front of him and stroked his forehead a few times. Silently, and her ice-cold hands shook at the same time.

After that she went again to the other side of the table, sat down there, her hands folded, and moved her lips silently until she lapsed into a rigidly painful demeanour with her pale face resembling one of those statues of suffering penitents which in the dim of catholic churches burden our hearts with so much dull pain.

"Karl", she said timidly.

The lame one raised his heavy head.

"Let me fetch my Holy Mother and the angels. Karl, am I right that you have nothing against it?"

Her voice had the ring of stirring love.

Exner rose up petulantly, because "nothing has come of the entire story again but women's gossip", took a few long strides through the room and then answered indifferently, "Jesus yes, certainly. For my sake, always", and hurriedly left the room. After a few minutes, the Virgin Mary with her two angels was standing again on the corner shelf above the table and looking down with rigid eyes into the room in whose darkness the small light hung on a thousand sweltering threads of light.

Towards eight o'clock, after their supper, both sought their bed.

Marie soon sank into a sleep and dreamt of blossoming mountains of light from whose bushes winged children fluttered down.

The lame one lay there with open eyes for a long time and let the day pass by him. Finally he emitted a contemptuous sound, wrapped himself in the sheets and went to sleep too.

But outside the night wind was playing with the breath of death.

18

But before the lame one could begin with the extraction of old boundary stones and the filling of the well, the residents of Steindorf on their own initiative began preliminary proceedings against him. Spies lurked around his homestead day and night. Letter after letter of invective was stuck to his door, to the wellhouse or fluttered by his window, thrown from an unseen hand. The children on their way to school stood shouting on the wall, pointing excitedly at his house and running away hurriedly when he showed himself with the cries, "He's coming, he's coming!" And when he pulled himself together to brave the rumours, strode armed with a heavy stick through the village, sat in the tavern, pressed passers-by on the path into conversation without pretext, then he must have perceived that he could not learn anything of the people's opinions and intentions. They stole away from him in order to shout threats at him from a safe distance, to spit or raise their fists at him. Intractably he backed into the net which their cowardly diligence had spun around him and lay in waiting until he could cunningly bring his plan to fruition. Only it brought him no success other than to fetch a few boundary stones from the far-off district of Petzdorf on a dark night and with great difficulty, and to hide them in the barn under the brushwood.

At the same time, he had to keep watch over his wife fearfully so that she did not get together with anyone. He managed all the shopping himself and was always in pursuit of the accursed letters of invective.

Marie never complained and raised no word of suspicion. She only fled horrified from the clumsy tenderness with which he now frequently stalked her. Otherwise she looked at him with a stiff mildness. She walked about with long, steady strides, her face wore a tense seriousness. With hard, overwhelming motions, like someone working in the very cold, she applied herself to every chore. If the wind banged a door somewhere or her husband's step rang out unexpectedly from the yard, then she started, ran with blanched face to the window and spied the path for a long time only to then go to work again silent and rapt like someone lost.

Only the lamp in front of the Holy Mother on the corner shelf burned without interruption, even on bright days, and on many a night when the lame one, torn by a nervous face from restive sleep, reached out to her, he found her bed cold and empty and heard through the door her monotonous, muffled prayer.

But she was not able to stop the rolling stone of retribution.

As a result of an anonymous denunciation, Constable Stief from Walsdorf came to the lonely farmyard at Freibusch one morning to interrogate the clod over the disappearance of the boundary stones and the cobbler, and to subject the house together with its close surrounds to a meticulous investigation.

Exner was deferential, friendly, stooping and bowing, saddened from aggrieved honour, became brutal, acted foolishly, said lies with an ingenuous, stupid demeanour, spoke truths with that uncertain voice and that evasive glance which characterise white lies, and outwitted the Constable completely, who became more and more morose, the more unpromising the interrogation shaped itself, and in the end, he only went on about this and that minor matter to give the lame one his due.

Marie's back ran hot and cold when she saw her husband jumping around in such smooth contempt for the truth with the guardian of the law. Several times she opened her mouth for a redemptive scream, but Exner's eyes forced her to make her statements along the line of his testimonies.

Finally Constable Stief made arrangements to rise from his seat at the table, snapped his notebook shut, and while he stretched the rubberband around it sedately and carefully, he said,

"That is a lousily accounted for story, you understand, my friend, and I can only say this much to you, some muck will yet fall on your head."

The lame one unintentionally stretched himself from his stooped attitude up into his full, square-built height.

"Just carry on as you are!" Stief flared and rose, pushing the chair back with his hand. "I've nabbed others like you, take note. Leave it well alone, the prosecutor will pick it out of their guts in due course."

He let his raking glance run all around the room, stroked his black moustache, looking at the floor, and then ordered,

"Now we will have another look!"

Overzealously the lame one sprang up and opened the door. In striding out, Stief insisted to him,

"Don't make a dance! Where have you put the stones?"

Exner asserted for the hundredth time that he could not give an answer to him because he had had nothing to do with the boundary stones, and asked him to take the trouble to investigate the entire house and everything that lay in and around it so that the vexatious suspicion could finally be lifted from him.

Stief did not let himself be misled, and if he also expected nothing from searching the house then he had the opportunity to practise on the hard-nosed man according to all the rules of the art, to soften and hope to find this or that which would unstick things and point him in a new direction. He climbed upstairs and downstairs, purred around everywhere with clacking tongue, beset him hard with ever stronger threats, finally tapping him on the shoulder in a dark corner and whispering benignly in his ear, now he could tell him, in private, he had a temper too and would understand to keep it secret. When they were standing in the shed by the pile of brushwood, the thought actually occurred to the lame one, whether it would not be better to aid the Constable's finding of the stolen boundary stones, for he had a vague hope of thereby leading the investigation down a dead end and in fact began to throw down bunch after bunch.

"What are you doing there?" the helmeted man asked gruffly.

"You should look to see if the stones are behind it", Exner answered and threw another bunch at Stief's feet.

"You — you — knothole, haha! Stief follows his nose, do you understand?" the Constable called contemptuously and crept through the little door into the open.

Exner followed him, and since he perceived that the investigation was at an end, he said,

"I'm very sorry, Constable, that you had to come here through the deep snow because of such absurd lies. When it put you out and it was for nothing!"

"Dammit, shut up! A royal Prussian Constable has no problem with that at all, do you understand!"

"No, no, don't be angry, Constable. I am just a dumb, simple man and don't know what authority is. I talk straight from the heart — adieu, Constable, adieu!"

He had accompanied him as far as the well house, made an awkward bow again and went to go into the house.

Suddenly Stief spat and shouted,

"Ugh! Disgusting! what is that stink in your yard. Like in a mortuary!"

"That's the water, Constable. Look, I dug thirty metres, tossed good money by the handful into that earth, and now the water has a taste that makes men and animals sick. That's how it goes for a poor man. Would you like to sample it? It isn't drinkable!"

Stief looked him steadily in the eye.

The lame one felt the membrane passing over his eyeballs and raised his hand to wipe it away.

"Come over here!" Stief ordered with a sinisterly pregnant voice.

After a short hesitation, the lame one obeyed. But now it seemed to him as if the well house was leaping up and down, and he looked at the Constable as if he was expiring.

"Yes, yes", he said nevertheless and went to the grey point in front of him.

Thank God! He had overcome it. Three steps before the shiny-buttoned chest, everything was as usual and he looked at Stief with well-feigned simplemindedness.

"Do you know something?" the latter asked threateningly and pointed at the well, "Do you know something? — I will ..."

He broke off however, grasped quickly in his pocket and cried,

"Hands out!"

The lame one threw a look at the nearby forest and saw how the trees began marching towards him, the ground thundered under him and a swishing filled the air. He recognised that no escape was possible and stretched out his arms with a crazy smile.

But Stief had suddenly thought of something else, dropped the handcuffs in his trouser pocket again, looked at his watch, whistled, blinked at Exner and with the words,

"Oh well, there is nothing at all to be found here", he wheeled around and walked away.

He had had the intention of arresting the lame one because it seemed irrefutably certain to him that the cobbler's corpse lay in the well. But the next moment, his scythe-sharp certainty had been dispersed by thought of the disgrace if a cat, a dog or nothing at all was found down the hole, and he struck off with the intent of first investigating the cause of the pestilential stink, and then doing with compelling authority what his hands itched to do. Besides, it was eleven, his stomach was empty and his throat was hoarse from too much talking. With hurried, long strides, he headed for the tavern. His sabre was hitting against the legs of his high boots. The rattling clapping gradually tailed off into the distance.

The lame one did not dare stirring. The shovelled snow huddled around him like a mob of lurking, white cats, springing up with every strike of the sabre, whisking about wildly and squatting down again. As the jingling steps became more and more indistinct, the snow calmed down, and when it was completely silent, the thousand white shovelled chunks lay motionless around him and goggled up at him like the dead faces of men buried up to their necks.

Exner had the certainty for a period that they would all begin screaming if he made any attempt to stir.

Finally he dared to turn around and saw Marie standing by the window, her crumpled face pressed against the pane as if she had died long ago, been raised by a stranger and rested against the window. He knew she had been frightened by the Constable's handcuffs, and to indicate to her that the raising and stretching out of his hands had been for no other reason than it being a quirky habit of his, he raised his hands to the well again and took a look at them as if he did not know that his wife was watching him. Then he began to move the lever with his right hand and stretched his left hand under the outlet pipe so that he gave the appearance of washing his hands. The pipe remained dry. Now he was flinging the lever up and down in furious haste. The well house shuddered, the piston rod groaned up and down. The water was not forthcoming. That's why, after a few hefty swings with the lever, he stood close by the well house and washed his hands in the air, stepped to the side, slapped them dry, went into the house, seized Marie around her torso and sat her down on the bench by the table.

Marie did not say a word, but just looked straight ahead.

It no longer seemed doubtful to the clod that she also knew, it was all out.

After he had sat for a while with his hands clenched between his knees, three plans had come to him. He must throw stones into the well to hide his crime. It was necessary to pursue the locating of the cobbler himself in order to remove the suspicion of criminality from himself. He must ditch and ignore everything without looking up or looking back, in order just to bring himself to safety.

He rose and immediately started on its execution.

In the shed, he threw the brushwood all over the place, carried the four stolen boundary stones out and smashed them into small pieces with the iron sledge hammer. He loaded these into a barrow and pushed it to the well. He left them there, lifted a fire ladder from the roof, fetched the other from behind the house, and bound them both together with cords.

After that he went into the house, changed his clothes and went into the village, cold and stony like a hard man striding to an undelayable affair.

He found old Freiwald at his winter work, the fabrication of kitchen utensils. When the clod entered the small room, the old man rose sheepishly, shifted his large glasses to his forehead and offered him a chair. Curt, outright, Exner set out his commission: the old well digger shall tomorrow morning see what the matter was with his well. The water had not been forthcoming for days. He, Exner, could fetch the well digger from Petzdorf, but Freiwald had dug the well of course and would be more thorough about the matter than someone else. The fire ladders were bound together, everything lay prepared, he could not be present himself because he had an appointment.

Freiwald made this and that excuse. The lame one restricted himself to repeating his instructions, gave his hand genially to the old man and left. On the village street, he suddenly did not know anymore what was happening. It was constantly like a roaring wind going through his body, and the sound of his steps seemed to cascade down to him from the surrounding mountains. He took his cap off so that the pounding from above would stop. The clamour in the air above him continued. So he decided to climb up the Eschberg. That is what someone did when such a thing happened to them. At the fork in the path where a steep path climbed up to the left, the other branching off to pass by Fuchsloch, he had already forgotten his intention again and strode to his paternal home. Half way there, under the alders of a pond, his brother Joseph suddenly stood before him. He was carrying half a sack of breadstuffs over his shoulder and heading for the mill.

After greeting him, the younger man asked,

"Now, Karl, where are you heading?"

The lame one was tempted to imitate his brother's soft, high voice, but stifled the urge and answered,

"To you. You will probably know how it's going with my one, and since I must keep an appointment in town tomorrow ..."

"Yes, how far along is it, how does it stand with the Lord of the Manor?"

Without paying attention to his interruption, the lame one continued,

"I would rather not leave Marie alone, as I never know what will happen with her. It's already too close."

"Well think, it won't be good, but yet ..."

"But yet", the clod considered the words and emitted an ill-favoured laugh. "What then, 'but yet'! Have I ever said 'but yet' when the interest didn't add up?"

"Now, Karl, look, I have a sick cow myself, and accordingly I actually have to go to Rolling tomorrow. In the end though, it's too far."

"I'm not an organ grinder, and what has your Rolling story got to do with me!"

"You don't need to have a temper again."

"Well, what would you prefer, to give me the thousand talers by the feast day of John the Baptist or for Kath to come tomorrow and stay with Marie."

"But, Karl, we are brothers. Must you always talk with a stick."

"Brothers! I know you! You would like it most of all if tomorrow I was hung at the gallows."

After this rebellion, the roaring wind began to hollow out the lame one's body again. A fear that he could not master took possession of him.

With fading voice, he asked,

"Joseph, for heaven's sake, for Christ and the Virgin Mary's sake! Do me the one good deed and send Kath to my place tomorrow. You don't know anything, anything at all, and I can't tell you anything."

Then it became grey around him, he heard and saw nothing more.

When he looked up again, he was sitting all alone on a stone and holding a ball of snow in his hand which he kneaded with stiff fingers. A gentle wind blew little drifts here and there from the snow covering so that they flew along for a stretch like silent birds and then settled down again. There was a hurried scurrying about him.

"Come on, keep coming," he murmured threateningly at the play of the snow, "keep coming!"

After he had said it for the third time, it occurred to him that he had revealed himself to his brother. Now nothing more remained for him but to flee immediately. He hurried home through the forest, threw himself at the wheelbarrow, took it into the field and shovelled it full of snow. Then he unbound the fire ladders. He could not untie the last knots, left everything lying, ran to the upper room, stuck his savings book in his coat pocket and then went up to the hayloft again to see how long the fodder would last for. The moonlight hung through the dormer, and with the wind, it was as if a white sheet was being blown in from outside. In the unsteady light, he bent down and grasped about in the hay. The longer he burrowed in the rustling stalks, the more inconceivable it became for him to abandon everything: the cows, the pigs, the house, the fields, the money. That skinny book alone rescued him above all. He, who wanted to subjugate Steindorf entirely, to have the Lord of the Manor on a string, he, who could fold everyone up like a penknife, if he wanted! Should he run across the street like a dog, hunted, impoverished.

In fury he piled the hay up with both hands and threw it at the moonlight. "Dog!" he screamed, "brute!" and terrible curses whilst tossing the hay continually at the dormer. The sweat was streaming over his face, his voice became hoarse, but he did not stop.

He kept bending down and throwing loads behind himself.

"My money! my money! my house! my fields!" His breath rattled even more.

Suddenly it felt like the floor was rising, a crackling ran through the shingles, a drumming hammered on the walls under him. Everything began to revolve, whirling it turned him, he received a blow against his head. Everything around him stood in sputtering flame. Then he collapsed.

A crashing and bellowing of cows goaded him early in the morning from the stupefaction in which he had lain the entire night.

He sat up in order to clear his mind. In the end, he brought together what was irrefutable.

He wanted to head for Landeck to withdraw the money from his savings account and then escape over the border to Bohemia.

Turbid, defiant, he rose, pushed his way through the hay and went down into the living room.

It was ice-cold. The grey light of dawn hung there. Nobody was to be seen. The beds in the bedroom were untouched.

Finally he discovered his wife lying in front of the table, coiled up like an animal.

He shook her.

She stood up, stumbled, went to the table, sat down on the bench and stared at the floor.

Then she lifted her eyes, let them glide over him and said mutely,

"There is nothing else left for you."

The lame one nodded silently.

As she looked up again, she noticed how he was becoming paler, earthly pale. All the time, he nodded his head and swallowed so that she could hear the bob of his Adam's apple.

Timidly he finally stretched his hand to her. She shook her head.

He let his arm fall and went, his head inclined to one side, hobbling out the door without turning around. In the house, he stopped for a moment, coughed a few times, spat and left the homestead with heavy steps.

Then the ticking of the clock was the only sign of life.

Marie stiffly turned her head and looked out the window. The forest stood like a vague wall in the morning mist. A dark ball moved towards it. That was her husband. Now he was disappearing like an angry ghost. — "Now he is gone", the young woman murmured and sank down sobbing.

PART THREE

19

The hand of her God weighed heavier than before on the poor woman. Whilst she lay and sobbed, the thought came to her of whether it would not be better to end her life. Was not God himself clearly pointing her to death's door since his visitations were not allowed to her? Perhaps her life was a jibbing against his will, a sin and to remain in it nothing but presumptuousness.

Her head upright, with steady eyes, she looked into these depths.

But was she alone? Would she tear her innocent child, so close to being born, with her into eternal perdition?

Just now, as she looked numbly at the terrible path like a beggar leans his head into the storm, the unborn child struggled in her body like a lamb struggles against the tether which will lead it to the butcher's block.

Without further reflection, she wiped the tears from her eyes and obediently, without a will, she let herself be pushed by the hand of God onto a path which she did not embrace. She kindled the fire in the oven, set out her breakfast and sank humbly into her hardship. Without looking the thought in the face, she carried on.

"As God will, keep still" and "God strikes with one hand and repays with a hundred", these and similar sayings of blessed ancient wisdom calmed her soul so that her fierce anguish was transformed into that dull, feverish calm with which the condemned listen from their dark prison to every noise outside.

Her husband had gone away in the direction of the lower field, so he could only have taken the path in the direction of Landeck. Of course, if he wanted to flee then he could only hope to go over the border before the police recognised the entire extent of his crime and struck out in pursuit of him. She began praying to God that He would let his flight succeed so that she and her child would be saved the shame. But to be certain, she climbed up to the summer room and looked in the drawers for the savings book. It had disappeared. The newspaper in which it had usually been shrouded lay in a bunched up ball in a corner. Thank God! At eleven o'clock at the latest, he could have taken the money from the savings account, at five o'clock in the afternoon, he would be over the border. Relieved and at the same time saddened that it had come to the point where she had to be gratified by such an event, she took herself into the living room again and her heart filled to bursting with all the agonising future possibilities.

The winter day had turned out clear. The mist had drawn itself up into the heights. The white light came quietly through the window, and every object looked as if intense moonlight was flowing over it. Sometimes a large snowflake fell through the air, slowly and waveringly like white blossoms edging swaying to the ground in the still quiet of a May day. Then there was again nothing to be seen but the billowing of this milk-white brightness in front of the distant forest.

"You?" Marie asked her God and her fate in the beautiful deadness, "you? ... you? ..." suffocating, help-less.

In the distance, steps rang out, nearing the homestead hurriedly. Marie stepped back from the window into the middle of the room in order to be able to examine the arrival as inconspicuously as possible and saw at the same time Kath, her sister-in-law, hurry past the well house to the front door. She was carrying a basket on her arm, was dressed in her Sunday best, and her cheeks were reddened from her quick gait. Marie hardly had time to step to the stove and, grasping a whisk, to give the appearance of busy activity, than the girl was also already, having arrived at the door, kicking the snow from her feet and then noisily coming in. White haze like a wolf streamed from her, waltzed over the floor and disappeared as it hid itself away under the bench.

In an instant, Marie knew that Kath must not be allowed to notice anything of what had occurred, in order to avert greater misfortune, and she replied wittily to the girl's greeting, "Yes, yes, the cold makes for quick feet!"

At the same time, she followed Kath, who went to the bench with her basket, with a deathly pale, mistrustful face and thought, 'what will happen now?'

"You're right, it bites right under the nails", the girl said and without turning around, she diligently took old clothes from the basket. At the same time, she talked hastily.

"Right, you're wondering why I bring an entire chest with me. Well now, I can't go through the village like this. You probably don't know yet, well no, it can't be. But he has just come home at Michaelmas from being a soldier, clerk Guste Seffe. Oh, how stupid we can be! But I can tell you ..."

Finally she gave up hiding behind words and looked back at Marie.

She sat on the bench by the oven, quite rigid and holding the whisk in her hand, stiffly like a weapon.

"Hey there, Marie!" Kath called stunned.

The young woman rose immediately, came straight over and began fingering Kath's work clothes with smiles,

"Good, pure wool, isn't it Kath. Oh, it holds! I once had a borrowed skirt, it was the purest ..."

She could not continue talking, the sounds were choking in her throat, she raised her face and looked despairingly at the girl. Then Kath rushed to her breast, and entwined, bodies shaking, they both stood there a long time.

When their hearts had settled, Kath drew her sister-in-law to the bench and began, gently cuddling, to stroke her limp hands.

Marie would have liked far too much to have known why the girl had come to her, but did not dare to ask from fear of betraying something.

"Karl is harsh to you, isn't he?" Kath began sympathetically.

"Well, you know all ..."

"And with the damned court all the time."

"That too."

"When is the appointment today?"

So, so. Then Marie had been mistaken. He had gone to Poland.

"Yes, did he say that?" she asked indifferently.

"Not to me, but to Joseph."

"No, no, Kath. I can tell you. He went to Landeck and is taking the money from the savings bank."

She had the feeling of being shrewdly picked out.

"How are you then?"

"Quite good."

"Don't you feel weak?"

"Oh God, now."

Thus they spoke empty words for a while while their souls secretly trembled like blades of grass standing in the wind of an abyss.

Suddenly Marie screamed out, "No!" jumped up and stepped to the table. Outside the old Freiwald walked past.

"Did you see that?" the poor woman asked and seized the girl's hand tightly.

Then the old man stepped over the threshold too and wished them a good morning with a bright voice.

Marie grasped his hand and asked quickly,

"Now, Freiwald, here too already?" to show that she knew everything.

"Well not already!" Freiwald laid his fur cap on the table and stroked the sparse hairs on his head. "But he is already gone. Hhm. No, no, not already. I should have been here at seven and now it's already half past. Well, it's good too that he isn't here. — But what have you done with the well? There's a hellish stink around the well house."

"Oh, because of that", it passed through Marie's head and she was overcome by a nameless fear.

"Marie! Marie! What is it!" they both called at almost the same time, since they saw how Marie's face became overcast with a grey pallor, and the girl grasped her by the arm.

"Nothing. It's alright. I was just feeling weak."

Kath and Freiwald exchanged compassionate looks. The old well digger thought to take from it that the girl meant, 'you'd be best to go to work.'

While he took his jacket off, took his time arranging this and that, picked and set like only an old man's life can neatly do, he talked from the spiritual depths of his soul to every grasp in verses which he bound with a sampling,

"It's actually a bad time for the work. — Because now in Winter, the earth spirit has the upper hand over the water spirit. — Against the strong source, well, there he can align nothing. — Never too much. — But the threads, the poor little threads! He is setting about them already. — And your well does not yet have the flow, and doesn't pipe, I like to say, in the right hole. — But however, the main thing, I find the pulse, — after that I can help it."

The women, though, were standing, listening to him and following his rummaging with attentive eyes.

"Yes, yes, you women, you have such a thing here!" with which the old man turned to them both and smiled kindly. "The stink for example. It could be a cat, a wandering thing which was going past and fell down. Sometimes we have to raise the boards, we must. That's quite okay. Yes, yes. But most of the time it is just the water alone which fouls and stinks. For the water is also living and springs and sits, all that. Dies too and fouls as well like everything which now is and now is not. In-between is the transformation."

Kath went and looked in the oven.

The old man understood the signal.

"Certainly, you're right, Kath. What doesn't go, we must push. But for the sake of a little sense, we just work. It's like the threads by which I feel further."

He had taken a pinch of tobacco and went cheerfully to the door,

"Now, here it comes in God's name!"

"Yes, yes, that's good. Comes. What use is everything!" Marie spoke out from her stupefaction and turned with violent exertion to the way out too. Only, she was barely in the hallway than she hastily turned around,

"Go on! I'll be right with you ... or wait — or go. — But don't come after me."

Her voice flooded nervously, confused, despite her effort to appear serene.

The old man stared at the door which had closed itself softly, and rocked his head back and forth aggrieved.

"Kath, take care of her, not everything here is as it should be. She will be a muddle or already is", he then whispered.

"Oh, it's my brother, true, but ...", the girl broke off bitterly.

"I mustn't make reproach. Old Freiwald does what he must", the well digger said to himself and lapsed into pondering.

After a long pause, he raised his head and when he had looked out the front door, he began again with muffled voice,

"It's becoming an ugly day! Grey and everything sunk. Look at how it snows, as if it wants to bury everything!"

With serious faces, they both looked into the winter morning whose clarity had already yielded again to a bleak light which was filled by the thick dance of large flakes. And although they heard nothing, it seemed to them as if they sensed a soft, melancholy humming, the weary, oppressive melody of the snowfall into whose spell they sank in deep silence.

Then a sound swam through the silence, came and went, like the groaning of a wounded animal skulking through a forest.

"Did you hear that, Kath?"

She nodded.

"Didn't it come from the living room?"

The girl had heard exactly that it had penetrated from the living room in which Marie dwelled, but shrugged her shoulders and remained silent.

"The stalls are there too", she finally answered mis-leadingly.

"Well, that would be possible too."

This whispered conversation was put to an end when Marie appeared again by the opened door. She strode upright, fortified. Her pale face carried the traces of blissful seriousness, looking like a warrior going from the benediction to the battle.

The old man and the girl had set the door outside in motion on hearing the sound.

Marie followed them.

When the ladders stood bound together in the well and the old man was on the point of climbing down, Marie sent her sister-in-law to the hayloft for fodder.

She herself wanted to return to the living room.

The old man nodded to her, then turned his back, made a cross and raised his right foot to the first rung. She was seized deeply by fear at that so her heart began pounding loudly. She did not have the strength to move, and the memory of standing on the same spot in which her husband had had to stretch his hands out to the Constable's handcuffs increased her fear so that it seemed to her that she was sinking into the ground with the humming.

Freiwald disappeared into the depths.

Motionless, the poor woman stared at the opening ten steps before her from which the ladder stared out. In order to not have to fall down and shake in mad fear, she turned her eyes to the falling flakes. They flowed together and drew nearer, and every time, if they touched, it seemed to her as if they were exploding with crackles and flashes. Everything around her swished and twitched and smouldered in billions of dazzling little points.

She riveted her eyes on the ladder before her again.

It slid back and forth almost imperceptibly.

The old man was still on his way down.

Now it was steady.

He was at the bottom.

Suddenly, the ladder moved with a sharp jerk to the side, a muffled sound rose from the depths.

Marie grasped both hands to her chest.

Now!!! — —

More and more distinct crunching of climbing steps. The man's cap. Finally his wrinkled, horrified face.

Marie tore her arms up high into the air.

With the cast out, shrill scream, "the cobbler!" she collapsed and lay there like a heap of discarded clothes.

20

Old Freiwald wiped the cold sweat from his forehead with a trembling hand and stepped away from the open well full of horror. After he had recovered a little, he safeguarded himself against the influence of the dead, spat murmuring three times into the well, then turned around and, invoking the Holy Trinity, threw three handfuls of snow behind him. With this activity, he was met by Kath who, hurrying back, looked stunned from the powerless woman to the trembling old man.

Finally she was capable of speaking.

"Now, but Freiwald!"

"Down there."

"Who?"

"The cobbler!"

"And dead?"

"Decomposed."

Then there glances sank into each other in horror.

Suddenly they started, seized by the same thought, and faced Marie, who lay there motionless, her pale face pressed into the snow.

In vain they strove through shouts, shaking and setting her upright to stimulate consciousness in her wilted body, then grasped her, Freiwald under her arms, Kath at her feet, and carried the apparently lifeless woman to the her bed.

There they began, more from fear than calculation, to rub the poor woman's body which they had released from laced up pieces of clothing. Marie lay for a long time as if she had really torn herself from death. Large tears fell from the girl's eyes and with an extremely stirring sound in her voice, like only living hearts can call to the dying, Kath begged Marie back to life,

"Marie! — Marie! — My dearest sweet Marie, wake up, wake up one more time so I can tell you how fond I am of you."

Finally the pale blue of her lips yielded to a gentle red, and her neck's artery stirred under the whitish-blue skin like a worm releasing itself from its torpor. Her breast also began to waver up and down. Otherwise the ill woman lay dead still.

"We're best to leave her to sleep in peace. That's the best thing now", the old man whispered, and while he turned his face half to the door, he betrayed that his thoughts were beginning to slide from worrying over the woman to the consideration of the terrible discovery.

Kath's soul stood on the same line between worry and horror, and she pondered aloud,

"There a corpse and here a life hanging by a thread."

The ill woman tore open her eyes, opened her mouth too, and then, as though lashed, her body hunched together, her eyeballs turned back in their sockets, her head thrust into the pillow. With a long drawn-out scream, the spasm ended.

"For heaven's sake, Freiwald, what was that?" Kath asked despairingly.

The old man observed the ill woman who groaned with closed mouth and dug her hands into the bed, and then replied,

"It seems to me, she is having contractions."

"Well ha, that is well asked-for and runs soon."

The old man immediately stomped out.

After a long hour during which the poor woman's life had often fluttered weakly before death's door, the fruit of her loins struggled free from her body.

It was a boy. The young mother lay breathing heavily in the rumpled bed.

When the midwife, a square-built woman with a man's face, held the child up to the light to inspect him for rightness, she shut her eyes and laid him in the cot shaking her head. For he was ugly, like the deformed image of a desolate dream. A grim kick of God seemed to have thrust him from the void into life.

His broad pinched head, wedged between the shoulders, misshapenly large, with the wrinkled face of an old man and small eyes under red bulges, sat directly on his short torso which had the proportions of a partly rectangular stone. His arms and legs were long like a spider's and knobbly at the joints. His fingers were fleshless bird's claws. Everything though was covered with long thinned out hairs, similar to those that buried moulds put out.

From time to time, the little monster emitted a buzzing noise ...

"Why didn't you fetch Patzelten from Walsdorf?" the midwife finally asked the girl, and her usually irritated look turned irate.

"Why?" Kath replied cluelessly.

"Because it's a changeling", the mannish woman said and threw a pointed look at the ill woman because she was still entangled in the superstition that such a child was punishment for hidden sins. She knew nothing of the sleepless nights, the soul's anguish and the endless indignities with which Marie had been served for her "one and only joy".

Kath sat on the bench by the oven and sobbed into her apron, stunned.

Outside the yard filled with onlookers, mostly men, who stood around gesticulating heftily and talking in each others' ears, casually stepping to the windows to look into the living room with timid curiosity, dispersing themselves as watchmen across the yard to then stare again into the open well, straining and thorough. The arrival of Constable Stief pulled them into a line. He sprang in extreme excitement into the yard, jumped down from his horse, threw the reins to an obliging man, stepped to the well, looked in it for a long time with a connoisseur's attitude and scratched behind his ear deliberating. After contemplating a while, he tore his notebook from his coat, wrote something in it, and then appeared, spurs rattling, into the living room.

The midwife had fled into the bedroom and closed the door behind her so that Kath had to meet with the zealous man.

His questions showered down on the timorous girl as if he was throwing sand in her face. She became so confused that she did not know the simplest things. With extreme effort, the fact came loose for him that the lame one had taken off at seven o'clock that morning in the direction of Landeck, probably to lift the money from his savings account. With surly grumbling over the thick-skinned pack of farmers, he finally stood up.

"Who are you?"

"Katharina Exner."

"Don't deceive me, otherwise I'll lock you up on the spot."

"Katharina Exner from Fuchsloch."

"I'm thinking, you are from here?"

"No."

"Now dammit, a wife lives with her husband."

"I'm not married."

"What, you want to deny that you're married?"

"Constable, I am just his sister."

"What then, 'of whom'?"

She broke out into tears and finally sobbed,

"I can't help it if my brother is like that."

"Ah, you, hmhm, well you could just have said that straightaway. Nailed up well! Forget it, we have him already."

He went rattling outside. The snow was thrown up by the hooves of the hack. He was gone.

After half an hour, he stepped into the living room again with the Chief Inspector. With, "Yes, sir", "Certainly, Mr Hoffmann", he stood at attention, stamped up and down, shouted in the yard and then gave a long report again over his methodical preliminary investigation.

In this unrest, the record of Secretary Dorn was slowly progressing.

"Do you know something, Stief", the Chief Inspector interrupted himself with these words, raised his head and smiled mildly, as was his habit.

"Yes, sir."

"Yes", Mr Hoffmann thoughtfully stroked his black moustache.

"What is the Major's order?"

"The main thing, however, is that we ... step here please — what is your name ..."

"Katharina Exner", Dorn growled.

"Right, so, yes. Indeed. I mean you! You should go out! Lord again!"

Kath left the room numbed, stumbled up the stairs and sank to her knees in the summer room by the window. Through the ceiling, she heard the men's conversation like the humming of a distant thresher. Then it broke off. She rose and leant her forehead against the windowpane. There Stief was flying like a tornado across the snow. Blown away he disappeared behind a wall. His helmet flashed a few more times. Then only the snow was trickling away again by the motionless forest.

Dorn's voice called her downstairs. The inquisition progressed. Finally everything had been taken down. The Chief Inspector rose and shook the dandruff from his coat collar with both hands. Dorn clasped the folder under his arm. Both looked around the living room again suspiciously and left without closing the door completely behind themselves.

Now the onlookers were in the yard by themselves again and bombarding old Freiwald, whose evidence had held great weight with the inquiry, with questions.

Kath sat on the bench by the oven and stared at her clasped hands.

The midwife ventured out of the bedroom again and sat down on the bench opposite her.

Outside, the onlookers' conversation was becoming excited.

"No water?" one asked shrilly.

"What I told you", a steady bass answered.

"Freiwald dug it, he must know", the doubter called belligerently. "How is it, Freiwald?"

"See my hand," the old well digger explained, "that's how dry it is, not a drop of water. A heap of stones, nothing else."

"That I don't believe, I have a well myself ..."

"Now stop there," Freiwald interrupted him, "it certainly had water, good, sweet, healing water. But now it's completely gone. For where such a thing happens, water disappears instantly. That lies in its spirit, because it's only for the living. For you see, men, water has a nature like fire! I'm going home, I'm not well actually."

He tapped on the window, nodded kindly within and walked away.

Slowly everyone dispersed from the yard.

The Constable Stief was fortunate. On the Landecker Ring, standing next to the entrance of the town hall, he arrested the lame one who was just going to escape over the border. Without resisting, Exner let the handcuffs be placed on him and hobbled in front of the Constable to the prison.

21

Evening came earlier than usual on this difficult day and surprised both the midwife and the girl. They had been sitting there wordlessly the whole time and mutually enjoying the certainty of their existence after the commotion. Each was suffused with the fate of this lonely house and neither spoke about it. Scanty words over the animals, the weather and events of the parish and its surrounds, heedlessly pushed back and forth, filled up the space between these introverted, simple souls. Then they would rise and look at the mother and child, and if they found them both asleep then they would step back carefully again and go to their seats.

Then both lapsed into pondering which merged into sleep.

Just the following morning, Kath awoke and found herself lying next to the oven with a bundle of clothes under her head.

The midwife, Mrs Klesse, was still huddled asleep on the bench by the table. A soft whimpering came from inside the bedroom.

The girl woke the midwife, and both went into the bedroom.

The pale glow of first light lay on Marie's pale face which lay turned up on the pillow, her eyelids closed.

"It was from in here", Kath said with a glance at the lifeless face, believing she'd heard a sound,   and hesitantly she lay her hand on the white forehead.

Then the ill woman began sobbing feebly. Kath threw herself on her and spoke words of comfort to her with tears. She talked from love, as Marie had already fainted again.

After a long while, the poor woman opened her eyes.

"Is it over?" she breathed anxiously.

Mrs Klesse nodded, bent down smiling and stroked the young mother's blond hair from her face, "All of it, all of it, my sweet woman."

"What is it?"

"A little boy."

Marie's face collapsed even more into anguished disappointment. Then she turned to the wall in silence. When she turned to them both again, her beautiful, blue eyes were full of tears.

"Is it true?" she then asked.

"Yes. But now you mustn't see him. You're still too weak."

"Thank God!"

Exhausted, she closed her eyes, and whilst her lips moved hurriedly in silent prayer, an ever deeper rapture came into her face.

For a long time, she smiled thus, for a long time.

In the meantime, the day materialised. All things became quite visible by and by as if they floated there from a distance. And with them, everything ran into the tested woman's soul, everything that had drained away before the terror of the birth stood by her bed, looked at her, began talking and asked, "What now?"

Then Marie became very afraid. She prayed. It did not give way. She shut her eyes, then it became greater. Because she had no idea what to do, she called for Kath. But when she appeared in the room, Marie realised that she was not able to ask about her husband and the consequences of finding the cobbler. She looked deeply at her sister-in-law and noticed a cautious joy in her eyes.

"Is he laughing a bit already?" she finally asked.

"Oh, he certainly laughs already, and how", Kath answered and stood and struggled with herself. Then she was overwhelmed, threw herself on her knees by the bed, took Marie's head in her hands and covered the pale face with hot kisses.

When the girl had left her and was leaning against the doorpost again, the ill woman asked sorrowfully, "Kath? ...", but it choked her and the words could not pass over her lips. Despairingly she looked at the bedcovers.

"No, no," she then said, catching herself, "I don't resent you it. It is a beautiful day, isn't it?"

"How do you mean?"

The girl looked aggrieved at Marie. The latter looked at her again for a long time and nodded amidst tears. Then Kath turned red and cried because the ill woman had recognised the joy in her heart.

"It's bad of me, isn't it?" she stuttered.

Marie reached from the bed, pressed her hand and dismissed her with her eyes. Before the door could close behind her, she asked if the door to the bedroom could be left ajar and the basket with the child placed on the bench by the oven, where she could see it from her bed. The girl did all that and decided from honest sorrow over her sinfulness to let nothing more of her love be noticed but rather to suppress it.

But Marie lay in her bed and realised how alone she was in her misfortune. It turned black before her eyes, and when she came to, her first clear look always sought the little basket. Then she decided to be strong in order to reach her child, and ate valiantly and slept, did everything that the midwife had ordered.

On the second day, the noise of bells sounded in the yard. Kath stepped to the window, wiped the condensation from the windowpane and looked out.

Jesus Maria! On the sleigh sat her brother, next to him the Constable, weapon in hand. The lame one, biting his lower lip, pale, his head inclined to the side, his eyes rigid, his hands shackled. A second sleigh followed with tinkling bells. A number of well-dressed men climbed out. At the head a hunched man, a monocle clenched in his twitching eye. Kath sank onto the bench, but jumped up the next moment and shut the door of the bedroom, ignoring Marie's weak words. Then she paced up and down the living room a few times. When steps came into the hallway, she huddled down haphazardly on the bench and pressed herself against the clock case. Straight afterwards the men entered ... The hasty traveller at the head. Behind him a limping man with a yellow, weathered face, who let his eyes glide over his misty glasses surveying the room, nodded contentedly on seeing the large table and immediately took a seat with a grand bow. While the Chief Inspector from Erlengrund, Major Hoffmann, and a man with a long, sparse beard were entering, the hunched man, who was obviously the headmost of them all, had surveyed the room and said to the white-bearded man,

"Makes a good impression, doesn't it, Medical Officer?"

"Very proper, perfectly understood, prosecutor", the latter replied with a deep servile bow.

But the limping man at the table responded,

"A loyal residence, completely loyal", and then dipped bashfully in the inkstand because the prosecutor was looking steadily at him.

"Steindorf, fifth of December 1893", he then said monotonously and let the feather fly across the paper.

"Now, Denzel!" the prosecutor interrupted him, turned around and looked at the scared girl by the clock case.

"Who are you?" he asked mildly into the desperate face of Kath, who thought she was going to be locked away and was so happy over the unexpected friendliness that she forgot to answer and laughed amidst her tears. Mr Hoffmann informed him on her behalf and then an excited conversation took place between the men, which was carried out in in broken sentences, sometimes in whispered tones, and was concluded by the prosecutor with the words,

"Therefore, please, gentlemen!"

Then they all hurried out. She heard the ladder shuddering into the well, indignant exclamations, the shed door creaking, the weak cries for help of Marie. It was all quite distant from her. She was not capable of stirring, everything flew around her. How long it lasted, she did not know. Now everyone came back inside. The Medical Officer was in deep conversation with the prosecutor.

"With the existing decomposition", he said, "nothing else unfortunately can be proven. Six weeks, as stated."

And in the middle of the living room, he made a long "speech", stroking his beard, whilst the limping man wrote everything down zealously at the table. The prosecutor was also questioned. Then it seemed to her as if she fell asleep. It went ahead all around her, but she did not understand any of the gestures or any of the words anymore. Once, tearing her eyes open violently, she thought she saw her brother standing before the table, and she wanted to scream, but was not capable of it. She sat in a lethargic state, like when we experience a horrible dream while sleeping and do not exactly know if we will awake.

Then someone tore at her arm. She came to a morbidly sharp awareness and recognised in all the faces surrounding her a threatening resolve.

"Where is your sister?" the prosecutor asked, disconcerted by the expression of animosity in her face.

"Councillor or whatever you are called," she answered firmly, "in there. But don't go in. She is dying, I can tell you, she is dying."

Threateningly she blocked the path to the bedroom.

She was forced to the side. But, endeavouring resolutely to help Marie to the utmost, she followed in their footsteps.

Marie was awoken by the rumbling footsteps. She opened her eyes unnaturally wide and attempted to smile.

She was questioned a lot.

Her face became more rigid, paler. Her hands were clenched on the bed. Her mouth fell silent.

Then the prosecutor pinched the monocle more firmly in his eye, bent down close to her ear and slowly asked quite loudly,

"Were you in an illicit relationship with the cobbler, Klose?"

The ill woman did not stir. Finally, long afterwards, she groaned almost inaudibly, "The cobbler ... th...e cob...", her eyeballs hung nervously in their sockets. Then the long eyelashes sank over them, mercifully covering her misery.

Denzel stroked his beard with his trembling hand.

The Chief Inspector shook the dandruff from his coat collar and turned with a pale face towards the door. The medical officer tended to the poor woman and explained that there was nothing to be done. The woman had fainted from weakness and loss of blood and there was no danger to her life "at present".

After that they all trod back into the living room, and the prosecutor called Kath to the table.

"Do you know if your sister-in-law had been in forbidden contact with the shoemaker August Klose from Steindorf?" he asked her, unfolding a soiled piece of paper on the table and carefully stroking down the countless creases in it.

Kath had meanwhile recovered from her fright and answered in the negative.

Whether she knew the shoemaker's handwriting by chance, the prosecutor continued insistently, and when she replied that except for a receipt, she had not caught sight of anything by his hand, he shoved the pressed-out scrap towards her and asked her to read what was on the piece of paper which had been found in the vest pocket of the dead man.

She wanted to draw it nearer to herself, but the white hands of the official did not relinquish it. The slip of paper was covered in distinct, large letters which were for the most part faded. With much effort, she finally deciphered the words, "...arest Marie — my life ... is falling apart ... love for you ... still ... Aug... Klose."

When she had read this, she felt the ground under her feet swaying. She steadied herself with stiff arms on the table so as not to fall over.

"It isn't true!" she then shouted too loud, and as the prosecutor mildly pushed her still further to honour the truth, she replied turbidly a few times, "No ... no ... no", and remained with rigid, averted eyes bent over like someone who looks with horror into vertiginous depths.

The men rose amidst excited conversation and left the room. Kath, paying no attention to their farewells, went and fell down on the bench.

The biting white light of the winter sun was falling through the window next to her.

She raised her eyes to the glass.

Then she saw her brother going away, his head sunk deep into his chest, huddled up.

She stared into the cold light until the whispering of the departing bells had perished in the silence. Then she rose amidst violent starts and stepped into the bedroom.

Marie lay there with open eyes, did not pay her any attention but continued raptly dabbing the knuckle of her left hand with the index finger of her other hand as if adding up something inconceivable. Finally she beckoned Kath to her and gave her a long kiss on the forehead, then she asked her with exhausted voice to again place her child so that she could see him through the open door, and lay there and did not turn her eyes from the basket.

22

We cannot help ourselves mutually. The most natural exertion for the welfare of others consists in the honest striving for the best in our lives.

Marie lay and remained silent. She told nobody about the processes in her soul. Even Kath did not touch with words the misfortune of the house. The discussion of the two, dwelling as though expelled in the forest's solitude, consisted in a deep look, a gesture, a kiss, a squeezed hand. Marie's recovery was taking place unmistakably, and even Kath was sinking deeper into her life when the last grim horror was taken from them and the black coffin with the bodily remains of the cobbler had been taken from the yard.

It suffused her with strength and even a sort of cheerful courage. Every activity slid smoothly through her hands, and when her brother Joseph came, the threads of her secret hopes continued to spin themselves. The good man now dared cautiously on tiptoes into the living room, whilst he had gone in the days of greatest stress with a heartening slap from her after a few fleeting words in the hallway, taking the way around the barn so that the poor woman would not recall earlier, better times by his sight. He looked at least once a week "to his right". When the two siblings had consulted thoroughly on the management of the household, they sat silently next to each other for a while until Joseph raised his head and smiling impishly passed on best regards to Kath "from a dear man" he had met by chance on the way. A few times, clerk Seffe, the son of a neighbour, enquired after Kath and now the good man also delivered messages to give his sister some cheer in these disconsolate weeks. In the sparring match that the girl's bashfulness then spawned, he could also speak of the happy turn in his long-standing love affair. He had now found the courage to ask for the hand of the Rollinger girl. Indeed, it stressed him a lot that everything could redound to his misfortune because the proposal had fallen on the day the cobbler was found, but the pious couple soon steadied themselves with the thought of their innocence and God's justness. But if in the end Joseph nevertheless always expressed doubt about the right to love amidst such a difficult fate then Kath called his attention to the fact that both would not have sought this love, that it on the contrary was to be looked at as a hint of a divine providence to hold out in sympathy with their unfortunate sister-in-law, and so they always parted with the mutual promise of leaving it to providence and meanwhile to neglect nothing in the stalls and house, in the barn and shed.

When, after this long absence, Kath went to Marie in the bedroom then the ill woman looked at the girl, nodding her head with a bitter smile as if to say, 'I don't resent you it.' But she was not able to force herself to an explanation of this behaviour, she just asked that the door be left open so that she could rest her eyes on her child.

The boy had been christened in all tranquility after his name had been gleaned by stealth from the young mother. The midwife had advised it because it was to be expected that the holy sacrament of baptism would exercise a beneficial influence on the soul and life of the little one.

Only he remained, even after he was absorbed into the community of christians, as spiritless as before. Most of the time, he lay there with closed eyes. He opened the baggy lids for short moments and blinked about. After his meal was concluded, he purred with pleasure like a tomcat.

He recompensed Kath's careful care with nothing. No, he became uglier and uglier. The mould-like down over his entire body had become thicker. His head covered itself with a bush of hair whose strands sprouted over his brows. The girl often looked at the kobold timidly from the side and thought with horror of the moment in which she would have to lay him in her sister-in-law's arms.

With every conceivable ruse, she put off Marie, whose maternal desire became more and more obstinate with the increase in her strength and sought by all kinds of ruses to get a look at the child. As final reasons, when the stock of excuses was exhausted, Kath brought Marie's weakness and the midwife's explicit prohibition together and always obtained thereby the appeasement of the upset woman who then desired sustenance every hour in order to strengthen herself quicker and so shorten the days of agonising yearning.

In the recent past, the impending Christmas had been decided on as the day on which Marie would stand up for the first time and be led to her boy. So the talk was of nothing else but the celebration of this holy evening, how the room was to be decorated, the Christmas tree, the child, and whether the little one would look at the lights. After such conversations, the young mother then lay with moist, contented eyes, her lips uttered ecstatic words, and the most blissful joy reddened her cheeks. Beside that she had troubling, nervous dreams and after waking asked fearfully to see her boy. When Kath denied her this, a deep sadness did not leave her for hours. The girl realised that she would not be able to resist for much longer now and hoped to obtain a shortening of the separation by days through a good word with Mrs Klesse.

But we humans only ever hold the threads in our hands, it is fate that weaves as it will and the day on which the yearning mother ran to her child came upon her without Kath realising it.

She stood by Marie's bed and took the emptied plate away. The young woman sank bank smiling and began to speak about the boy.

"Is he laughing already?" she asked.

"Well, he is beginning to now. When I stroke him, he purses his lips sometimes."

"Who does he look like?"

"That ... you know, I can't see it well at that age."

"But his eyes."

"No, I won't say anything. You will see."

"Now! Dearest Kath, do me a favour!"

The girl shook her head earnestly.

"Stay in bed, Marie. There's a time for that. He won't run away."

Marie touched the bedcovers lightly with her arms which were already filling out and raised them up triumphantly,

"Look, I can't stand it! — Kath!"

Then she folded her hands and looked at them with eyes in which you could see her soul kneeling.

The girl put the plate on the chair and bent over the poor mother in the anguish of sympathy,

"Sweet Marie, just wait a little, okay. Look, Mrs Klesse must come first."

She kissed her and, against her will, tears came into her eyes. Full of sorrow, she pressed her face sideways into the pillows to hide the betrayal of her misery. But as she lifted her forehead, a fervent tear must have fallen on Marie's face. With a hard shove, the frightened mother pushed the crying girl off her and looked sharply into her face.

"Kath ... Kath! ... why ... why are you crying?" she then asked haltingly, pondered for a moment and then continued turbidly,

"Do you think I didn't see that and in a day and a night things that make my hair stand on end and my heart harden like a stone! You! Ha! If I didn't have my God, from whom I know more than all of you ... Kath, say it gently, I won't be hurt, my dear God has me right in His hand."

Kath had already wiped the tears from her eyes and laughed poignantly,

"Sweet Marie, one should not be weak of heart when a mother must beg for her child so. Look, if it was up to me then you would have had him a long time ago. But what use is that? It would strain you to pick him up. Who knows? Now and what would become of the poor, dear boy without a mother?"

Marie lay for a while and looked with large, unseeing eyes. Meanwhile it grasped her soul with the deep, blurred sounds of a distant, restless water.

With deep breath, she shook it off, stretched out her arm and squeezed Kath's hand with devoted, thankful pressure,

"You're right, what would my boy be without me! Look, I won't say anything anymore, it will come to be. — Oh, and when I'm well ... everything will return again, see, the heaven is my witness, if it isn't followed up by me ... what do I say then? — Go and sing me a lullaby, 'bye, baby bunting' or 'hush, little baby'. You haven't sung once yet."

Kath left.

Soon after the cradle was swinging back and forth creaking on the floor, the boy had not been taken from the basket in days. The girl sang gently with sorrowfully shaking mouth. The restrained anguish lent the tones a poignant depth. Finally the song faded away into silence and Kath crept quietly to the shed to fetch wood. The latching of the door disturbed Marie from her rapture. She turned her head. The song remained silent. The living room was empty. The clock ticked in the silence, "Come, come, come, come." Tempting like a little silver voice.

Then the yearning for her child overwhelmed her. The wind mumbled dull threats in the snow outside. But Marie felt herself rising. Already her feet were touching the floor. Her eyes measured the distance to the cradle. It stood rocking by the oven. White linen lay over the sleeping child. For a moment, she thought of Kath, who would be affronted by her disobedience.

But just to throw a glance at him! Just a solitary kiss! And lift the linen. Quick, quick! Kath's steps!

A kiss ...

She caught sight of the changeling, tore the linen to her mouth and collapsed wordlessly. — — —

Kath found a body next to the cradle, rigid, laid out, stretched out by the torture of the calamity. She grasped Marie by the armpits and hauled her over the threshold of her bedroom. Her heels struck like dead wood. Then she finally lay the unconscious woman on her bed. But she would not let go of the linen from her cold fists, nor from her clenched teeth.

"That will be your death, poor woman", Kath spoke mutely.

In her helplessness, she knelt next to the bed and prayed.

Then Marie opened her eyes, tore the linen from her mouth with a jerk and stared blindly at it. Then she looked with a goggling glance at Kath.

"What use is praying now, hahaha!!!"

With gratingly raw laughter, she turned away from Kath, looked at the white wall and did not stir.

Shuddering, Kath went out and shut the door in fright behind herself.

After a few minutes, she heard her sister-in-law screaming again, laughing hard and inanely. The convulsing laugh of despair.

23

The girl's fear was quite unnecessary. The door, which she had kept shut for a long time by the iron boss in the middle, was not flung open. Her poor sister-in-law did not rush in with deliriously confused eyes and flying hair to strangle her and the changeling.

The heartrending laugh was not heard anymore from the bedroom. Yes, she did not even hear anymore that agonised moaning breath with which the depths of the human body perpetuated its life. It was silent, completely silent.

And after Kath had listened a little, she ventured to open the door a crack.

It was silent, completely silent.

In fear the girl banged on the latch so that it snapped sharply.

Marie did not stir. With her face turned to the wall, her right arm stretched tightly on the bed, her hand formed into a fist, she lay as though in a seizure.

She was probably dead.

"Marie! Marie!"

And then, when she stood quite close and the raised her urgent cry louder, close to the bloodless ear, the woman finally pushed her head over and looked at her rigidly with motionless, cold, large eyes. For a long time and without a word. Her face was like a wall, without any soul. Everything that the girl wanted to say in compassion to comfort her died before the horror that infused this deathly stiff countenance.

"God's grace on you", with this heartfelt wish, Kath crept out on tiptoes helplessly.

Marie, when she was alone again, stared at the ceiling for a while. Then she slowly turned her face to the wall again so that hardly a crease in the bed stirred.

She did not say anything more, which Kath also wanted, refused to take in any nourishment and lay in the same rigid state, with face turned away, for a day, two days. For she hated the life that had betrayed her over everything, and her yearning was directed at death.

The cold of winter forced itself through the plain windows, but she did not draw her bare arms under the covers. Her senses seemed extinguished so that she did not feel pain. On the fourth day, her arm was blue and limp. Kath could move the head of the arm back and forth like a dead one. With force she tried to infuse her with a spoonful of soup. Her mouth remained defiantly shut and her eyes watched contemptuously through a crack.

Kath cried, begged, threatened. The death-seeking woman's teeth did not part.

After long exertion, Kath pulled the arm out from under Marie's head and she sank back limply onto the pillows with turned up face and closed eyes. In nameless fear, the girl rushed outside, through the yard in the snow and waded aimlessly out into the field in which there was no one but the wind which skimmed up and down the snowed-in wall and played with the flakes.

"Help," she screamed, "Help! She's dying, she wants to die! Good people, help me!"

No one heard her. Finally the befuddlement of her compassionate anguish left her.

With wobbling knees, she waded back and found Marie in the same posture again.

In the evening, Joseph arrived. A maid followed him, laden with stores.

"It's all too much, Joseph, too much. Oh, you're a godsend!"

The mild, gentle man was still standing on the threshold when Kath called that out to him without answering his greeting. Then she told him everything.

"That mustn't be. That would be the murder of another, that mustn't be", he said hastily after listening to the tale which had been made yet livelier by exclamations and frightened gestures.

They came to an understanding through glances by the poor woman's bed and talked to her with urgent, imploring words.

Only her pallid face did not stir, her eyes remained shut, her mouth clenched shut as if it was not a human lying in the bed but the weathered stone statue of that woman who stands in deepest anguish under the cross, taken from its pedestal, and now, the covers pulled from its cold body, stirring the sympathy of kind souls.

Finally Joseph's fury overcame his love and he pried open her mouth violently with the spoon handle while Kath briskly poured milk into it.

Choking she ejected all of it.

"Why ...? Don't you like me?" she asked coughing.

Those were her only words, then she lay as ever. Only when she heard them gently shuffling out did she turn around with feeble haste and fasten on their forms with an avid look. Kath noticed it and pushed Joseph out quickly, carefully closing the door behind herself.

Yearning groans followed them both.

"Did you hear that, Joseph? That's the first time in four days, the first sound. She is dying like silent Ender from Stillergrunde, dying from the soul which is poisoning her stomach! Now she has spoken, now it'll go exceedingly downhill. I can't stay alone. If you don't stay then I'll run away in the night, and if I flee, who knows where in the snow I'll suffocate."

Joseph sat down cautiously on the bench.

"Yes," he said after pondering a bit, "it isn't good to be alone, not even for two. A third ... but who'll come here to the dead well, as people are calling it already, nobody wants to who holds their life dear."

After he had fallen silent, Kath waited a long time and looked at him tensely, expecting certain help from him. But he looked gloomily at his clasped hands, started suddenly and sent the maid away.

When they were alone, Kath asked impatiently,

"What now?"

Joseph looked sadly at his sister, but he did not give her advice, as he was too occupied by the misfortune.

So the two sat there with lowered heads. The darkness came, the wind sighed in the fine branches of the little plum trees. The child began to scream. Kath gave him his bottle and consoled him cooing. The night lay in the room in which the only sounds of life were the two helpless persons' long, heavy breaths. Now the grey stains of the windows also lapsed into the black, and it seemed to Kath as if she was walled in to an unlit cell of such closeness that her breath beat back warmly from the near wall into her face.

In fear she began praying loudly. The man joined her with his deep voice. They said Lord's prayer after Lord's prayer, then every prayer they knew, and the Lord's prayer again without counting, without rest on and on. Their voices became dry, hoarse, failed. Kath fetched water. They began anew, monotonous and soft. Neither knew anymore what they were saying, but they did not stop. They exhausted themselves, became numbed, just so as not to have to think of the terrible death which the tortured woman was forcing on herself in her bedroom.

When the first dawn light of morning swam into the night, the hard will of the death-willing had been broken, and with her last strength, she cried for life.

The prayers hurried in with a light and saw Marie, drawn tightly into a knot, struggling with confused motions against her existence whilst her mouth made slurping motions amidst inarticulate noises.

"Quick, warm some soup, quick, quick! We'll try again!" Joseph urged.

And when he raised her head and Kath brought the spoon close to her lips, she emitted a cry like a hungry animal and stretched towards the sustenance.

While she ate, she cried, stammered words of thanks and curses; threw herself back and gasped. It was all because she recognised that she had succumbed to life.

Then the day sank from the roof.

Joseph went home.

Kath watched after him thankfully.

Sleep had come over Marie and rocked her towards life in its deep silent waters. She bore it with a sorrowful smile which did not disappear from her face.

She slowly recovered. In the beginning, she still ate with reluctance. But soon she was calling with a feeble, misty-eyed voice for sustenance and endured the sun's light without signs of pain.

Otherwise she looked at everything indifferently and did not ask about anything in the present, or anything from the past.

Her face was so regular in its persistent pallor, so solemnly unmoving in the depth of overcome misery; her eyes so still and clear, yet so completely without a shimmer of life; the pounding ardency so completely removed from all her gestures so that it often occurred to Kath that she was looking at an incomprehensible apparition on a solitary stone, sitting far from all men, with which she had once dwelt, with which she had once lived, laughed, suffered and cried, who had now completely lost all memory of the earlier existence; whose eyes now saw differently, whose soul thought differently, whose heart yearned for different things.

She was leading a very active life inwardly.

When, sitting in bed, she had imbibed her meal, she remained a long while in helpless rigidity and gazed bitterly somewhere as people tend to do who are filled with remorse over the pointless battle against naturalised errors. Then she opened the lids of her eyes wide as if it served to transform something intangible, to take in something eternal as fare.

This distant look took her so captive at times that she forgot everything else. Then she let the proffered meals go cold. When Kath returned after some time to fetch the dishes, she found the food untouched.

"Now, Marie, eat up!" she reminded her.

"Eat," the beset woman responded with soft, wavering voice, "eating, always eating. The unhappy eat from bowls, the miserable drink from glasses. Eating, eating. — To be human ... like a thin straw is turned out ... eating and always eating, you don't know anything else, you people."

And from the heights to which her glance had turned, she let it sink heedlessly down on Kath and looked into that distance again, becoming silent.

Even Joseph, who had been summoned by Kath, did not get "anything sensible" out of the tested woman. She talked detachedly to his face too, slippery words which his soul was not able to grasp.

"Now, what is that about?" his sister asked him when she had returned to the living room again.

The quiet man looked aggrieved into the distance, shrugged his shoulders and stroked his forehead, sighing. The girl thought he wanted by that to say that Marie had gone mad, but asked once more in the interests of certainty,

"Do you mean she's lost her mind?"

"Not yet that actually, Kath — not yet. But it could happen. For where have you read such things, and I — and even her, Marie? It sounds like the wind, like flowing water, like when it undulates in a forest, it takes hold of you, but nobody can understand it."

"Take care, Kath," he began again after pondering for a long time, "such people carry the spirit to where it shouldn't go. Don't laugh or be silent with her, her soul is in horror of other things. Take good care of her."

24

While all this was happening, the case against the clod progressed. The prosecutor had found sufficient evidence to inaugurate an investigation against him over the murder committed on the cobbler August Klose. A number of hearings had already taken place. The entire affair had become more confused than clarified by them. Nothing pointed to the relationship which had existed between Marie and the unfortunate shoemaker and which, in the prosecutor's view, must have been the grounds for the lame one's criminal act. The accused had recovered from his low spirits and was behaving quite differently in his frequent hearings.

Sometimes her remained in a silence which resembled derision, other times he gave a story long and detailed to the best of his ability, a story which obviously mixed truth and falsehood. But he always showed himself ready to swear a hundred holy oaths over not having touched a hair of the cobbler's head. One time the prosecutor attempted to explain the clod's deed as eliminating the cobbler as a witness to the boundary crime. But the further he carried through with this assumption, the greater the contradictions arrived at with the established facts, and all the previous findings turned out to be problematic if the handling of the case in law were to be accomplished by these means. The examining magistrate finally convinced himself of what he had held to be probable from the beginning on, that the father of these deductions, a young assessor who possessed more in the way of vanity than a legal mind able to fasten straightaway on the right course in such a confusion of possibilities, had fundamentally erred. So it came to be that after a weeks-long digression one entered with all intentness again on the first track and considered the wanton relationship of the young wife to the dissipated cobbler to be the turning point of the entire drama. To that the faltering statements of the accused still came across. Not as if he was indicting his wife, no, he only made himself clear in curses against his friend, the cobbler, and then recounted the episodes which implied a deep marital conflict. From this position, the lame one was not to be brought out by any trick.

The main prosecution witness, Marie, could not be interrogated because of her condition.

Finally the Chief Inspector Hoffmann reported, "that no medical objections stood in the way of her interrogation anymore", and one day the persons who were already acquainted with Kath stepped into the living room of the solitary house by Freibusch. The hasty man with the lynx eye behind his monocle asked her for Marie, whilst the limping man laid his folders on the table and Major Hoffmann took a look at the wooden deer heads on the wall.

Kath answered timidly, her sister-in-law was certainly healthier, but still lay in bed. They opened the door, convinced themselves that the room was exceptionally narrow and ordered the table and chairs in the living room close to the bedroom's entrance.

That all happened in rumbling haste.

Marie sat up, looked quietly at the line-up and nodded her head.

"Why are you nodding?" the prosecutor asked, lifting his chair into the bedroom and taking a seat.

"Because I understand my misfortune."

This and everything else, the poor woman spoke with a certain, steady voice.

The official act began with the usual questions about name, age, birth, criminal record, etc.

"You know what an oath is!" the prosecutor spoke.

She smiled dismissively and then said,

"No!"

Stunned, the questioner glanced towards the Chief Inspector who shrugged his shoulders, then set off on her with hard words, and when she could not dislodge the contemptuous smile from that beautiful, pale face, he sprang up and spoke in the living room with a hushed voice to Kath. Returning, he whispered with the Chief Inspector. Both men leant back and looked sharply at Marie for a long time.

"But the eyes, the eyes are too collected to me", the prosecutor then murmured to Hoffmann, who nodded in agreement.

"The whole exterior in general", he opined and stroked his black moustache meaningfully.

Marie acted as if no one was present and sat there with lowered head, not stirring.

"How long have you been married to your husband?"

The prosecutor took up the interrupted interrogation again without swearing her in.

"Not at all."

"So you were living as his concubine?"

"Yes, yes, I was his concubine!"

"But", the Chief Inspector fell on her answer hastily, "you were demonstrably married in the registry office and church."

The prosecutor touched Hoffmann's arm with his hand, as a sign that he was leading the interrogation.

"Married," Marie began, softly nodding her head, "well yes, yes, I married him. For better or worse, or worse. Whoever marries, the individuals bind to each other. And it's crazy to bind a bird together with a stone. See, you men, that which God called me to cannot be done. For that reason, I was not married."

"But, Mrs Exner ..."

"I'm not called Exner and not Marie, I have no name anymore. That was everything. It lies by the door like the snow which the wind plays with. My life, the great illness that it was, I have survived, am well and dead."

"I beg you, Mrs Exner, we believe all ..."

"Yes, I have also begged, but now I am begging no more. Now my attitude is a saw and my tongue a hammer. You good men, like the knuckles around a dice shaker, cast us so."

The prosecutor looked at the Chief Inspector Hoffmann with a glance that said, 'she really does seem to be crazy.' Then he rose and went into the living room. As he entered, Kath followed him with the changeling in her arms and placed herself on a corner of the lower end of the bed in which Marie lay.

Kath was confused, smothering the child with caresses and always shoving the dummy back in his mouth, although the little unlovely boy protested against it with shrill cries.

Mr Hoffmann bent down to the prosecutor,

"I don't see, where it can lead."

The latter polished his eyeglass with his handkerchief and murmured,

"I'll go for the lot."

Then he turned to the ill woman and gave his rough voice a gently assertive tone.

"But now, Mrs Exner, show some reason. This child sprouted from the marriage with your husband, didn't it?"

During all the preceding, Marie had remained in her position. Only with Kath's entrance had her head sunk somewhat lower onto her chest. Her eyes directed steadily at her hands, she sat absent-mindedly. Even the prosecutor's question seemed to have left her untouched. She did not stir. The index finger of her left hand just stroked the back of her right hand, searching over the protruding tendons.

Then she nodded as though in a dream, and with a wavering voice she began talking monotonously,

"Reason ... oh yes, you men! The goat has its horn and men have their reason. But what help is the goat's rammer when it is taken by the tether to the slaughter, and what use is man's reason when it comes over him like a butcher's knife! — the eyes cry, the soul despairs."

With a long, sighing breath, she paused and was silent for a while, as though collecting her strength.

The prosecutor saw that the madness still reigned over her, remembered having read in an essay somewhere that it was best in dealing with psychotics to wait for an attack and decided not to stop Marie, in order to deal in the following lucid moment with the necessary question over her relationship to the cobbler Klose. He nodded to the poor woman encouragingly. She turned her face to him a little and looked up at him with lowered head from her gleaming eyes, then she began again with wavering voice,

"And it's a double: this child. Man, are you a father and do your children laugh? Then you are in heaven. For when a child laughs, the world stands still."

Going into raptures, she threw her head back and threw her hands in the air.

"Oh you are my dearest little girl, my little brave one, and where are you? Don't you hear, your mother is calling: where, where, where? The wind falls and the sun gets up when it's morning. The bird flies from its nest. But when will you get up, when go, when fly?

Dead before birth, dead before living and beautiful like a red finch in spring and like a starling in its first brooding."

She said it all singing like a hymn.

But as she took up her old, weary posture and her eyes sank down, she caught sight of Kath and the boy in her arms. Then her face became even paler and a horror shook her body.

Suddenly, deathly despair in her eyes, she got ready in her turbid ferocity to rise.

The men sprang up and calmed her down.

"I'm going, I'm putting an end to it", she murmured continually, springing up. "If you ... the father in my name ... haha ... father ... a beautiful father ..."

Then she turned silent, but only to flare up after a few moments screaming,

"Oh, you cursed faith!" — — —

She continued talking to Stier,

"Like the cuckoo in the forest, calling everywhere. It calls — oh, how it called me! I strike out from the path, down from my beautiful path, over sticks and stones, through holes and rippling water until I do not know anymore where to nor where from ... and always it calls: cuckoo ... cuckoo ... cuckoo ..."

Her voice had become softer and softer. The last word could only be read from her lips. Sunk back, her blue eyelids shut over her deep-lying eyes, she paused as if she wanted to sleep.

The prosecutor now thought his time had come. He edged up gently and directed all kinds of questions about the cobbler at her. Her pale face remained unmoving. He unfolded the hapless man's note and lastly accused her of having a wanton affair with him and that the child was probably the fruit of this sin. All of that to get her hackles up. Marie did not alter her desolately numb face at all. Suddenly she tore herself out of the invisible clutches and commanded with an imperious voice and a drilling glance into emptiness,

"Ha, Father! You, haven't you had enough yet?! — Let go of me, I have not troubled you!!"

Then she again lay deathly pale, motionless, wilted.

The three men of the court realised that nothing was to be started with the unfortunate woman, and they hurried away, deciding to repeat in the following days the attempt to obtain a succinct testimony from her.

But Marie acquiesced completely for days, hardly touching her food and holding her face constantly turned towards the distance. Her lips were open as though drinking. An invisible current emptied into her eyes, making them stiller, removing their turbid glow and sinking deep into their hollows. On the fifth day, she fell into a sleep from which she only awoke after twenty four hours.

She straightened up and called for Kath, who was soon standing before her bed and waiting in astonishment.

"Now I'm conscious, what will I do?" Marie said to her after a long pause, laboriously as though it caused her great effort to scrape her thoughts together.

Kath was unable to speak, because she was frightened by Marie's eyes. They were turbid, like a dormant water in deep mist, without sight as it were.

"Look at me always here," she said, "it's stupid that I'm not walking. But it isn't worth it anymore. That too: the shrub doesn't get scraggy all alone, and no water swallows itself. That too: whoever strikes themself, still has something. But me? — — On the path that I went along, I saw a man who was like a blossoming shrub ... he was mine, and I did not take him ... give me your hand, Kath, and don't be frightened."

The girl did so.

"Now, yes, yes, girl," Marie then said with a feeble smile, "it must just be, why, I certainly don't know. Go and bring me my clothes. Then pack your things together – you are thanked for everything that you have done for me – and leave me alone."

Deep pity darkened Kath's eyes with tears, but she forced her anguish back out of compassion and answered,

"No, no, Marie, you're still too weak. Stand up if you think you're not. But I'm not going away. All the work at once would be too much for you."

After thinking awhile, Marie rose and Kath helped her get dressed. When she raised her right arm to put her jacket on, the poor woman cried out weakly.

"I don't have full strength anymore in my arm. That's from lying for so long. It'll probably come back again."

"You will have frozen your blood."

"In bed?"

"Well no, not in bed. Did you know that you let your arm lie outside the covers for perhaps four day and nights?"

"Oh, then anything was possible."

Then they stepped through the door.

Marie walked into the middle of the living room, and as she looked all around herself, she began to sway. If Kath had not caught her, she would have fallen to the floor. The woman leant her head weakly on the girl's shoulder. She stayed in this position for a long time while her eyes looked down large and haggard. Anxiously Kath finally lifted her head and saw a crazy expression in her face.

"What's with you now?" she asked at the same time.

Instead of giving an answer, Marie took a step back and pulled Kath with her.

"Look!" she stuttered and pointed with her wavering arm in the air.

"What is it now?" the girl asked again full of fear because she could not see anything at all.

Marie straightened up forcefully, went to the table, remained seated for a long time indecisively and then looked at Kath, shaking her head.

"No, no," she breathed, "don't worry yourself. The invalid is stilled ruled by her weakness. When you go, I'll pick up."

In order not to excite her anymore, the girl fell silent and went about her daily tasks distressed.

Marie followed all her activities with her eyes. It seemed quite incomprehensible to her, quite pointless, what she saw then, and she said disappointedly to herself, "That is life, so that is ..."

But when Kath took the screaming boy in her arms, the woman could not keep her eyes open. The raw sounds of the unlovely boy hurt her so that she began trembling and fled with averted face into the bedroom where she buried her head deep in the pillows.

But with the entire strength of her foundering soul, she held onto the decision to make a last attempt, and after a few days, she was in a state to hold the child. She laboured with empty face, went about softly like a being without a soul, without love, without hope, dead, but busy like a machine. She had noticed that her dreamy talk troubled Kath. That's why she controlled her feelings and seldom spoke and then only everyday things.

After Joseph had also convinced himself that his sister-in-law's spiritual state was no longer cause for worry, she finally attained the transfer of the household management entirely to herself.

"You will only have to send me water. A barrel full every two days will be enough."

"Yes, yes, Marie," was Joseph's hearty assent, "and as soon as it's gone, come to us with bag and baggage."

With that his large workman's hand stroked her faded cheek awkwardly.

"Oh, you dear fellow, I won't use up your time anymore. I thank you for everything that you have done for me. I'm too weak to give it back, I can only thank you. And now keep well, for me being alone is best."

Kath sobbed on the neck of her sister-in-law, and even the man's eyes stood full of water. The woman had become somewhat paler. Her lips trembled. But she could not cry. For the well of her soul had run dry.

"Go, go! Dear girl, you're fortunate!"

She stroked Kath tenderly over her red parting. Then she forced both of them gently out the door.

25

Now Marie was sitting alone and soon did not know anymore why she had yearned for it.

As the renunciation of death had come to her because it was no longer worth her while to die, so too was her life becoming something that was not worth her while.

She bore her soul forgotten within herself. Only the dark path through which this existence had gone astray was staring into her inner being. Alone too at this grim gate, her thoughts no longer called for her unfaithful mother who had deserted her in her need. For she had died away like smoke in the cold, and a peace had taken its place, which empowered Marie to see everything, to hear everything, to perceive everything without asking after the meaning and intent.

The black timbered ceiling still hung as threateningly as ever over the room, but the farmstead did not harbour the happy chirping of the goldfinch in its midst anymore.

"Shoo!" the solitary woman, after she had observed it attentively for a long time, called to flush out the bird which was perhaps searching on the floor of the cage for scattered seeds.

"Shoo! — Shoo! — Shoo!" she repeated a few more times indifferently and observed at the same time the pattern of her blue-printed house apron.

When nothing stirred, she took the wire house down and found the little bird lying dead on the floor, its red-ringed head pressed in its puffed up feathers. It had been allowed to starve. For the misfortune had advanced in silence.

"Dead", Marie said slowly, then went and threw the cage complete with bird into the snow.

Then she sat down again and her hands lay strangled in her lap. She felt the security of having nothing but her silent breathing going in and out.

The child awoke. She warmed the milk, tasted it, gave it to him to drink, cradled him in her arms, always humming the same dead tone between her teeth, and had neither loathing nor sorrow.

Because the boy did not want to sleep, she sat and rocked the cradle with her foot. At the same time, she counted the pots in the cupboard, the nails in the wall, and before she rose, she noticed a hole in the plaster.

"The plaster has fallen out with the change in temperature", she said and went to work as if it could not be otherwise than that such a discovery would spur someone on. She swept the room, fetched fodder, washed crockery and did the laundry. She did everything precisely, silently, sharp as a trained animal. Clattering bowls, her days ran through the house. Her nights were an empty daze.

She saw all that had come before, all the shattered desire, all the striving sweetness, the disintegration of all her hopes. But the bloodless recollection never aroused anything which would have torn her up furiously or left her huddling in tears. All her life lay in her like a little heap of wizened leaves which the wind had swept into a dead corner.

Only when Kath and Joseph brought the water did the weak swells of remaining existential angst begin to smoulder.

Unshakable hurt constricted her throat with the entrance of these two dear people, sorrowful stuttering broke up the words of her turbid conversation, and when they left again, the poor woman knelt on the bench, pressed her forehead against the windowpane and looked with the dull bitterness of an outcast at the traces of their feet in the snow until the wind had smeared everything.

Then she bent down again to the dust of her work. With every visit of the pair, this painful fit repeated itself. The hardship climbed so that in the end it drove her away. Kath and Joseph at one time found the entire house empty. Only the changeling purred from its pillows. After a long search, they found Marie in the shed cowering behind the pile of brushwood. Pale, scared, shaking over her whole body, she let herself be raised, led into the living room, looked around for a long time with dull eyes and suffered with a distressed smile of helplessness all the questions over the reason for her puzzling behaviour. Finally when both, dispirited, wanted to get to work again, she said timidly,

"... the brushwood ... the brushwood ..."

Nothing more was to be prised from her.

With each water trip, the same scene repeated itself. Only Marie's hiding place changed. Sometimes, probably when she had been surprised by their arrival, she contented herself with creeping under the bench or the table and turning her face to the ground. She had to be drawn out with friendly coaxing and finally with the use of force, and, intimidated by the worst, she then remained pale and shaking in a corner.

"I can't help myself. A fear just attacks me when you come", she said one time unbidden and looked past them in dumb misery.

Thus her life slowly decayed like an uninhabited house. For her soul, which had gone missing in the torment of a burdensome fate, was rambling in unknown places and did not want to return.

Marie's face lost all expression, her voice its tone. Her skin became like crinkled linen, her hair, brittle and lacklustre, had retained nothing except the fullness from its previous golden beauty and was now more like the pale, fine grass in late autumn forest-clearings. Her lips could barely still cover her teeth, her body withered. Wilted and delicate like an atrophied girl in the first years of her maidenhood, she moved however with the uncertainty of old age. Indifferent towards herself, apathetic towards her environment, she always walked about in the same clothes which had become far too large for her and now shuddered on her scrawny body.

It was as if she was separated from the external world by a desolate girdle of such dimensions that all tidings of that life stirred in her desolation only as the play of incomprehensible noises and colours. This absence of soul from a living body could not be explained any other way.

She could stand for hours by the cradle of the hungry boy, listening to his discordant screams and watching with avid tenseness, to then turn around suddenly and stuff the oven full of wood.

She forgot to feed and milk the cows, and when the animals bellowed and stamped in anguish, she ran to the window and looked out tensely as if someone had called her, or tore the door open to let in someone expected. The shadow of her hopes never materialised, but nor did she lose her dull temper. After every disappointment, she went to the bench and continued indifferently knitting a stocking which was just a long tube because it never occurred to her to start the foot.

For Christmas Kath brought into the solitary house by the forest a tree, supplies of food, apples and nuts. After two days, everything still lay untouched on the table. The woman had hacked up the little tree and burnt it in the oven.

Finally Joseph led the completely neglected cows to his own stalls. When Kath made as though to also take the changeling from the cradle, Marie clawed the girl's arm with her thin, pale fingers and looked at her with threatening wildness.

Only in the depths of her eyes did a last shimmer of inspiration smoulder, a soft radiance of timid expectation. It also perhaps ordained Kath to lay the child back in the pillows again and to make a last attempt at her unfortunate sister-in-law's salvation. She went to Mrs Wende, told her everything and asked her to visit Marie some day. It would perhaps be easiest for her, of whom the pathetic woman "had always thought highly", to dispel the silent madness which had borne down on her.

The Lord of the Manor's wife said neither yes nor no and showed Kath out. In the process, they both met Wende, who, musing to himself, wanted to stride past, but started at the sound of Kath's voice and looked at his wife angrily.

"The Exner Kath was asking after little piglets," Mrs Wende said hastily to her irritated husband, "but I told her that we've had no luck with the sow this year."

Wende shook his head approvingly, murmured something into his brown beard and continued on.

Mrs Wende hid from herself and her husband that her heart was ready to help the unfortunate woman out. From herself because she could not cast off the reproach of having been partly guilty for this horrid fate. From her husband because he would never have allowed her to set a foot in the house of his adversary, especially now as the entire legal process had not taken the turn he had expected but had found an all too abrupt end. More discontented than before, liverish and perverse, he had the business firmly under control. His sharp, covert eyes watched suspiciously every excursion of his wife, whom he suspected in his summary hate of a secret sympathy with the Exner clan.

But how simple it is. This dissimulation increased Mrs Wende's drive towards the path of compassion even more and, when the favourable accident was certainly quite close to fulfilment, she lumped together the appointed clothes, secretly baked pastries and cakes and picked out meat and sausages from the stores. For she thought from remorse of bringing her consolations in the form of the usual "weekly visit" in the Grafschaft.

Finally it behoved. Early on the 23rd of March, the Lord of the Manor left the yard to take part in his role as school superintendent in Leschkowitz in a meeting on school matters arranged by the county council. His wife learnt from the multifaceted arrangements and the assurance, repeated unnecessarily often with the most threatening airs, that his return would follow in two, at most three hours, that he would be away the whole day and she was already starting on the preparations for her excursion when his carriage had barely disappeared creaking behind the first fold in the ground. She soon found herself on her way. Snow still lay around, but it was brittle and of a grungy white, and had partly disappeared from the southern slopes. The eternal life of nature was metamorphosing once again and beginning to prepare for its most magnificent form. The grey clouds of winter gaped apart. From the blue sky, the unending lap of God, the first dreams of spring were falling down to earth and surrounding all things and beings with a bright shimmer. The forest trees of Hedwigstein and the Rollenberg appeared sharp and defiant like soldiers before the battle. The young saplings in the fields stood sweet and shamefaced like girls before dressing. Their branches glistened and gleamed in the joyful light as if they were golden hair.

From time to time, a wind picked up, like a roaring horn blast answered by an indistinct echo from distant valleys, the rattling of an approaching army's weapons.

Then the air was full of restrained songs, and around everything the frisson of approaching delight rippled more clearly.

These signs of the approaching resurrection surrounded Mrs Wende on her way to Marie.

For that reason, the impression which the unfortunate young woman complete with her surroundings made on her was like a shock which completely upset her well-thought-out plan of conferring her wisdom. The little yard was studded with brushwood, strewn straw and hay. The hallway was unswept. Under the stairs to the loft, tubs and barrels lay, dry, falling apart, stacked on top of each other like old junk. The hoops protruded.

Despite several knocks, nothing stirred in the living room, which on entering seemed as dead as the entire house. Stinking, stale air filled it. The cradle in the middle was covered with a dirty sheet. Around the oven, a messy heap of straw lay and pieces of straw were also dispersed all over the floor.

The Lord of the Manor's wife hesitantly closed the door behind her, waited a little, finally straightened her bony figure and for good luck, wished, "Good morning."

No one stirred. Only, behind the cradle, a noise wavered regularly back and forth. After taking two steps deeper into the room, she noticed a thin, female being which lay on its knees and was cleaning the legs of the bench with a dry cloth. Mrs Wende thought it was a housemaid which the pitiable woman had employed to help.

"Where is the lady, girl?" she asked, and when the person did not pay any attention but steadily wiped up and down with the cloth, the estate owner's wife finally called out as loud as she could,

"Are you provoking me, can't you hear!"

After a pause, the person ceased her activity, looked enquiringly at the cloth as if she was not quite certain if it had spoken and then turned around.

It was Marie. Even more wizened, even more un-kempt. She wore her dress strangled around her body the way you tie a bundle hastily. Now she laid the cloth down with exaggerated caution and looked straining up and down at Mrs Wende.

"Well, hey, Marie! You are being horribly diligent. The entire house could be carried away and you would not stir. Come here now and give it a little rest."

Marie remained in the stance of someone who, veiled in impenetrable night, is surrounded by noises that they cannot understand. In the end, she narrowed her eyes as if to penetrate with her glance into a quite far-off distance.

"Hey, Marie, hey!" the Lord of the Manor's wife tried to get through to her again.

Marie rose quickly, ran around the room excitedly, collected a handful of straw, then stopped perplexed and looked around.

Mrs Wende had placed her basket on the table and settled down in a chair.

"Now come over to me," she said to the lost woman amicably, "you can always do the cleaning later."

Marie's face lost its rigid expression and softened. She advanced like an obedient child and took her place opposite Mrs Wende, still holding the straw clenched in her hand.

"Look, I've brought sausages with me, pieces of meat, a few cakes and pastries. The baking didn't turn out well for me though. It's nothing with beer yeast. Eat up well now, you're far too down."

Whilst, saying all that, she emptied the basket into a bowl she had fetched, Marie sat silently there, listening raptly. Her hand, freed from the compulsion, let the straw fall. Mrs Wende took her seat again and, in expectation of a reply, directed her eyes at Marie, whose body tilted forward and looked straining with turbid look at the Lord of the Manor's wife as if she was not sitting there clearly and distinctly before her but was enshrouded in a deep darkness, barely visible.

Mrs Wende was troubled and at the same time seized by this strange behaviour. But before she could get in a few new words, Marie gave up the effort to penetrate the shadows of her shattered life, rose, wiped the condensation from the windowpanes, sat down again and folded her hands in her lap.

The light fell glittering over the table.

"The — sun — shines — beautifully — — very beautifully", she said arduously after looking at it for a long time, with a ring to her voice as though it came from the draw of a bow by an unskilled player across a violin which had lain for years unused in a case.

The Lord of the Manor's wife construed these words correctly as a sign of an incipient sympathy and, in order to deepen it, asked after the child's progress.

Marie listened to her former mistress's words with interest, like they were the sounds of a foreign language.

No understanding showed in her pale, exhausted face or in her turbid eyes, but rather, after a while, a look came into her countenance, like a sleeper's smile when they are tickled.

Mrs Wende repeated her question, jogged her arm in the end and pointed vigorously at the cradle. Then the poor woman finally stood up as though under the impact of a push, went to the changeling's bed, stripped the cover off and then stood as though turned into stone.

The child had become even thinner. Its wrinkled face resembled more that of an ancient man and was completely overrun by grey hairs as if it was covered by mould.

"Now hey, what are you doing with the child?" the Lord of the Manor's wife asked, tempted to rip the child out of the cradle.

At these loud words, the little being tried to move its arms. But it was so weak that it could only wave its wizened hands. At the same time, it cooed weakly. But its folded eyelids did not lift, only the eyeballs underneath appeared to be shaking.

"But Marie!" Mrs Wende began again, filled with indignation over the pitiful condition of the unlovely boy.

Alone, the lost woman did not stir. With stiff arms propped on the edge of the cradle, her shoulders hunched up, her head stretched forward dully, it seemed as if she was hanging in the air by strings, a bundle, not human anymore.

Her face bore an expression of brutish anguish.

"It'll die of hunger. Don't you see?" Mrs Wende called her again.

Marie hung motionless over the abyss of her life. The Lord of the Manor's wife went and handed the boy the bottle which it lashed onto so hungrily that half the sucked milk flowed out again from his broad mouth and ran down his emaciated throat.

"Drink, drink, dear child," Mrs Wende encouraged lovingly, having forgotten all shyness before this grotesque ugliness and now only seeing the needy manworm, "keep drinking, poor, poor boy. Yes, yes, we'll give you more. Don't worry."

She spoke sweetly, fondly, with that deep pity of a mother's heart which sounds almost like happiness fulfilled.

Then Marie unexpectedly emitted an agonising scream which did not seem to want to end.

Mrs Wende embraced her, felt her entire body shaking, led her away from the child to the window, sat with her and propped her up until the old peace had again taken possession of her.

But it was not the same rigidity in her anymore. A wall seemed to have been broken through, and with a pleading look, full of inexpressible laments, she looked fixedly at her former mistress.

"When you're calm," the latter soothed, "no, no! Don't be frightened, you're with me. Don't worry, your husband won't be getting out so soon, no, no, he's doing time. They have added up his years because of the boundary stones. And if he runs that out then he'll perish because of the cobbler. Don't worry", she kept repeating anew, stroking the wilted face which buried itself in her breast and embracing the body which shivered softly with every word like a tree before a wind blowing from afar.

When Mrs Wende fell silent, the poor woman lay on her side, and her breath became heavier and heavier, more fearful.

"Sweet Marie, you're always crying. Let yourself go out. We're all okay with you, the entire village. There is not one, house by house, farm by farm, who wouldn't feel sorry for you. Especially old Freiwald. Pity that he's dead. Think, they buried him last week."

Thus the good woman comforted her, and because Marie seemed to visibly hold her overflowing breath at mention of the old well digger and seemed to be becoming calmer, she thought it best to tell her the old man's story. He had received a blow to his core, probably from the discovery of the cobbler.

For from that time on, he became unwell without any apparent ailment. At the end, his soul was smiling, free of pain or struggle, like a still water flowing over into the unknown well which soaks up the rivulets of all human life evermore. His last words had been best wishes to her.

During the telling, Marie had straightened up. With the final sentence, she moved firmly away from her old mistress to the table, and it seemed as though she was pondering what had been said.

The Lord of the Manor's wife saw that her visit had not been in vain, decided to return at a convenient time and went away, since Marie did not want to pay attention anymore.

26

But Marie felt that her spirit was heading back into its old residence. The longer she felt, the clearer it seemed. Still completely preoccupied by the burden of its secret wandering, shaken by its homecoming, it brooded in its chambers while all the memories pressed towards it from without somewhat like a horde of people striking against the closed gate of a city at night in a confused tumult. Like a dark cloud, however, her consciousness lay over this last cleavage in her life.

She had sight again, but did not see anything yet; sensed, but indistinguishably; perceived, but did not apprehend.

Meanwhile she sat at the table in the unease of a person before an approaching departure, laid her hands together, took a few steps into the room, turned back and looked at the foot of her struck forward leg whose tip quivered back and forth gently with her stormy heartbeat, looked through the window, turned away and lapsed with expectant breath into an empty acquiescence.

Thus hour after hour elapsed.

Towards the end of the afternoon, the changeling began to scream hoarsely, fell silent as though suffocating, struggled on purring timidly. Then his short breath sounded like a tough mass was churning in his little chest.

Marie looked down at herself and realised her neglect, stood up, washed herself, combed her hair and put on clean clothes. During all that, she had the feeling she was clearing away the last obstacles. When she had adorned herself, she felt that impregnable feeling of thirst and hunger borne by the palpitations which beset the nervous before a decisive act. She drank in eager draughts from a jug of milk.

With the rest, she went to the cradle to feed the child. He lay whitish-blue and silent. His eyes were deeply wrinkled up, his wide mouth open, his wizened little hands lay spread out motionless.

She grasped him, and since he had limp coolness to him, she laid a blanket over him so that he would warm up.

Meanwhile the evening twilight had come, and a sheaf of red light flowed through the window over Marie, who was startled by it and thought by it that someone had moved up behind her and touched her. She waited a little to see if the light would talk. But it spread itself indifferently into the room, flowed over everything and finally turned into wreathes and patches which lighted up and then vanished. But Marie did not trust this play of light and shadows, rather she sat down at the table and observed it all with suspicion.

"Wait for it. — Wait for it", she said covertly to herself. Somewhere, in the bedroom or under the table or behind the oven, something was crouching and waiting to ambush her. — It is already here. When it gives a bit of an appearance, it is a shadow. She knew exactly that it was a matter of life. Slowly it shuffled across the floor with the noiselessness of a cat.

"What do you want?" she asked to scare it away.

The shadow moved further along towards her. Then she got frightened. "Who are you? — I didn't do it!" But the grey animal did not let itself be stopped. Now it was already so close that she saw its sides trembling with stifled breath. In order to save herself, she climbed onto the bench. — At once everything went dark and she knew she had died. When she pondered in nameless fear what would happen now, since she lay alive in her grave, someone laughed at her as if mocking her. After a while, she dared to open her eyes a little. Then she saw a tiny little Virgin Mary standing next to her. She sparkled by herself and puckered her face scornfully.

"Did you laugh at me?" she asked the saint, already furious but still submissive. The figure just nodded its head stiffly and the light went out. Then a spell subsided in Marie. — She suddenly recognised herself again, saw where she was and knew everything that had happened to herself.

In despair at God, her soul had gone missing within her; in indignation, she awoke in this moment to the laughter that God had made over her. With that a blow came over her heart like when a bell sounds a storm warning.

Without thinking she rushed to the shelf in the corner and brushed the wooden figurines into her apron.

Then she went into the yard and sought in the uncertain light of the descending night the high wall of snow before the barn door. She waded in there, trod a deep hole, stamped the figurines down into it with her feet and threw snow over it.

As she lifted up ball after ball with her hands and pressed them down, she uttered that great indignation which her existential pain had become,

"Death on death. — The kick to your heart so that it breaks like mine. Torturer — torturer — torturer ..."

Now it was accomplished.

A snow cone towered over her buried God, and with gasping chest and flashing eyes, the woman stood before it. Then she went back inside. With rigid eyes, she stared at the window which stood like a pale patch before her in the black night.

She did not light a candle. She did not lie down to sleep. She waited for a long time for a wild miracle which she thought she had invoked by her curse. But when nothing happened, she went with shaking knees into her bedroom, fell face down on her bed, buried her hands despairingly in the pillows and fell asleep, exhausted.

After a period, she gave a jerk.

A thudding bang had struck the roof of the house.

The walls were still shaking when she jumped up. And as she now grasped the timbers, the trembling was shared by her inner being, was alone for a while in her while everything around her seemed to smitten by lifelessness and then began slowly to stream out from her, but not as if it was only a movement, rather as if it was a second incomprehensible being. She felt it gliding down in herself, running out of the bedroom and through the living room. It opened the door, slammed it and began soon after, out in the hallway, to call for her with the voice of a frightened child,

"Mother! — Mother!" so that she sallied out to see who was there.

When she entered the hallway, her little girl, her "duckling", was outside, blowing into her frozen-blue hands and constantly stepping from one foot to the other so that her blond hair ran together deeper and deeper over her face.

"Why didn't you stay in heaven?" Marie asked in astonishment.

The girl lifted her eyes and looked at her helplessly.

"Did he chase you out because of me?"

The child just nodded disconsolately.

"Now in the night ... in the cold, really?" she continued questioning incredulously.

Instead of answering, the girl broke out into pitiful sobbing.

Then Marie became intoxicated with fury.

"Come in, come! Your dear mother will help you", she said, finally controlling herself with effort, and led the child, whom she watched pattering beside her, into the living room and closed the door behind her so that the entire house creaked.

With that the changeling awoke from his paralysis and screamed grouchily.

These tones penetrated the blond girl. She was becoming more and more unreal.

"Girl, Greta, don't be frightened! — Calm down! — Calm down! — I'll keep my child ... I need no other!"

With her foot, she kicked against the cradle.

But the changeling's voice became louder and louder and threatened to absorb her child completely.

Then Marie pressed the blanket firmly over his face, fetched still more pillows from her bedroom, laid over them with her body and remained so for a long time, until the unlovely voice had completely ceased.

She carried the pillows with dancing steps back into the bedroom. Then she lifted her girl into the cradle.

She did not need to remove the body, for her her dead boy was her duckling.

Now she lit a candle and moved a chair over to the cradle to lull her treasure to sleep, her treasure who was so tired from the journey out of heaven through the cold clouds to the earth.

Now everything was as she had wished it with her yearning and her sorrow.

Her foot rocked the cradle while she sang,

> Bye, baby Bunting,
> Father's gone a-hunting,
> Mother's gone a-milking,
> Sister's gone a-silking,
> Brother's gone to buy a skin
> To wrap the baby Bunting in.

She sang without stopping and rocked the little bed swishing. Her eyes blazed, her face had shrunk, wrinkled deep by wild delight.

Exhausted, she had to make a pause. She grasped the corpse's face and found that it was ice-cold.

"How cold you are! We'll start a fire. Then you'll get warm."

Soon it was crackling in the oven.

She waited a while and then checked how much progress the heating had made with her treasure.

Still ice-cold. — — —

Dismayed she bent down over the deathbed and pondered for a long time.

Suddenly she flung herself up.

"Oh, now I know! The earth has killed you. And me too. — Light — light — light! — everywhere up to the ceiling, out to the roof, glaring light! We'll burn the night to the ground. After that we'll be delivered from everything, we and all mankind."

She sprang out joyfully, hauled pieces of wood over, layered four pieces around the cradle, laid kindling underneath, lit it and sat down again by the cradle.

Soon her world in all four directions was in flames. On her face lay a blissful radiance.

But her song had an ungovernable force.

> Bye, baby Bunting,
> Father's gone a-hunting, ...

she sang until her last breath.

When the horrified residents of Steindorf arrived, the song was long burnt up. A flurry of sparks climbed into the air from the collapsed timbers and lost itself in the heights like the swish of a beating wing.

Then everything sank down into ashes. — —

But the night remained with earth. For it would not let it be taken away.

It gives birth to men. It takes them away again.

And between the night's rise and fall, the hourly chimes of human existence swing in a quite narrow space.

Their tone is eternal desire in miserable struggle and bitterest sweetness.

About the Publisher

Our mission is to provide translations into English of the complete works of neglected Major European writers. We do not cherry-pick works that seem the most marketable, but rather seek to provide a complete collection of each writer's works so that readers can follow the writer's development and decide on its merits for themselves.

http://www.facebook.com/KANitzPublishing